Redeeming Kyle

REDEEMING KYLE - 69 BOTTLES #3

Zoey Derrick

Praise for Claiming Addison and the 69 Bottles Trilogy

"I could go on and on about this book, but I'll leave you here… and the fact that buying a copy of this book should come with a complimentary change of panties…" 5 Stars Shurrn - The Smutsonian

"Holy smokes batman! Where is the fire extinguishers? This final book in this trilogy is scorching hot. Must have significant other around when reading this book!" - Beta Reader on 69 Bottles Trilogy

"Simply AMAZING! Definitely a MUST READ for 2015!" 5 Stars Stephanie - Stephanie's Book Report

Praise for Craving Talon

"Absolute smutty perfection!"
5 Stars Shurrn - The Smutsonian

"Fluidly and beautifully written…"
5 Stars Amazon Review

Acknowledgements

Z-Team: Thank you to my beautiful Street Team. You ladies are the best and I love you for everything you do.

Rachel - My BFF, my Numero Uno Beta Reader. Thank you for always being ready, able and willing to read my raw craziness and for loving every word! P.S. Tell your husband he's welcome!

DawnMarie - You are my queen pimp! Thank you for telling everyone about the Trio, for listening to me whine and for helping me tell the world about 69 Bottles.

Mandy and Lorraine: Ladies, without you, this book wouldn't be in everyone's hands. You're amazing at everything you do. Stay Raw!!

To my beautiful Beta Readers: Lisa, Danielle, Vickie, Kali, Liliuokalani and Amy - Thank you for your kindness and willingness to read my mess of a beta copy. Your feedback has been instrumental in creating the story in your hands. Your love of Addison, Talon and Kyle is amazing. Thank you for everything!

To Emily - your words, your encouragement, and your love of my work keeps me going and it keeps me pushing my boundaries. Thank you for being such an inspiration.

For my Fans - Thank you for always wanting more, for reading, and for reviewing my work. Without you I'd have no reason to keep going. Thank you for loving my work.

To Rachel, a.k.a. Parajunkee - Your creativity is an inspiration. Your work is beyond amazing, Thank you for the cover of Claiming Addison and for everything you do to bring my stories to life.

To Stephanie - Thank you for loving my story so much you told every one about it. Your love for Addison, Talon and Kyle inspires me to write more.

To Shannon - Seriously, you're the freakin shiz. No words can say how much I appreciate you and everything you do. I think you have a lot of woman to fight over to stake your full claim on Talon and Kyle!

Christine and Kelley - I HEART YOU! *Grins* That is all!

Stop Right
There!!!!

Now that I have your attention...

If you have NOT read Claiming Addison - 69 Bottles Book #1 AND Craving Talon - 69 Bottles #2, please stop right here.

I want you, the reader, to have the best possible reading experience and in order to do that, you need to first read Claiming Addison and Craving Talon.

Book 3 - Redeeming Kyle, is a continuation of Craving Talon. Starting this series with this book means that you will be lost, you will not understand what is happening therefore spoiling your reading experience.

Thank you for taking the time to read this notice. If you've already read Claiming Addison, proceed with caution. *Winks*

A WARNING FOR READERS!

I, Zoey Derrick, am not responsible for the following:

Husband/Boyfriend/Significant Other Breaking.

The cost of batteries required for reading this book.

Broken Vibrators.

Loss of sleep

Broken fingers

Or

Panty washing.

Read One Handed!

XXOO! Enjoy Craving Talon!

Zoey

For Schadoh - Keep your head up everyday. You're a brave and beautiful young lady. Thank you for being my biggest fan!

chapter 1

When I wake, I know it's early, but I also know I slept a long time. Not wanting to wake my men, I crawl out of bed and head for the bathroom. I decide that I need a long soak and this tub is far too big to go unused. So I fire up the water and let it fill. I go in search of a hair tie. I don't know why, but I look into the baggie and I see something strange inside. It's a tie, or something that looks like one, mixed in with all the others. When I pull it out, panic races through my veins. Where did this come from? How did it get here? I sit down on the side of the tub very slowly. Putting my head in my hands.

"Breathe, Addison," I tell myself. If this is in here, it's not in me, and if it's not in me that means… "Oh god."

"Baby girl?"

I jump at the sound of Kyle's voice; I didn't hear him get up. "Oh god," I groan. Panic rises and my breathing spikes.

"What's wrong, Addison?" He kneels down in front of me.

I hold up the hand that has the ring, my birth control ring, in it. "Where did this come from?"

He shrugs and shakes his head. "I have no clue, where did you find it?"

"In with my hair ties. It's not for my hair."

"Then what is it, baby girl?"

Oh god. I don't know if I can tell him. God, I don't want to discuss this. "It's nothing," I say.

"You promised honesty, Addison. You're lying to me right now."

I start crying. "Not lying, just, oh god Kyle, this is my birth control." I bat my eyes to try and slow the flood of tears. Oh god, emotional, crying, bitchy- fuck.

"What do you mean 'birth control'?" he asks, completely innocent.

I look at him and fight the urge to scream as the panic continues to rise. "It's called NuvaRing," I tell him in a shaky voice. "It goes up there; it's full of hormones that act as birth control. I put it in and then three weeks later I take it out, I bleed and put a new one in. I need to know how long this has been with my stuff."

I can see fear and panic creeping over his features. "God Kyle, please, no, don't, damn it, don't. I need someone to be strong for me right now. Please don't panic, I can't, I can't handle it."

"Baby girl, I'm sorry. I just, we haven't..." He falls onto his butt.

"Kyle, breathe. Please. I..." I have to tell him, "Kyle, I have issues with my uterus."

He looks at me, waiting for an explanation. "I'm on birth control only to regulate my periods. Without it, I bleed maybe, twice a year. I have cysts. Do you understand what that is?" He shakes his head. "They're little bubbles on my ovaries that over time can turn hard.

These cysts completely block one of my fallopian tubes and limit the functionality of my ovaries. There are also a lot of hormonal issues and other areas of my health can be affected too. One of my ovaries only functions about twenty-five percent of the time. Without birth control I have a less than five percent chance of getting," I swallow hard, "pregnant."

"So there's no way…"

"I didn't say that. I don't know. It's all going to depend on how long this has been out of me. Which is why I need Talon. Can you go wake him for me? I don't think I can move right now."

I don't know how he does it, but he manages to pull himself together. He turns off the water behind me and leaves the bathroom.

I can hear him in the bedroom. "Talon, come on, big man. Addison needs you to wake up."

"Huh, what's wrong?"

"Nothing, she just needs to talk to you. She's in the bathroom."

"Okay, give me a sec," Talon tells him.

I put my head in my hands while I wait for Talon to come into the bathroom. God, Kyle freaked out, I don't think I can handle Talon freaking out on me too.

"What's going on, angel?"

I take a deep breath. "Do you recognize this?"

I show him the ring. "Yeah, I found it and put it into your hair ties bag."

Thank god. "When?"

"Oh, um, Vegas I think, when we packed you up."

Oh fuck. "Kyle, can you bring me my phone, please?"

"Angel, what's going on?"

"It's not a hair tie. It's actually called a NuvaRing, it's my birth control," I say softly.

He kneels down in front of me. "I don't understand."

"This goes inside of me, and it releases hormones into my body, then after three weeks, I take it out and within a few days I get my period." Kyle shows up with my phone.

"When were you supposed to take it out?" he asks me.

"Sunday morning, but I couldn't find it. Then with the Bryan Hayes thing, then yesterday- I just forgot about it. I was going to have one of you help me, but everything just got so messed up. But I couldn't find it because it was gone and it's been gone..." I look at my phone, "for over two weeks." Panic soars once again.

"But we haven't used condoms." I put my hand on his cheek.

"I have problems, with my ovaries. My likelihood of getting pregnant is less than ten percent."

"So you're not..." I can see the panic I feel reflected in Talon's eyes.

"I didn't say that, though I wish I could." I look back at my calendar. My period usually shows up Tuesday night, or sometime Wednesday. "I need a test, but it might be too early." The tears flow again when I see Talon with complete panic on his face.

Kyle kneels down behind Talon. "Talon, are you alright?"

He doesn't respond. He just sits there. His body is radiating panic and ready to freak out. I put my hand on his cheek. "Look at me, big man." He doesn't move. "Come on, big guy, I need you to look at me." Tears streak down my cheeks. I can't stand to look at his panicking face; I need him to look at me. "Come on, baby, look at me." Finally his eyes meet mine. "Hi there." I smile. "You with me?" He nods slightly. "Can you talk to me? What are you thinking?" He looks down again. "No, no, keep looking at me."

His eyes come up, meeting mine, and they're thick with unshed tears. "I'm scared," he breathes.

"What are you scared about?"

"I'm not sure I'm ready to be a father," he says in a whisper.

"Aw, baby, we don't know that. We don't know one way or another. Until we know for sure, we cannot panic. Please, I can't." The tears flow harder and faster, "I can't stay strong for the three of us." I look past Talon to Kyle.

"Talon, no matter what, we're all in this together," Kyle says as he rubs Talon's back. "You're not in this alone, neither is Addison."

"What if it's yours?" Talon asks.

"Honestly, it doesn't matter to me whether it's yours or mine. If she's even pregnant, we're still all in this together. We've made a choice to be a threesome; everything we do involves all of us, no matter what," Kyle says. His strength is like a shot of adrenaline straight to my heart.

Talon loosens up a little bit too. "Kyle's right. We can't make assumptions until we know for sure."

"How do we do that?" Talon asks.

I give him a small smile. "I need a pregnancy test."

"Where do I get one?" He's eager.

"Breathe, big man. I will send Tori or someone else to get one."

"I'll go," Kyle says as he stands up.

"Relax, cowboy. There is no guarantee that the result I get today will be accurate. A blood test is preferable, but I don't want to take the risk of it leaking to the media. So, if we're going to get one, I'll need at least two. I'll take one today and I will try another one on Thursday or Friday. My period usually starts on Wednesday after I take out my ring, but I only had it in about a week before it fell out. So my body is probably screwed up."

"Okay, let's get you a couple of tests," Kyle says.

I nod and look to Talon. "You feeling better?" He gives me a tiny lift of his lip. "I'm going to slide into this nice warm tub. I need to relax."

"Can I join you?" Talon asks. "I just want to hold you," he whispers.

I look up at Kyle who nods. "I'll go talk to Tori," he says.

"Are you sure?" I ask.

He leans down and kisses my forehead. "Absolutely," he says and leaves the bathroom.

I reach for Talon's hand. "Come on." He stands up with my help. I step over the side of the tub and stand in the middle. Talon steps in behind me and slides down into the water.

"Come, angel," he says and I sit down in front of him. He wraps his arms around me, under my breasts, and pulls me back closer to him and holds onto me like he needs air to breathe. I settle into him, his hold and his touch surrounding me. I lay my head back on his shoulder.

chapter 2

Kyle is back within fifteen minutes and Talon hasn't moved. He has his head buried in the crook of my neck and I love the fact that we're wrapped up like this. Kyle stands over us. "Join us, please," Talon requests.

I smile at Kyle and nod and he steps out of his pants and t-shirt before joining us in the tub. He starts to sit down opposite us. "Come here, and turn around," Talon says and Kyle turns around and sits down between our legs. He hesitates to lean back.

"You won't hurt me," I tell him, wrapping my arms around his chest and pulling him back against me. Once he's settled against me, I wrap my legs around him, keeping him pressed tightly against my body. He leans his head back on my shoulder and Talon kisses his head, and then buries his face back in my neck.

We don't move, staying like this for some time. We hold on to each other and it's pure bliss. I nearly forget what we're facing right now. What Kyle said, about us being a triad, a threesome, and how no matter what, no matter whom, it doesn't matter. The idea brings tears to my eyes again.

Kyle shifts and I let him go. He turns in the tub. "What's wrong, baby girl?"

Talon's hands begin rubbing along my stomach, but there is nothing sexual about it, it's strictly comforting. "I'm scared. I'm nervous. I'm, god, I don't know. So many things are running through my mind." Talon lifts his head.

"Lean back, Kyle," Talon says and he does, getting awkwardly comfortable, so many legs. "Go to him, baby, lay with him."

"Where are you going?" I ask quietly.

"I'm going to see if we have what we need to try and find out. We're all going to make ourselves crazy if we keep fretting over this and I can't take it anymore." He stands up as soon as I'm pressed back against Kyle and his arms and legs are wrapped around me. "I'll be back in a few minutes." He leans down, kisses my forehead, then kisses Kyle's, before stepping out and wrapping a towel around his waist.

"Is he okay?" I ask Kyle.

"I think he's freaking out, but I think he recognizes how much you and I need him, so he's trying to be strong."

"What about you, cowboy?"

"I'm freaking out. But," his hand rubs along my stomach, "either way, I'll be good. I just need to get past the unknown. That's all." I put my hand on top of his and we lay there. My early wake up, my panic and emotional drain catches up and I nearly fall asleep before Talon returns. He has a bag in his hand.

"She got like, four boxes. What did you tell her, Kyle?"

"I didn't know what to get, so I'm assuming she grabbed a couple different brands."

Picturing Tori in a drug store, buying pregnancy tests for me, almost makes me laugh. Almost. "What do you say, baby girl, should we give this a go?" I nod and he unwraps his legs from around me, giving me room to stand up. "No, stay, let me get some towels," Kyle says as he climbs out.

"Talon?"

"Yes, angel?"

"How are you doing?" I ask.

"I'm better now, I think. I just need answers. My mind will run a thousand and one different scenarios and I need to turn them off."

"Even if it comes back negative, we're not necessarily in the clear. You do understand that, right?"

He gives me a small smile. "I do, but at least it's something I can work with. If it's negative, how long will we need to wait for another test?"

"I'm going to say a couple of days. Maybe Friday. Unless my period shows up between now and then." He nods. "If it's positive, we'll figure it out, I promise."

He leans down, kissing my head. "I know we will. We always do," he says as Kyle comes back with a stack of towels, one is wrapped around his waist. He sets the rest on the sink and he hands one to Talon, who opens it up for me. I stand up. He wraps the towel around me and begins rubbing me dry.

Once he's done, I kick them out. "I'll let you back in when I'm done. I can't pee with an audience." They leave reluctantly and I sit down, peeing on a stick, my heart rate rising further with each passing second. Once I'm done, I put the little cap on it and lay it flat on the counter. It's one of those digital ones, so there is an hourglass flashing. I open the door. I want to climb back into the bathtub but they're both sitting on the bed.

Zoey Derrick

I walk over to them and they both wrap their arms around me. Holding me to them. "I have a better idea," I say and I step around them and climb onto the bed, dropping my towel in the process. Talon gets up and comes around the bed to his usual spot and Kyle lays down behind me, his front to my back. "Turn around, big man, let me hold you." He rolls over and backs up. I push one arm under his head and the other under his arm and I rub my fingers along his tight stomach muscles. Much the same as Kyle is doing with me.

"How long do we have to wait?" Talon asks.

"About three minutes or so," I say and kiss him between his shoulders.

"Want me to go look?"

"No Talon, I don't want you to move right now. I just want to lay here between the two of you."

No one says anything for about fifteen minutes. "Okay, I can't take it anymore," Kyle says.

"Okay, let's go." I move to sit up.

"Let us look, angel. You stay put."

"I'm freaking out just as much as you are, you know?"

"I know, but let us look first," Kyle says. "We will be right back."

"Guys, what's going on?" I call out after what seems like an eternity but is really just a couple of minutes.

They both come back onto the bed. Kyle slides in behind me, Talon slides in front of me. "Look," Kyle says as he shows me the stick. 'Not pregnant' stands out like the biggest, brightest, sign I've ever seen.

Relief washes through me. "My god," I breathe. I look at both of them and they both seem a little sad. "What? You're not happy about this?" I ask.

"We are and we aren't."

"Whoa, wait a minute. Not ten minutes ago the two of you were somber ducks, now you're disappointed that I'm not pregnant, or that the test says I'm not."

That conversation, the one we had back on the bus, when they were talking about my nipples, Talon's slip, plays through my mind. "I think you'll be sexy as hell when you're pregnant." Kyle says as he reaches back to set the test on the table, then comes back and wraps his arms around me.

"I'm scared shitless, but I think, while lying in the tub I realized that while the prospect scares the living shit out of me, I might be a little excited about the idea of one day having a baby with you." Talon smiles. Though it's not his normal bright smile, it's better than what it was earlier.

"What if it's Kyle's?" I tease. He wraps his arms around me, between Kyle and me.

"I don't think I'll care, or even want to find out."

"Gah, you guys are maddening, you know that?"

And in tandem they both thrust their hips at me and I can feel their erections. One probing in the front, the other in the back.

I lift my leg and wrap it around Talon's hip. "Are you going for trying to knock me up?" I ask and they both thrust again. I groan. I feel Talon shifting his hips again, and this time I can feel the head of his cock probing at my entrance. Kyle shifts, reaching for something. When he comes back he has a bottle of lube in his hand. I moan and Talon dips the head of his cock inside, just teasing, just barely stretching me.

Talon cups my breast in his hand and I can feel Kyle stroking his cock, lubing himself up. "Oh fuck," I groan and feel Kyle pressing against my tight ring. Talon releases my breast from his fingers and he reaches under my leg, lifting it. Giving them both access to my inner most parts.

They're both probing gently as I writhe. Talon's mouth finds a nipple and he licks, then sucks it into his mouth. I moan, relaxing and opening for them.

chapter 3

We spend the next two hours like that. Talon and Kyle trading positions and loving on me as hard as they can. That is until I can no longer keep my eyes open. I'm exhausted and I have so much work to do, but I fall asleep in their arms.

When I wake up, there are two boxes, along with all of my luggage, stacked in the room, but the guys are nowhere to be found. Obviously they packed me up, but I needed to go through that stuff. Shit, what am I going to wear tonight? What the hell time is it anyway? I roll over to look at the clock. "Shit." It's nearly two and we have to leave by four. I stretch; my body is deliciously sore from their treatment of me earlier. I soak up the aches, but my stomach is rolling. I swallow hard. God, I hope I'm not getting sick. Then the image of the 'not pregnant' test comes to mind. Relieved, yes. Disappointed that it wasn't positive? I'm surprised by the realization that for some reason I wanted it to be positive.

For just the briefest of moments, hope blossomed. When you've spent the majority of your adult life on birth control dealing with the problems that I have, that tiny ounce of hope was enough to wash all doubt away. It would certainly explain a few things. Like the fatigue I feel. I was tired after only being at the mall for an hour yesterday. Eating rejuvenated me, but it didn't last long. I'm glad they came to meet me because it was the boost in energy I needed to keep me going. Hell, I passed out on them last night.

To top that off, I feel bloated and my breasts feel heavier. I'd chalk it up to normal, pre-period behavior, but rarely have my breasts been a factor. Then again, Talon was latched onto them for the longest time this morning.

I stretch and the nausea rolls through me again, but it passes quickly. I head for the shower.

"Baby girl?" I hear Kyle call from the bedroom.

"In here," I holler back. I just finished putting on my bra and panties. I found them laid out for me on the bathroom counter.

"Hey, you doing okay?" he asks from the doorway of the bathroom.

"Yes and no," I tell him. It's true. I still don't feel at a hundred percent; add to that the disappointment still plaguing me. When I was in the shower, I couldn't help imagining what it would be like to be pregnant, and that of course brought me back down emotionally.

"What's wrong?" Kyle asks as he comes to stand behind me, wrapping his arms around me and kissing me on my neck.

"Yes, I'm okay, and no I'm not. I'm not because I'm not feeling the best. I haven't really been feeling great since we got here, but I just chalked it up to the fact that I've been so tired."

He looks at me in the mirror, his blue eyes meeting my too bright green eyes. "What can I do?" he asks and I'm not sure I have an answer for him.

"I don't know, to be honest. I'm not sure if I'm catching a cold, or what, but I just feel achy."

"Did we jump the gun with that test this morning? Maybe you're getting your period. Or..." He drifts off, but there is no hint of fear in his eyes and I'm comforted by that. Maybe what they said earlier still stands true.

"What if I am? What if we just took the test too soon?" I see a flash of fear in his eyes, but it dissipates quickly.

"You say that like you're disappointed. Talk to me, Addison," Kyle whispers softly.

"At first I felt relief because, well hell, we've only been together a few weeks."

"Is that the only reason you felt relief?" he asks quietly.

"Honestly, no. I was relieved because I don't know if I'm ready for a baby, but then the disappointment started to set in. I've spent so much time convinced that getting pregnant is impossible, so the chance that I could be got me a little more excited than I thought only to find out it was negative. Then after you and Talon saw the test both of your attitudes changed, shifting everything. It was like you were both relieved and it became okay to talk about it again. But the disappointment started ringing. I don't know if I can have children, and I've been so wrapped up in my own career that I never really thought about it. But I'm also scared to death."

"Do something for me, baby girl?" Kyle asks softly. I nod. "If you're not already pregnant, and you want a baby at some point, you know damn well that Talon and I would make it happen. No matter what. So try not to be disappointed, I'm sure there is some way we can make it happen."

I feel like crying again. Just the fact that he holds me just a little tighter to his chest, comforting me, is enough to make me want to burst into tears.

I manage to keep it together and Kyle leaves me so I can finish getting ready. I decide to wear the outfit that Talon bought me before the Minneapolis show. I pair the black tank-top jumpsuit with the lacy overlay that's actually a dress and my black calf height three-inch heel boots. The ensemble looks great. I leave my hair down so that it's wavy and free flowing down my back. We're taking the buses to the mall since we're leaving immediately after this little shindig for Chicago. The band has an early morning radio appearance and it will take us a good seven hours to get there. This event is due to be over around eight, but it will realistically be more like nine to ten before we get out of there, on the buses and finally on the road.

When I leave the bedroom, Talon and Kyle are both talking with Mills while the rest of our luggage is being loaded onto hotel carts to be taken downstairs. Mills smiles at me, but keeps talking. Talon turns his head, smiles widely and goes back to talking to Mills, probably about tonight.

"Addison?" Kyle calls and I look at him. "We need someone to introduce the band tonight. Normally I'd do it, but…"

"You want me to do it?" I ask with a smile.

He nods, "If you feel up to it."

I smile wider. "I'd love to."

While they finish up their conversation I grab my iPad and load up my email. I can look at it on the ride over. Once Mills, Kyle and Talon are done talking, we get ready to leave. "Thanks again for packing me up," I tell my guys, and they both smile.

"We tried to wake you a few times and we weren't exactly quiet while we were doing it, but you had no intention of waking up," Talon says and he comes over to me, wraps his arms around me, and kisses me. "You look amazing, angel."

I blush. "Thank you. You should like it, you picked it out."

He smirks. "I did, though I had more ideas about how to take it off of you than what it would look like on." I feel his hand brush across my nipple and it aches slightly. I flinch. "Whoa, you okay?" His face grows concerned quickly.

"You weren't exactly gentle with them this morning." I give him a secret smile. "Not that I'm complaining, but now I'm paying the price."

"I'm sorry, angel."

I tap his nose with my finger. "Don't be. It's alright. If you both behave, I might let you make it up to me," I tease and Talon releases me. Kyle is there to quickly take his place.

"I agree. You look amazing. Feeling better?"

I do a quick assessment. "Yes, actually."

He smiles. "Good."

"Alright guys, time to go." Mills tells us as he comes back into the room. Kyle and Talon take my hands in theirs and we leave the room.

Zoey Derrick

Once on board, I go back through my emails. "The guys went out last night?" I ask, though my voice is more accusatory than questioning.

"Yeah, well, they stayed late at the mall, there's a couple of bars up on the fourth floor. Why?" Talon asks.

"Because they made the news."

"Oh no, badly?" he says.

I smile. "No, just some splash pieces on where they were. They appear to have behaved themselves."

"Which is more than I can say for the three of you," Dex quips as he comes on the bus. I blush, of course, which only eggs Dex on a little more. "You would think, after handling those two, you wouldn't blush so much. Unless they're boring in bed. In which case, you know where to come for a good time." Dex flicks his tongue at me.

"Oh I have plenty of fun, fuck you very much," I tease Dex.

"Ooh she's feisty. Tell me, boys, how do you wrangle her in?"

"Stuff it, Dex," Talon says, and the look on his face is pretty stern.

"No, seriously, how do you do it?"

"Drop it, Dex," Kyle warns and Talon and Kyle exchange a look. I can't see it, but it is a little too encouraging to Dex.

"Oh come off it, why don't you two just get a room," Dex snorts. Talon and Kyle exchange another look. "Oh shit...oh my god, you already..." Dex looks from me, to Kyle, then to Talon, and back to me. I, of course, blush even redder. "About fucking time," Dex says as he throws his bag onto his bunk. "I mean seriously, none of us give a shit what you're sticking your dick into." He laughs and sets about straightening his bunk.

"Well, I guess that cat's out of the bag," I grumble. Just then Peacock comes up behind me.

"Heya Red," he says with a smile.

"Hey Eric. You okay?"

The look on his face says it all; it's strained. "We still need to have that talk, don't we?"

He shrugs. "We have plenty of time." He smiles and gets himself situated and Mouse isn't that far behind him. Tori steps onto the bus with a large black duffle slung over her shoulder.

"Hey Tori, let me show you to your bunk," I say. She nods and we slide past the boys. Dex wiggles his ass at me as I pass and I smack it, hard. Which makes my hand sting, Talon and Kyle laugh and Dex starts spouting something about harder next time. A creepy chill runs through me.

chapter 4

Once we arrive at the mall, Tori, Kyle, Rusty, Beck, Mills and I all go inside, leaving the rest of the guys at the bus. Our goal is surveillance and to meet with the rotunda coordinator. When we enter the mall, it is a few hundred decibels louder in here today than it was yesterday when I walked through.

The hallway from the door going into the mall is lined with people screaming and shouting. Some of them get really excited when they see me. "Maybe we should take her back to the bus," I hear Tori say to someone and I turn around.

"No, I have a job to do. I am Addison the employee, not Addison the singer right now. Let them cheer."

"Addison, we're only concerned about your safety."

I look around the room. There is event staff stationed about every ten feet along the barricades holding people back. "I think we're good."

A short, stocky woman carrying a radio and a clipboard quickly approaches us. Kyle stands between her and I. "I'm

Kyle Black, are you Annie?" She nods. "We spoke on the phone."

"Oh of course, Kyle."

"This is Addison. If you can't find me, she's your next in line." I shake her hand.

"It's a pleasure to meet you. I'm going to assume you're the Addison they're shouting about right now," she says rather loudly, but her voice doesn't carry far because of all the noise.

"That would be me. Sorry about that."

"Oh heavens don't be. We love this. Though the stores on the other hand, not so much." She laughs. "We have a back door the band can enter through and then it's a much shorter distance to the stage. Which is on the other side of the elevator there." She turns and points. "We cut the autograph line off at five hundred. We've only guaranteed the first two hundred to be able to get their autographs. Pictures are up to you guys to handle. Allow them or don't, but we do have a photographer here, hired by Vicious."

I look at Kyle and I can tell that we're both thinking the same thing. "No pictures, at least not directly with the band, individually or as a whole," I say and Kyle nods. I look to Annie. "I'll make the announcement when I introduce the band."

"Perfect, we have event staff set up to funnel the line and provide additional crowd control. I have to tell you, this is the largest turn out that we've ever had here."

"You're kidding?" Kyle says as he takes another look around. The sound doesn't quite match the number of people I'm seeing.

"Nope, and we're still funneling people this way. Though we're about to cut them off."

"About to?" I interject.

"Come, you'll see," she says as we walk toward the stage. I notice how the guards surround us in a circle formation, scanning the crowd. I don't know why but it makes me nervous.

We get closer to the elevator and from the path that we just walked, going left and right is a narrower pathway and on either side of the shrunken path is a sea of people.

"Look up," Annie tells us. I do, and I nearly fall over. Stretching four floors high are people, leaning over the railing, looking down. I side step just a little, my hoard moving with me, and I can see out in front of the stage, leading into the amusement park area, are more people.

"Do we have a count for this?" I ask.

Annie looks down at her paperwork then picks up her radio. She calls to someone and they answer back, though I can't hear the response. She looks at me. "Over seven thousand total."

"Jesus Christ," Kyle spouts.

When Kyle and I get back on the bus we're completely pumped up and excited. "What's up with you two?" Talon asks with a smile.

"Oh my god, just wait until you see. There are over seven thousand people in there."

"Whoa, what?" he says as he sways backwards.

"Easy, big man," I tell him. "It's insane, but the mall has cut off your autograph line at five hundred, and only two hundred are guaranteed. We're also eliminating pictures. We don't have the time. They can take pictures as you're signing the photographs, which look amazing by the way." The band has publicity photos to hand out at these events.

"I didn't expect this many people," he says dumbstruck.

"What I think he means is that the gravity of how popular they are is just now setting in." Kyle bumps his shoulder in to Talon and smiles widely at him. "You've hit super star status. Get used to it."

"I don't think I can ever get used to it."

"Good, because this way it won't become an expectation," I say with a sweet smile. "Don't need it going to your head," I tease.

He and Kyle both laugh. "Too late for that," Kyle adds in.

"You two are too much sometimes," Talon says and I laugh.

Talon kisses my forehead as he goes to walk away. "I need to go prepare the guys."

I smile at him. "Go get 'em, tiger."

"Do good luck rituals apply for personal appearances?" He wiggles his eyebrows.

"No, now go."

"Ladies and gentlemen," I announce into the microphone and the crowd slowly dies down. "How's everyone doing tonight?" I ask and they get all excited again. The acoustics suck and the noise just bounces all over the place. I put my hand out, pushing them up and down to encourage them to quiet. They settle back to a dull roar. "In case you don't know, I am Addison Beltrand and-" the loud roar of the crowd cuts me off once again. I do believe I blush. "You're all too much, but I am not the reason you're all here at the Mall of America tonight." They roar again with excitement. "It is my proud honor and privilege to introduce to you 69 Bottles."

The crowd gets wilder than before, but they settle quickly. "Ladies and gentlemen, I introduce you to Mr. Dex Harris on drums." I turn, clapping as Dex takes the stage behind me. "Mr. Eric 'Peacock' Caldwell on the bass." Peacock steps up onto the stage, I notice now that his peacock mohawk has a fresh coat of color in it. "Mr. Calvin 'Mouse' Richardson on lead guitar." With each introduction the crowd gets louder and louder. "And last, but certainly not least, front man Talon Carver."

I immediately wish I'd put earplugs in. Talon comes out on stage, comes up behind me, kisses me and goes to stand behind his assigned spot. I quiet the crowd again. "Just a few short announcements before we get started. The guys have agreed to sign as long as their pictures hold out, however, in order to accommodate as many fans as humanly possible, the following rules must be obeyed. Stay in line, if you leave, you lose your spot. It doesn't matter if you have friends that are holding your spot or not. Number two, because 69 Bottles wants to honor as many fans as possible with autographs, we will not be allowing photos with the band or individuals. You are allowed to take pictures of them while they are signing for you. And lastly, be respectful, not only of the band, but of the people around you." I turn to face the guys. "Gentlemen, are you ready to meet your fans?"

"Hell yeah!" They all shout in unison and the crowd goes nuts.

The guys step down off of the stage and take their seats behind the tables that have been set up for them. I watch as Mills, Rusty, Beck, Leroy, Casey, Troy, and Bruce surround them. I turn back to the front of the line and nod to the security guard. Kyle is handing out the pictures as they come through in groups of five and the band begins signing their lives away.

About ten minutes later Talon shouts in my direction. "Yeah?" I shout back.

"Come here."

I want to roll my eyes, but I don't. I go stand next to him and lean into his ear. "What, lover?" I watch his smile widen.

"Have you worked out your autograph hand?"

"No, why?" I ask as I look up in to the face of a girl, who reminds me a lot of me when I was a teenager.

"Addison, can I have your autograph?" the girl asks me.

I smile. "Absolutely."

After that I somehow find myself joining the band and signing autographs for the fans that ask. I start off sitting on Talon's lap until someone finally brings me a chair and then I sit between Peacock and Talon. I'm technically not a member of the band so I don't sign their publicity photo, but I spend the next two hours signing whatever else the fans have for me to sign. Occasionally I look over at Kyle and he smiles widely at me, giving me encouragement to keep going.

All one thousand of the publicity photos have been given out and the crowd still hasn't died down. The band has signed every last one of them. I feel so bad that I started massaging Peacock's hand at one point because it was cramping up. After two hours all of our signatures look like chicken scratch and our time is running out before we must leave for Chicago.

"Make an announcement," Talon whispers to me between fans.

"About what?"

"We'll walk the rails. Sign their books, pictures, whatever."

"No, just do it. Don't announce it. The sight will create a rush of people to the rails. Sign the ones in the hallway on the way out the door, nothing more. They'll get another chance, someday." I smile at him. He wants so badly to please them all. "Talon, we don't have time to sign for everyone. Maybe someday we can do a longer signing here, but for today we have an hour to get out of this building and back on the bus."

"Okay," he says sadly.

'Don't be sad. Be proud. One day you will be running out the door the minute it's over." I wink and he nods.

He stands up and takes the microphone from its stand. "Ladies and gentlemen." The crowd finds it in themselves to scream louder. "I just want to say what an honor it has been being here tonight. On behalf of myself, Dex, Peacock and Mouse, thank you from the bottom of our hearts. I'd also like to thank Kyle Black and Addison Beltrand for being amazing at what they do." The crowd cheers and is still cheering when we all leave the stage.

Talon starts signing autographs along the barriers; Peacock stays with him while Dex and Mouse go to the other side of the hallway. Amidst their signing, they're calling for me. I oblige those that ask and sign a few on my way out the door too.

chapter 5

Troy picked up dinner for all of us from one of the restaurants in the mall and we spend the first hour or so on the road enjoying our dinner. It was nice to come back to food. I didn't realize how hungry I was until I started eating. I'd ordered a salad and then ended up eating Talon's french fries too. He laughed when I kept taking them but then he and Kyle continued to hand feed them to me.

At least I was stuffed when I was done. I wished I'd ordered a burger, but a girl's gotta watch her figure, right?

When we were done eating I hung back, waiting to see if Peacock wanted to talk, but he said that another night would be better, he's tired and wants to crash. After dinner, Dex and Peacock headed to their bunks for the night. Mouse lowered the table and strummed his guitar while Talon, Kyle and I squeezed onto the couch behind the driver to watch Mouse play. Talon and Mouse talked quietly about the different songs that Mouse played for us. I didn't recognize any of the songs, but the music was hypnotic and it wasn't long before my eyes grew heavy and I fell asleep with my head on Kyle's lap and my feet in Talon's.

Sometime later I wake up to the guys quietly arguing over who is going to carry me to bed. Kyle ends up escorting me toward the bedroom while Talon stays behind to hang with Mouse. I notice Tori's curtain open as we pass and see that she's sitting up on the bed reading. "Thanks for tonight," I tell her as I lean against the wall of her bunk.

"You're welcome. I've never seen a crowd like that, well, just this one time at Comic Con." She smirks at the memory. "It was actually pretty fun."

"Good, did you eat?"

She looks at me. "I did. Thanks."

"You a heavy reader?"

She laughs, "Yeah, I read all the time. Especially in situations like this when I'm left to my own devices a lot."

I laugh, "Ironically, I've read less since getting on this bus than I have in years. What are you reading?"

She laughs. "It's a rock star romance."

"Oh my god." I burst out laughing.

"I'm a sucker for a happy ending, but I don't like where this one is going. It seems the chick is going to end up with the bodyguard."

"I think I've read that one. I was rooting for the lead singer."

She snorts and I hear Kyle snicker. I forgot he was behind me. "You good, baby girl?" he asks and I nod. "Okay, don't be too long." He kisses my forehead and ducks into the bedroom, but he doesn't close the door.

I turn back to Tori. "Everybody loves a bad boy," I say with a smirk.

She laughs again. "You can say that again."

"Well, I'll let you get back to it. I'm going to bed."

"Hey, I've been meaning to ask you about this morning."

"Thank you by the way."

She nods. "How'd it turn out?" she asks sheepishly, like she shouldn't be asking.

I shrug. "Not sure yet. Going to wait until Friday and try again."

"Keep me posted, okay?"

"Are you asking personally, or professionally?"

She gives me a half smile. "Both."

"You'll be one of the first I tell." I wink and bid her good night.

Before I go into the bedroom, I hear Mouse and Talon both playing and Talon's super sexy voice is wafting quietly through the bus. I know that Peacock and Dex sleep with ear buds in, usually watching a movie, so the playing won't bother them. I love listening to Talon, and adding Mouse into the mix is quite awesome too. It takes everything I have not to go back to the kitchen just to watch and listen.

Exhaustion wins out and I go into the bedroom. Kyle is lying on his side of the bed; his iPad in his hand and lying on my pillow is my e-reader. I smile because he was listening. I strip out of my outfit, which is really comfortable. I ditched the shoes as soon as we were on the bus though. Nothing like heels and a moving vehicle. "You read my mind," I say softly as I climb into bed. "Thank you." I lean over, kissing him gently. A display of appreciation and it stays exactly that.

"A penny for your thoughts?" I ask as I snuggle into him. He wraps his arm around me as I lay my head in the crook of his shoulder, slide my hand across his stomach and hitch my leg on his. I look up at his iPad and am surprised by what I see. He's looking at pictures of Talon and me that are popping up from tonight.

"I'm just thinking about how lucky I am."

"Then why do you look so sad?"

"Scared."

I lift my head to look at him. He puts the iPad down and his blue eyes meet mine. "About what, cowboy?"

He doesn't say anything to me. The hand that was holding his iPad moves between us and his fingers rub along my stomach. I want to cry. Not sure if it's a happy or sad thing. "One minute, I want it to be, the next I start thinking about my mom and the way that she is, what happened with my dad, Dan. It scares me because of what happened in Dallas, Kansas City, how to protect you, how to…god, there's just so much."

"I wish I could take your worries away, and maybe I can, we just don't know yet. Until we know one way or the other, all the worry is for nothing. I'm scared too, but in truth, I'm more scared about you and Talon, and how you're both going to handle this."

He brings his arms around me, rolling onto his side. I bury my head in his chest and he holds me, rubbing my back. "God, baby girl, I didn't…god, I'm being selfish right now, I'm so sorry."

"Stop, you're not being selfish. I guess for me, I can't freak out until I know for sure, which means my period shows up or a doctor tells me. A test, sure, that will help put me in the right mind frame, but with my issues, I am so worried about everything but what will happen in nine months." I tell him into his chest.

"I guess I just don't understand what your issues are, which was what I was actually reading when you came in. I changed it because I didn't know how you'd handle it," he whispers.

"Show me what you were looking at," I tell him. "I'd like to help you understand."

We spend the next twenty minutes or so looking at the website he's on. He raises questions and I answer them as best as I can. I think by the time we're done he understands because he asks me if it hurts me and I explain to him that I get occasional sharp pains, but they don't last and that the primary issue is my hormone levels and it's the reason for the birth control.

After that we snuggle into each other and I fall asleep wrapped in his arms.

Sometime later, I don't know when, Talon comes crawling into bed. His waking me sends me to the bathroom. When I crawl back into bed I realize it's after one in the morning.

Talon's arms are waiting for me and I snuggle into him. Kyle quickly snuggles behind me. "Did you guys have fun?" I ask as I get comfortable.

"We had a great time. We finished out a couple of songs and started in on a couple more."

"That's awesome," I tell him.

"Thanks, angel," he says and before long I fall right back to sleep.

"Addie?"

"Hmm…"

"Are you coming with us to the station?" It's Kyle.

"What?"

"The radio station, are you coming?" I groan. He chuckles. "Stay in bed, panda girl. It's okay."

"No, I have to, I need to work."

"No, baby girl, you don't. We got this, I promise. We do it all the time."

"Alright," I groan.

"Sleep, baby girl." He kisses my forehead and before he even leaves the room, I'm right back to sleep.

chapter 6

Chicago's concert goes perfectly. The crowd was unbelievable. The band went out after the show. I practically had to push Talon off of the bus. He wanted me to come with, but I told him that he needed to spend some time with his band, which is something he hasn't done enough of.

By Thursday morning we're on the road to Cincinnati and a hotel for a couple of days. The owner of the venue we're playing added another show, Sunday night, and provided us with hotel rooms. Which is great because I don't want to be on the bus on Friday.

Fatigue seems to be a growing issue with me lately and I'm starting to mentally convince myself that I'm pregnant. Too many signs are starting to fit together.

I tried to talk to Peacock again and he said he wasn't ready.

Sam finally called me Thursday. We talked for a few minutes, but I could tell she was itching to ask me about Dex and I let her go. I accepted her apology for the issue back in Phoenix but I don't think she fully understands what she did wrong. She also told me that she wasn't going to be moving in with me. That, apparently, she and bitch-face had a heart to heart and they're better. She's actually been staying at her apartment more and mine less, which is great because I don't want to have to throw her out. I wonder idly if she really did work things out with her roommate or if she understands the gravity of what happened, and knows that I would still push her to stay with me if things are really bad there.

Talon spends a lot more time with Mouse and the guys. They're putting themselves knee deep into writing for the new album, leaving a spot for 'To Be Free'. I'm proud of him for stepping into his band role and out of our bed, though the bedroom activities haven't faltered in the slightest.

Talon being with the band is giving Kyle and I a lot of time together just the two of us. During our time together I realize that we're able to talk about anything, though we haven't had any more baby talk since Tuesday night. But I can tell there is something going on with him and I don't know if it has to do with tomorrow morning or if it's something else.

We spend our days and evenings doing our thing, but when the sun goes down, I'm all theirs. Despite my growing fatigue, I can't resist these two no matter how hard I try.

When we arrive at the hotel in Cincinnati, I'm wired for some strange reason. Once again they haul off all of my clothes and once we're upstairs I start going through them. Picking what I want to keep. My garment bag has doubled in thickness with the outfits from the guys in Minnesota and because they're great show outfits, I decide to keep them with me. We'll also be spending quite a bit of time in Philly next week, then a night in Boston and finally on to New York for two weeks.

The PR work for the band has been minimal. They're keeping their noses clean and the headlines regarding me are dying down. Cami continues working with Bryan Hayes' people on the duet and more than a few artists have come out of the woodwork seeking my voice. Which is awesome. Cami has kept her promise about not asking me about what I want to do until after the tour, which I still don't know. Everything seems so uncertain right now.

By the time dinner arrives in the suite, I've gone through my clothes, packed up three boxes to ship back to LA, and reorganized everything. Despite sending back three boxes, I'm still using all of my suitcases, but one of the suitcases has clothes specifically for New York and can go under the bus.

Talon, Kyle and I sit down around the table in our suite to eat. The table is loaded with comfort food. Talon has spaghetti and meatballs. Kyle has peanut butter and jelly sandwiches, like four of them, plus a massive bowl of french fries to be eaten by all and I have good ol' macaroni and cheese.

"Did you finish with your clothes?" Kyle asks as we start eating.

"I did. I have three boxes to send back to LA. One suitcase, my old one, has stuff for New York in it, so it can go under the bus, and then I've put everything else in my new suitcases and the garment bag, along with my purse and messenger bag."

We go back to eating in a comfortable silence that quickly grows uncomfortable. "What's on your mind, guys?" I ask them about halfway through the meal.

Neither one of them says anything; they just keep eating for a couple more bites. "Oh come on, out with it. You're making me crazy."

They both laugh nervously. Then Talon looks at me and asks, "We were wondering if you'd want to take the test tonight?"

"It says that first morning pee is best."

"So you could take one tonight and get a different result tomorrow?" Kyle asks.

I shrug. "I don't know, just going by what the box says. We have like, eight of them, so yeah, I guess I could, but why the rush?"

"I have to leave at five tomorrow morning for the radio spot. I don't know for sure when we will be back. I don't want you to take it alone, if Kyle comes with us, and I don't want you to have to wait until we get back. And neither one of us wants you to take it and then we have to run off to the radio station."

"But even if it comes back negative tonight, I'll still be taking one in the morning to be sure. Well, either way I'll take one again, so I don't see why not." I shrug and take another bite of my mac 'n cheese. Deep down, I know what it's going to say and my not wanting to take one is rather selfish. I'm afraid that if I take it and it's positive, it's either going to go really well, or it is going to go badly and I'll end up sleeping alone. At least in the morning, they'd have all day to get used to the idea.

"Did we have plans tonight?" I ask as we're finishing eating. We've all eaten nearly everything, though I feel like I'm in a carb coma between the pasta and the french fries, but I don't really care.

"No, we just wanted to spend the night with you," Kyle says with a small smile. "Which is why the comfort food. We figured it would be a great pajama and movie night."

"I think that's a great idea. But I'd really like to take a bath."

They both perk up a little at that suggestion. The master bedroom has a nearly full size Jacuzzi style tub in it. More than big enough for the three of us to fit. I push back from the table and stand up. "Where you going, panda girl?"

I give him a small smile. "I have to pee. I'm going to start the tub, and then I'll take the test and climb into the tub. I will leave it on the counter until you guys come in and join me. I will cover it up, so it will be your choice to look or not look before getting in the tub, sound fair?"

They both nod, hesitantly. I put a hand on each of their cheeks. "Look at me, both of you." They both look up at me and I can tell that they're nervous. Not so much as they were on Tuesday, but it's still there. "The result changes nothing between us," I whisper. "Promise me? No matter what, it changes nothing."

Talon and Kyle both turn their heads to kiss my palms. "I promise." Talon is the first to answer. I give him a small smile.

"I promise," Kyle breathes.

"Come in when you're ready," I say and leave them there. I go into the master bedroom, stripping off my t-shirt and jeans as I go. Finally shedding my socks and stepping into the large bathroom. I go straight for the tub. Turning it on, I test the water and let it start to fill up. There are two faucets pouring into it, so it won't take long to fill up. It has jets and warmers and all that kind of stuff but I leave that alone for now.

I go for the bag with all the other tests that Tori bought and pull out another digital one. Which is what most of them are. I open it and sit down. My heart is pounding and I have stage fright momentarily. Fear, excitement, nerves, anxiety, all of it running through my veins as I'm finally able to go. When I'm done, I put the cap back on, set it on the counter, and take one of the washcloths off of the shelf. I throw it over as the hourglass continues to blink. I grab another washcloth, along with my body wash and walk toward the tub. I slink down into it. Soaking up the warmth, letting it engulf me, comfort me. I shiver with chills as I sit there looking at the counter like a big neon sign is going to pop up in front of me when the test is done. But of course, nothing happens.

Not until ten minutes later when both Talon and Kyle walk into the bathroom, naked. I watch as Talon reaches for the test under the washcloth, but he picks up both, keeping the test covered. Looking at me, his eyes are haunted when he tells me, "We look together. We're in this together." As he and Kyle step into the tub, Talon sets the test down in the corner.

chapter 7

Kyle takes me in his arms and I wrap my legs around him. His cock is hard and heavy, pressed between us. Talon slides up behind me. I am completely and totally surrounded by my men. Talon's legs are over Kyle's and I can feel his erection pressing against the small of my back and it turns me on to no end to know that regardless of what's looming on the edge of the bathtub, these two are still so turned on by me that they're hard as stone.

I lift myself on Kyle. Reaching between us, I position the head of his cock inside of me and I moan with pure pleasure as I slide down on him. Talon's lips are kissing my shoulder, his hands are sliding along my hips, up my ribs and around to my breasts. His touch is hot, but they're tender. Kyle's mouth takes mine. We're not moving; we're just being, connected in our most intimate places.

I can feel him twitch and my muscles contract around him. Talon's fingers continue milking my nipples, tugging and stretching them. I writhe against Kyle and he pulls back from our kiss with a hiss. Talon begins kissing my neck, up behind my ear. I can feel him nudging me to move. I turn and he takes my mouth with his. His hands haven't stopped moving and I can tell from his kiss that he's eager.

I flick my hips against Kyle who is now caressing Talon's cheek as he continues kissing me. Kyle's hand slips down Talon's neck and disappears. Talon groans and I can feel Kyle stroking on his cock. Desire ignites and I start to move against Kyle, with each stoke of Talon's cock I grind down. I can feel Kyle's cock buried deep and my pussy clenches around him. Talon releases my lips as my orgasm begins to build hard. Talon pulls his hands away from my nipples and then he reaches for Kyle's cheek.

Talon urges him forward and quickly claims his mouth. Watching them kiss brings my orgasm closer. I move harder and faster against Kyle and his hand moves faster against Talon's shaft. I can feel all the muscles surrounding me and inside of me tighten. I'm the first to go as I grind harder and faster against Kyle's cock. My orgasm explodes, my body trembles. I'm barely coherent enough to hear and feel both my men explode. Kyle erupts inside of me. Talon releases into Kyle's hand.

There is a hum and ripple across the water that pulls me out of my post orgasmic haze. "What's that?" I mumble.

I feel Kyle chuckle against me. His cock, still inside me twitches and I moan. "That's the filtering system."

"Oh," I say and open my eyes. Neither of them has moved much. We all wear the same glossy eyed looks. I slowly slide up, off of Kyle and he pouts.

"He likes being in there."

I laugh and cup his cheek. "I love having him in there."

He kisses me chastely. "I love you," he breathes. Once I'm clear of Kyle, they both back away, giving me a little bit more room to sit on the bench. My orgasm has me relaxed, but it doesn't last when my eyes fall to the covered test on the corner of the tub.

"How are we going to do this?" I say as I pull my knees up, wrapping my arms around them, holding them to me.

Both my guys turn toward me, their knees touching my butt, reiterating their need to be touching me. "How do you want to do this, angel?"

"Hand it to me, covered with the washcloth. We can all watch as I uncover it."

"Okay, baby girl."

I shiver, chills running through me again, but I'm not cold. I'm freaking out. Neither guy moves. They're both looking at me. "What's wrong, angel?"

I put my head back on the side of the tub. "I'm scared, I'm freaking out, I'm anxious, I'm ten thousand and one things all at once. I want to get it over with but I'm afraid to look. I'm afraid of what you guys are going to do. How you're going to react."

"I can tell you how I will react," Kyle says quietly. "It doesn't matter. I am going to hug you, and kiss you, and hold you regardless of what it says." Kyle sounds positive that this will be his reaction, but I can hear the fear in his voice. A fear that is either of the unknown or of what we've talked about regarding his past.

"That is if he can beat me to it," Talon says quietly but there is a lightness in his voice that I didn't expect. "What are you going to do?" Talon asks me.

"I'm going to cry." Like it was waiting for me to say it, a tear slides down my cheek.

It's on Talon's side so he wipes it away. "Let's do this," I breathe, fighting the emotional rush coursing through me and trying to keep my voice strong. Talon reaches for the test. He brings it over to me and I reach for it with a very shaky hand.

I notice that Talon's hand is steady. Kyle reaches behind the washcloth, grabbing the test itself. "Pull off the cloth when you're ready, baby girl."

I take a shuddering breath as another tear streaks down my cheek. I feel like I'm ready to explode, I reach up, pulling on the cloth and Talon lets go. I close my eyes.

All I hear are shocked hisses from the two men who love me. I start crying. I have a feeling that love is about to be tested.

"Angel?"

"Baby girl?"

"I can't. I can't look," I sob. Neither one of them say anything to me. I just feel them stand, the water sloshing and shifting around. I start crying harder. I hear the drains kick open and the gurgling of water as it escapes its confines. The water settles as they both step out.

"Grab a towel," I hear Kyle say to Talon.

The water drains out quickly and I start to shiver. A towel is thrown down on the bottom of the tub. Then I hear the tub creak with feet and arms sliding under my knees, forcing my arms to let go. I do and an arm comes around my back and I am lifted from the tub. I feel a kiss against my forehead and I know its Kyle. His mustache is trimmed tight, where Talon's is scruffy. I lean into his chest. The tears are still flowing.

I am walked into the bedroom and then laid out on the bed, on a towel. Immediately there are towels drying me off gently. I can't stop crying and I don't know the answer to the million-dollar question.

Once I'm dried off, I hear the towels hit the floor and the bed dips as they climb into bed with me. That's when I am given my answer.

chapter 8

Gentle hands, four of them are pressed gently against my lower abdomen. Just above my pelvic bone. The hands are met with gentle kisses. "Oh god," I sob. My whole body is shaking with fear. I put my hands over my face and try to turn over, but gentle hands stop me.

The hands come away and I am showered with more kisses along my stomach. The kisses quickly turn heated and open mouthed. Talon begins kissing north toward my breasts, and Kyle slides south, past my smooth mound. "Let us show you how we feel about you," Talon murmurs against my breast. His tongue slides warm and wet across my nipple at the same time Kyle's tongue meets my clit with a similar lick. I shiver and sob.

"I can't..." I manage to get out. They don't stop and I quake again. "No, please, stop," I sob. "Please, just hold me." I cry harder.

"Okay, angel. Okay, shhh, we're here." With mouths and hands gone, I roll over onto my side. Talon gently wraps his arms around me from behind. His hand comes to rest on my stomach and I cry harder.

Kyle lies down in front of me and he pulls my hands away from my face. "Come on, baby girl, hold me," he whispers softly and I let my hand slide across his stomach, once I reach the other side, I tug, asking him to roll toward me and he does. I bury my face in his chest and I let loose. Holding my two beautiful men.

I'm pregnant. I'm pregnant because of my stupid birth control, I'm pregnant because, damn it, I screwed up, this is all my fault. I was careless, I was…I sob harder. God, what they must be thinking right now. We've only been together a few weeks, a few weeks of pure bliss, absolute heaven, and now their woman is pregnant. I'm pregnant.

"Baby girl. You need to calm down." Both Kyle and Talon's hands begin gently massaging my skin. Kyle's hand on my back, Talon's on the front. "Breathe, baby."

"Angel, we want you to calm down. This isn't good."

God, I feel like throwing up. "Addison, look at me," Kyle says softly. "Come on, baby girl." I feel his hand move and touch my chin. "I need to see those gorgeous green eyes, can I see them?"

I lift my head until I know I can see his eyes, but I can't open them. "I'm so scared," I breathe.

"Look at me, baby girl. Look at me so you can see the smile on my face. Look at me so that you can know that we love you. Come on, baby girl."

"Please angel, we need you, we need to see you," Talon pleads.

I begin to bat my eyes, working out the tears that are lingering. I know I haven't seen the end of them, but I need to try and be strong. My guys need me. Damn it, Addie, open your eyes.

When I finally get them to open, I can see Kyle with a beautiful smile on his face. "Hi panda girl."

"Hi," I croak out, emotion choking my throat.

Talon slides back slightly and I roll onto my back.

"Hi, angel." Talon's smile mimics Kyle's

"Hi, big man." I look at Kyle. "Cowboy?"

"What, baby girl?"

"Are you really okay?" I ask him.

He smiles and gently rubs his hand over my stomach and I shiver. "Right now, yes."

I fight back the tears that threaten me again. I look to Talon. "Are you?" I ask.

He responds by touching my belly and interlocking his fingers with Kyle's. I start crying again, this time the fear is finally replaced with tears of happiness.

The guys stick to their word and we have a cuddling movie night. Though they're both in pajama bottoms without shirts, I am snuggled into one of Talon's t-shirts and nothing else. I wanted to complain about that, until I understood why they didn't want pants on me. They held me with gentle hands on my stomach and I was extremely comforted by that fact. I was also comforted by the fact that we didn't talk about it anymore. We were just us.

I fell asleep about halfway through the second movie, I couldn't tell you what it was, but I wasn't that interested in it. The guys got more excited about it than I did. But considering we ended up watching some romantic comedy movie first, I didn't complain.

When I wake up both of them are gone. Talon and the band have a radio spot this morning and I think Kyle probably forced himself to go. I do what I said yesterday and take another test. I've heard of false positives and negatives before, so I figure what can it hurt? After I do that business, I climb into the shower and I notice once again that my breasts are tender and feel heavy, and though they don't appear to have grown any, they feel like they have.

Once I'm out of the shower I look at the test, expecting the same result and since I didn't actually see the first one, I want to see this one for myself. It says 'pregnant' on the digital display and I cry again, but this time, it's not so bad.

It's after eleven when I get a text from Kyle

Kyle: Hi b-g (baby girl) Radio spot went great, How are you doing? Feeling? We will be back in a little while, making a couple stops. X

Me: Hi Cowboy - I'm well, I don't know actually, still in shock I think, but feeling so so, still tired, been up since 9. Have fun, c u soon XO

Kyle: I love your kisses. I love you. XXX

Me: I love you. Tell T- Hi, give him a kiss from me.

Kyle: will do baby girl, relax, order lunch. See you in a bit.

Kyle: wait, don't order lunch, we're bringing you lunch. C U soon.

I laugh. He honestly seems okay about all this, at least for right now. Ironically, I would have thought Talon would have been the one to break down and lose it, but I'll take it at this point. I know that if anyone freaks out, the other is going to pick up the pieces.

I spend my time in bed, waiting for the guys to come home. But I'm not idle. I get to work on a couple of press releases for the week we're in New York. With the recording of 'Your Eyes', the duet version, and 'To Be Free', the label wants an announcement to be made from 69 Bottles. No problem, I got this. I smile to myself.

When I'm done with that, I send it off to Cami for proofing and approving, since we actually have time for this press release and I'm not working up a scandal piece.

Cami's emails haven't stopped flowing with a wealth of information regarding the Bryan Hayes duet. I finally break down and ask her how the label offers are coming. Her response is pure Cami style.

Giirrrll, let me tell you. I've not been in this business very long, but what is happening right now is beyond anything Trinity or Vinnie have EVER seen! We're actually checking the label offers against the labels we don't have offers from because, well, that will take a lot less time. Some of the more lucrative ones we're negotiating further, hoping for the best contract and the best financial outcome for you. Also with the best schedules for you. Some labels are pushing for albums and tours before the year's end. That's extreme and not something we're willing to subject you to.

So how are you? How are the guys doing? How's the tour? Where are you now, Cincy or Philly? I've lost track, though I'm sure at some point a headline will pop up.

BY THE WAY!! EXCELLENT job at Mall of America on Tuesday. Social media was abuzz with it for most of Wednesday, speaking of which, you need to tweet more. Oh and I heard the radio spot this morning - inter webs, what a beautiful thing - Talon sounds great, happy even. What have you done to that boy? How's Kyle?

Okay duty calls, I gotta go. We'll chat soon.

Cami's email sends a turmoil of emotions through me. An album and tour by the end of the year? No way. That gets me thinking about all things baby. I open a Safari window and go to Google, typing in 'due date..." Google does its thing and completes 'calculator'. I click on it and the first site that pops up is a website called BabyCenter. I click it as I pull my paper planner from my messenger bag and take a look. Then I put the date in.

December 10th is what it says my due date is, I scroll down and it tells me... March 19th, date of conception. I look back at my planner. My eyes grow wide. "Albuquerque, New Mexico... OhMyGOD!" I growl to no one because I'm the only one here. That was Talon's comment about...Oh for fuck's sake. The irony can't even begin to be explained. The night that he brought up my nipples, breasts and the unspoken thought of getting me pregnant. Jeez, could there have been a bigger sign?

I quickly become addicted to reading about what's going to happen to me and my body, and what's going to happen with the baby. I'm barely four weeks along. When I read through the symptom checker I'm surprised by how much I'm feeling already. When you do that, everything seems to become a symptom. I also come to the conclusion that my fatigue is only the beginning. I yawn, adding to the issues with my being tired. All I've done is shower, get dressed and then sit my ass on the bed looking at the computer and I'm ready for a nap.

chapter 9

After I'm finally able to pull myself away from all things baby related, I log into Twitter. My followers have grown substantially and it makes me smile. I read through some of the @ Mentions and see a lot from Minneapolis and the Mall of America event. Many of which have pictures attached from the signing. Most are of Talon and myself side by side and everything is positive. Which, in my experience, is a first. There are some mentions of Chicago and then some of the upcoming shows in Cincinnati.

About the time the tickets for the second show went on sale is when my videos started going viral, so I wonder how many of those tickets were bought because of that? I don't really care, all I know is that the second show sold out faster than the first one did. It makes me smile.

I have, surprisingly, several celebrities tweeting about me and my videos. Some actors and others musicians. When I click on a lot of their names, many of them are following me, so I start to follow them back.

I decide to Tweet… "Hanging out in Cincy, Ready for Saturday night's show." It is immediately retweeted dozens of times, and more mentions come in, 'can't wait to see you on stage', 'can't wait to meet you', and a lot of 'I'm so bummed I didn't get tickets.' It's pretty cool to see people interacting with me.

I play around on social media a little bit more, then turn to my Kindle and start looking at books. There are countless pregnancy books in digital format, the one book I want, 'What to Expect When You're Expecting' I want in actual book form. I want to be able to share it with the guys easier and it would probably be better as an iBook, bigger and more interactive.

"Addie?" I hear Kyle shout from the sitting room of the suite.

"In the bedroom," I holler back and look over at the clock, it's about two.

"Okay good, stay there," I hear him holler back.

I raise an eyebrow in confusion, but I do as I'm told and wait, impatiently, for them to do whatever they're doing. I close up my laptop and put it, along with my planner and iPad back into my messenger bag. I can smell something, but I can't quite put my finger on what it is. Then Kyle comes bounding around the corner to the double doors of the bedroom. "Hello gorgeous," he says in a salacious tone. "We have a surprise for you. How are you feeling?" he asks as he comes to sit on the bed next to me.

"Pretty good. Hungry and tired, but good."

He smiles. "Well, come on then, we can solve the hungry problem." He stands up and holds out his hand for me to take, I do and slide off the large bed.

When I stand up I get dizzy and have to sit back down. "Whoa, baby girl, what's wrong?" he says softly as he kneels in front me.

"I just stood up too fast. I'm alright."

"Come on, you need to eat," he chastises softly. "No more of these long periods between meals, okay?"

I nod and he stands again. Helping me up. This time I don't get dizzy or fall over. He escorts me to the sitting room. As we round the corner my nose is assaulted with something delicious. "What is that?" I ask.

"What you come to Cincinnati for."

I look at him, then we come around the corner and there are three cups and three large bowls sitting on the table. One of the cups is facing this way and it says "Skyline Chili" on it. "Oh my god, you didn't?"

They both laugh. "We did. Come, eat, angel," Talon says and I take a seat.

"Have you had Skyline before?" Kyle asks as he sits.

"Once, a very long time ago. It was amazing." I take a deep inhale through my nose and am assaulted with spices and deliciousness.

"We just got you the cheese, hope that's okay?" Kyle says.

"Mmm, that's perfect." We dive into eating and it is the most delicious thing I've had in a long time.

Neither one of the guys say anything as I eat my way through the massive amount of food in front of me. Before you go getting all 'piggy piggy' on me, I don't eat it all. I lean back in my chair and put my hand on my stomach. It's distended from the amount of food I just consumed. "That was amazing. Thank you both," I say softly.

"You're welcome." I notice now that I've consumed more than them. I've always been a big eater but it took me nearly three days to finish off the bowl the last time I had it.

"We have more for you," Talon says with a smile.

"Okay?" I say hesitantly.

He lifts up a gift bag from beside his chair. "We thought maybe you could use a new book to read." Kyle smiles and Talon hands me the bag. I start wracking my brain for any new books that have come out recently.

I pull the tissue paper out of the bag and reach in. I pull out three different books wrapped individually in more tissue paper and set the bag down on the floor and the books on the table. I reach for the first one. "Wait." Talon stops me and he takes the book from me. "Start with this one," he says and it's a thick book, but not overly heavy and when I unwrap it I'm shocked to see the exact book I wanted in paperback about an hour ago. 'What to Expect When You're Expecting'. "We thought maybe you'd like to read up on what's going to happen to you over the next nine months," Talon says with a smile.

"Thank you, I was just looking at this on my Kindle and thought I'd rather have it in paperback, but Talon?"

"Yes, angel?"

"You didn't buy this, did you?"

He smiles wildly. "I wanted to, but Kyle talked me out of it and he did it while I left the book store."

I smile. "Good, because we can't tell anyone yet, okay?"

"Why?" Talon asks.

"Because, most people wait until fourteen weeks to tell people, I'm only four weeks into this thing. And they say it's bad luck to tell too many people too soon."

"Okay," he says somberly.

"You want to shout it from the roof, don't you?" I ask him with a smile. He nods. "You can, soon, just not right now." I wink at him.

"You should have seen him in the store. You're lucky you only got three books. He was ready to buy them all."

"Oh jeez, I'd never have been able to read them all." I laugh.

"I know, that's why you only have three," Talon says, gesturing for me to pick up the next book, and I do. Unwrapping it I find a pregnancy journal. I flip through it and it has week-by-week sections for diet, feelings, and health trackers etcetera.

"Okay, this is awesome," I say with a big bright smile.

"That was all Kyle," Talon says with reverence. "He thought you'd like to track what you eat and do, and keep track of all the changes."

I look at Kyle. "Thank you, cowboy." He blushes slightly.

"The next one though, is *all* Talon," Kyle says with a smirk.

I unwrap the book and bust out laughing. "We don't need any help in this department," I tease as I read the cover of 'Kama Sutra for Pregnant Couples.'

They both laugh with me. "I know, but I thought it might be fun," Talon says with a bright smile on his face.

"Well, it's is a definite possibility, only problem is there are three of us."

Talon laughs a little harder. "No, that just means we can try two a night."

"Oh my god!" I squeal. "You're so bad." I sober up a little bit. "But seriously, thank you, guys," I say as I take both of their hands in mine.

"Anything," Kyle says.

"Anytime," Talon adds.

My heart swells to the point of explosion as these two look at me with all the love I know they feel.

The rest of Friday is spent with me being pampered by the two of them with a bath and dinner. No fighting, just talking. We talk about the stuff I read on the internet, I tell them about the estimated due date and they're both excited. I also go on to tell them about Cami's emails and all of the social media stuff over the last couple of days. We eventually curl up for another movie that I don't make it twenty minutes into before dozing off.

chapter 10

I'm awoken Saturday morning with severe nausea. I quickly climb out of bed, but I'm not quiet or careful about it, and as I'm bolting into the bathroom I hear both guys calling my name.

I grab my hair, pulling it back just as I vomit spectacularly straight into the toilet. "Baby girl?" I hear Kyle, but I can't look away. He crouches down next to me and starts rubbing my back. I wonder idly why, now that I know I'm pregnant, I suddenly vomit the next day. Then I remember the nausea I've had.

"Angel?" Talon calls as he comes into the bathroom.

"Go away. You guys don't need to watch this," I manage to get out between heaves.

Talon comes to kneel on the other side of me, replacing my hand in my hair with his while Kyle continues rubbing my back. "I'm alright," I say through a couple more heaves.

When I'm finally done, I reach up and flush the toilet and put the seat down. I sit rather clumsily on the lid with my head in my hands. Both of their hands are resting on my thighs. "I just need a minute." I was woken up so abruptly but it's taken until now for my body to catch up.

"What can we do, baby girl?"

"Toothbrush and a bath," I say and Kyle stands, walking toward the tub and then the water starts running. Talon doesn't leave my side while Kyle sets about drawing my bath. Neither one of them say anything to me, which is okay. I don't know what to tell them and I'm certain they don't know what to say. "I feel better." Which isn't a lie. Once I was done retching it was almost instant relief.

"That's a good thing, right?" Kyle asks as he comes to stand next to me. I look up at him and he's naked, and for the first time, he's not hard and it makes me sad to see it. I glance back down and Talon, naked also, is soft.

"It's a good thing," I mumble. "What did I eat last night?"

"You had that bar-b-que chicken wrap thing and french fries," Kyle tells me and I start to remember.

"Do we need to get you to the doctor?" Talon asks.

I shake my head. "No, I'm pretty sure this is morning sickness. I'm alright, I just need to relax for a few minutes. Drink some water and with any luck, go back to sleep."

"You got it, angel." Talon stands, holding his hands out for me to take them. I move slowly, afraid I'm going to make myself dizzy again. Both of them escort me to the tub and help me step in. I pull my t-shirt over my head and I hear hisses from both of them as they take in my nakedness.

I sit down gingerly in the tub and look back at both of them. What was once soft is now getting hard and I am comforted by the fact that my body still turns them on. Though there are no visible signs of pregnancy, they know what's inside. I move past their cocks to their faces, both eager. "Come on," I say quietly and they both step in.

Talon turns me, pressing my back to his front. Kyle looks at me, desperation to be held is playing in his eyes, but I can see worry. "It's alright, I won't break," I reassure him and he turns, leaning against me. I put my head back on Talon's shoulder and Kyle puts his head back on mine. I wrap my arms and legs around him, holding him to me. I soak up the warmth of the water and their bodies.

I can tell that Talon is hard as stone, pressing against my back, but there is nothing sexual charging the air.

When we climb out of the tub, I am quickly dried off, and I brush my teeth to get rid of the taste in my mouth before a clean t-shirt is pulled over my head. It's one of Kyle's. I can tell because it's smaller. Talon's shirts fall onto my thighs whereas Kyle's, though still big on me, barely covers my sex.

The brushing of the t-shirt against my nipples makes them harden and ache. "Take the shirt off, please," I groan. "It hurts."

Kyle goes for the hem and pulls it over my head. "What hurts, baby girl?"

I want to cry, not because of the pain but because this is only the beginning of what's to come. I'd felt the heaviness in my breasts a few days ago and brushed off the soreness caused by Talon's all too eager mouth and fingers, but now reality sets in. "My nipples," I whisper, hoping to avoid giving away the flood of reality running through me.

"What can we do?" Talon asks.

"Put me to bed. Cuddle with me," I whisper back, still not trusting my voice.

They lead me into the bedroom and lay me down first. I roll towards Kyle's side and Talon slides in behind me, then Kyle lies down gently.

After about ten minutes of cuddling I've finally mustered up the courage to ask a question that's been bugging me for two days now. "Why won't you touch me?"

I can feel them both stiffen around me. "We touch you all the time," Kyle says stiffly as his hand rubs along my stomach.

"That's not what I mean, and you both know it. You haven't touched me since Thursday night and that was with a test we hadn't seen. Since then, nothing. Do I turn you off now?" The tears threaten to spill over and I don't care, I let them go.

Kyle turns to face me. Putting my face in his hands, his thumbs wipe away the tears. "We don't want to hurt you," he explains.

Frustration boils to the point of explosion. "I'm no different than I was on Thursday before we took that test."

"It's just, its different now," Talon says behind me. I try to turn and Kyle releases my face.

"Why, because instead of wondering, which was okay, you know the truth and despite everything you've done and said, it's all of a sudden not? That doesn't make any sense."

I sit up, a little too fast, but I recover quickly and slide out from under the covers, crawling to the end of the bed before I slide off. "Nothing's changed, nothing will change, that's what you both told me and now... now it seems as though it has."

"Angel, please, calm down."

"No Talon, I won't. I need to understand why all of sudden I'm no longer attractive to you, why you don't touch me."

"Does this look un-attracted?" Kyle says as he pushes the blankets down his body, revealing a beautiful hard-on that's glistening at the tip. "Addison, you're fucking gorgeous, you're smart, and you're fucking sexy, maybe even sexier now that we know you're pregnant. Our not touching you has nothing to do with you being unattractive, it has everything to do with the fact that I am scared shitless, Addison. I'm scared of hurting you, I'm scared of hurting the baby, and I'm scared of everything that's happened this week. It wasn't on my agenda to get you pregnant, but it's happened. We-" he gestures between the three of us, "made that choice to take the chance because we didn't consider the consequences of what could happen. We slipped up once because we didn't have anything, but none of us went back to using them again. And now... now you're pregnant."

"Do you think I trapped you into this? To get something out of it, to make you stay in my life?" I say as straight and emotionless as I can.

"Oh dear god, no," Talon says. "That's never been a thought in my mind. Angel, we played this game together, we got into this together and we stay in this together."

"Addison," Kyle says softly. "We know that you never intended for this to happen like this. I know that it's way too early in this relationship, but I cannot change what's happened. I cannot take it back, I refuse."

"Then why? Why haven't you touched me, made love to me?"

Neither one of them say anything. I walk over to where my pajama pants are sitting and I pull them on. I go back into the bathroom for Kyle's t-shirt and despite the tenderness, pull it over my head. Neither one of them have moved since I left the room. "Bottle cap," I say and they both hiss.

"Please, angel, don't."

"I already have."

"Addison, you're upset, we get it, but you can't shut us down like that. Please, we need to talk about this," Kyle says.

"I tried. You both clammed up like I stole your tongues. Obviously I turn you off, otherwise you would have made a move, said something, done something, but you didn't. You both just sat there. This is not easy for me. At all. I am pregnant; I am pregnant because of a choice we all made together. If you can't live with that choice, love me for that choice, or show me that you love me after that decision has been made, then I don't know what else to do."

Talon sits up on the bed, climbing up onto his knees. "Take it back," he begs. I cock my head at him. "Take back your safe word," he demands. "That phrase is sacred and we will not dishonor it if it is your wish, so take it back so we can talk."

"I take it back." I reply reluctantly.

"I'm scared, Addison. I am so fucking scared of the future, of everything, of the fact that you're now pregnant. I'm scared of who I will be as a father, and a lover. I don't fucking know how to do this, Addison. I don't. I need your help, I need your guidance and I need your understanding. This is so fresh and new for all of us. I want to worship your body from head to toe. I want to make love to you like I need air to breathe. It's a goddamn necessity for me to show you how much I love you. I'm afraid to touch you, because I don't want to hurt you. I'm afraid, god, I'm afraid to be inside of you, afraid I'll hurt you, or the baby. Can you understand that? Can you understand why that's scary for me?" I nod at Talon's confession. Tears are streaming down my face in thick waves.

"We did it before we knew. We've done it countless times since Tuesday, and then you just cut me off. It's not fair because it makes me feel like I no longer turn you on, that you no longer want me sexually. It scares me, Talon."

Kyle climbs off of the bed. His cock is still hard and heavy, sticking straight out from his body and he comes to stand behind me. He hooks his thumbs into my pajama bottoms and pushes down. Then he comes back to the hem of my t-shirt. "I know this hurts. Please let me take it off." I uncross my arms and he pulls it over my head. Like lightning Talon's mouth is stroking fat, wet, languid strokes across my nipple.

A shiver of pleasure pulses through me as I fall into Kyle. His arms wrap around me. "We want you, baby girl. We need you. I didn't know how to do this after we found out. We started to and you stopped us. It hurt, but I stopped because I knew that wasn't the right time." His hands caress along my stomach. "We didn't know how you felt about it. We failed to communicate with one another."

Kyle begins kissing my neck and down my shoulder as Talon's tongue meets my nipple once again. Despite the soreness in them, the mix of pain and pleasure sends ripples of lust throughout my body.

"Take us, angel." Talon looks up at me through his heavy eyelids. "We're all yours," he hums as he takes my other nipple into his mouth.

I bring my hands up to his cheeks, urging him up. He follows my urging until I am face to face with him. "I can't. You and Kyle need to prove that nothing has changed."

chapter 11

Kyle pushes me forward toward the bed and I follow his lead. I am quickly sandwiched between the two of them. Talon's mouth is on mine in another heartbeat and Kyle's lips trace along my collarbone. I melt into their touches. A part of me wants to make them stop. I feel like I've tricked them into this.

"Stop…" I breathe.

"Baby girl?"

"I need to know…are you doing this because you want to or because I've guilt tripped you into it?"

Talon takes my head in his hands and looks me straight in the eyes before he says; "You can never guilt us into loving you. I am doing this because I love you, and because I need you." His lips crush mine and I wrap my hands around his neck, holding him to me. I can barely breathe, so I back away. I turn in the circle of their arms and face Kyle.

"I've wanted this since Thursday night, I just didn't know how." I cup his cheeks in my palms.

"Just like any other time before," I whisper and he too kisses me hot and hard. Talon's hands begin tracing along the curves of my body and I shiver, goose bumps racing, nipples hardening painfully and my knees go weak.

"Come here, angel. Lie down, let us show you." I can't resist his request and I climb onto the bed toward the pillows. All of the blankets are shoved off of the bed and the majority of the pillows too, except the one under my head.

They both come on either side of me. Kyle's hands caress along my stomach. "Your body is changing already," he says with a small smile and I look down. Laying like this I can see where my stomach doesn't sink like it used to. It's minor and in a different position it wouldn't be noticeable. "It's hard," he says as he gently presses into me.

"Protected," I breathe. Both of their hands begin exploring my body, while one goes up, the other goes south. Hands, tongues, mouths with open kisses. I am awash in sensations as they continue to caress me. They both come to my breasts at the same time, looking at me, seeking my approval and I nod slightly.

Ever so gently their tongues lick across my nipples and they harden instantly. Pain and pleasure shoot straight to my core. I am ready and wanting them with every ounce of their love, with every inch of their bodies. My back arches and I moan as their mouths and tongues slowly work at my nipples.

I can feel gentle pulling and sucking and I know that pleasure and not pain is their goal. The hands farthest south begin to roam, caress and touch. Eventually leading to a hand cupping my mound. Mouths sucking gently have me wound up so tight that when a finger strokes my clit, I nearly explode. My back arches again and another hand spreads my lips, seeking entrance to my core.

"Argh!" I grind against their hands massaging me. "Don't stop," I moan and they both increase their pace. I move my hands to between their legs and I take hold of their cocks, one in each hand. Stroking them. Talon unlatches from my breast and growls.

"Fuck!"

I continue stroking their cocks in my hands as they continue their finger massages on me. Kyle releases my breast and comes up to claim my mouth. My body trembles and I'm close to exploding for the first time in days.

Kyle swallows my cries as I explode around massaging fingers. My orgasm makes my toes curl. I need them both so bad.

I can't open my eyes and I feel Kyle's cock come out of my hand and I moan at the loss. Then I feel him lift my left leg and the bed dips under me. He lifts my legs and positions the head of his erection right at my entrance. "Please," I beg and he begins sliding inside. I'm so sensitive from my orgasm that my muscles clamp down.

"Open for me, baby girl," he urges and I take a relaxing breath, and he pushes in further. I continue stroking Talon's cock as Kyle slides inside of me. I'm panting with desperate need. A need to be thoroughly fucked by my men. Kyle starts to slide in and out of me. Talon's cock disappears from my hand.

"No," I groan and I hear them both laugh. I look to Talon who is sliding off of the bed. He opens the bedside drawer and pulls out a bottle of lube that he stashed there at some point. I watch as he begins massaging it onto his cock and I shiver. I'm going to get both of my men.

Kyle's pace increases slightly. I watch as Talon finishes up with the lube then grabs the bottle, bringing it with him. But he doesn't come back to the bed near me. No, he climbs up behind Kyle and I groan with pleasure knowing that Talon is going to claim him. Then I feel disappointed and I pout. Talon laughs. "Relax, angel, you'll get to have me too."

That causes my back to arch and Kyle stills, buried deep inside me as Talon begins to work at preparing Kyle to take him. Kyle leans forward, his lips landing on mine, giving Talon all the access he needs. It's my turn to stroke his tongue and swallow his moans of pleasure. The pressure inside me grows momentarily and Kyle groans, and shivers. "Relax, cowboy," Talon whispers. "I got you."

Kyle pulls back from our kiss and I can see the pain and pleasure rocking through him and I can feel his cock twitch inside of me. I put my feet down on the bed and begin to thrust my hips. Working his cock while Talon works his way inside of him.

Kyle's arms begin to shake from the pleasure and pain of holding himself up. Talon slides home then pauses, giving Kyle the moment he needs to adjust. Then Kyle starts to move inside of me, sliding in and out of me while working Talon's cock at the same time. It takes but a millisecond and I explode again. Kyle groans as my pussy clenches and my orgasm burns through me.

"That's it, cowboy, milk my cock, fuck her," Talon grunts as he begins thrusting his hips into Kyle. The rhythm is felt within me. Though I can tell Kyle is restraining himself, either from coming too fast or from pushing too hard and deep into me. It doesn't matter because the head of his cock is working at my g-spot and I'm nearing my third orgasm.

"I'm, ah fuck," Kyle cries out and I feel him explode inside of me. Hot wet spurts of cum coat me from the inside. Talon growls out his orgasm as he pumps into Kyle harder. I come for the third time.

Kyle collapses onto me, but still holds himself up off of me, not wanting to squish me. I kiss his cheeks, his jaw and then finally claim his lips. I know that Talon is withdrawing from within him. When he's done, I watch him disappear into the bathroom on shaky legs. Kyle slowly pulls his still rock hard erection from my pussy and I whimper at the loss. There is nothing better in the world than being connected like that. We slow our kisses and he slowly backs off of me and lies down on the bed.

I can't believe I'm still so fucking horny. I sit up and very quickly climb to my knees, taking Kyle's cock into my mouth. I can taste the delicious combination of him and I drying along his shaft and it turns me on even more. I begin making love to his cock with my mouth and he grunts, shudders and moans as I continue assaulting him. "That's mine," Talon says from behind me and a ripple of excitement rocks through me. I release Kyle's cock from my mouth and look at him. "Grab a pillow, angel. I'm going to take you from behind." My eyes roll up into my head with excitement as I grab a pillow, holding it to my chest. "I want you as flat as you can be," he says and I make an adjustment with the pillow so that it is firmly under my chest as I lower my hips to the bed. "That's it, angel, just like that.

Talon climbs up behind me and I look at Kyle who is watching Talon position himself. While he lays there I watch as he strokes his cock. It's fucking beautiful and I shiver in anticipation as Talon lines up the head of his cock with my core and gently pushes into me. I feel tighter from this angle and Talon feels bigger. My pussy is sensitive from my orgasms and pleasure shoots through my veins straight to my core.

Kyle climbs off the bed and picks up the lube. "Oh god," I moan. I know that Kyle is going to take Talon and disappointment runs wild. "I need to see, I need to watch," I breathe.

Talon glides his hand along my spine. Gentle caresses. "I promise, angel, I will make you watch him fuck me, but not today."

That's when I feel Talon's finger playing with the rim of my ass and my orgasm erupts once again. Shaking through me, shattering me.

It takes me a minute to realize that Talon has stopped and he moans. I look behind me and I can see Kyle behind him. Talon leans forward, bracing himself on stiff arms above me. "Ah fuck!" Talon groans as Kyle's hips thrust in and out in small movements and I can feel the perpetual motion in my pussy. Somehow I find leverage and begin moving against Talon as Kyle pushes inside until he is sheathed completely.

Kyle in Talon and Talon in me. It's enough to send me over the edge once again. Then they both begin thrusting. Kyle pushing Talon forward and deeper inside. Talon holds back some, taking Kyle, not wanting to come so soon. "Fuck me, this is... argh, god damn it!" Talon continues with a string of expletives as Kyle thrusts harder and faster into him. It doesn't take long before an orgasm is rocking through me once again.

This time, when I explode, I bring my two beautiful men with me, shattering and collapsing onto the bed, exhausted, I fall asleep before Talon even extracts himself.

chapter 12

"Baby girl? Come on, sleepy head." I feel soft lips against my forehead. "You need to wake up." More soft kisses against my forehead and cheeks.

"Go away," I grumble.

Kyle laughs. "I love waking you up. You're so cute. But it's one thirty and you haven't eaten yet today." My stomach gurgles and he laughs. "That's what I thought. Come on, lunch is here."

"What's for lunch?" I mumble, trying to wake up.

"Grilled cheese, chicken noodle soup and french fries." My stomach rumbles again. "God, I love you," he says on a sigh. "Come on, let's feed you."

"Have to pee," I say sleepily.

"Well then, come on, you might want some clothes too." I look down at my naked body.

"Oh," I snort. "They're over rated."

He laughs a deep belly laugh. "They are, but Mills is out in the sitting room."

"Well that sucks. Everything alright?"

He smiles. "Everything is great. Talon told him."

"No, no, no, we can't..."

"Relax, baby. He had to, you know Talon, he's being overprotective of you already." I roll my eyes. "My sentiments exactly. He wanted to talk to Tori, but I convinced him that she's your bodyguard, and you need to talk to her."

I give him a thank you smile as I step into the bathroom.

When I come out, Kyle is still there. On the bed are my grey pajama pants that are wide legged and my favorite because they're flannel and so comfortable. With it is one of my camisoles and I shudder. "I thought this might be easier than a t-shirt," he says. He's being so sweet. "Though I brought one of those too. One of my super soft ones." I touch the material and it's really soft, almost the same softness as my flannel pants, but the size will force it to rub against my nipples and I don't feel like putting on a bra. I pull the cami over my head and the brushing sends little stabs of achy twinges through me. It's not painful, just uncomfortable. Once it's in place and I move around, there is next to no rubbing.

I smile at him. "It works." Then I pick up his soft grey t-shirt and pull that on.

"I like you in just the tank top better," he grumbles as he wraps his arms around me. "You feel like a soft panda bear." He smiles and kisses my forehead. "Come on, hungry girl, let's go eat."

When we come around the corner in the sitting room, Talon and Mills are deep in conversation but Mills looks up and smiles widely at me. Talon turns toward me. "You okay, angel?"

"I'm good. Hungry." He laughs and I sit down. Kyle joins me. Mills and Talon go back to their conversation, and I look at Kyle as I take a sip of my soup. It's heaven. "We need to get a ten gallon drum of this stuff," I say and take another bite.

He laughs. "I'm making a mental note. Get the girl chicken noodle soup and lots of it."

"Sounds great to me." I dive into my soup with gusto, not wanting it to be gone, but desperate to fill up my stomach. Then I move on to the grilled cheese and about half of my french fries, which Kyle promptly eats the rest of.

"How are you feeling?" he asks as I finish up my lunch.

I give him a half laugh. "Tired again."

"Is this normal? You're sleeping a lot," he says with concern.

"I think so, from what research I did yesterday it's one of the primary symptoms. My problem is I keep giving into it and falling asleep. I need to keep busy, keep myself awake. Work through it kind of thing."

"But it's good to give into it, right?"

I smile. "It is, but it's affecting my eating pattern, as well as my ability to work. I think the next couple of weeks or so will be rough, but once we get to New York, with the crazy schedule, it will be easier."

"I just wish I knew how to help. I feel like you're doing this alone."

I look up at him with tears threatening. "I'm not doing this alone. I have you and I have Talon. You're taking care of me, feeding me, loving me. I'm not doing this alone," I tell him and bring my hand to his cheek. "Please don't fret, or feel like I'm alone. I'm not. It may be my body, but what you and Talon are doing makes it all that much easier for me. Just don't treat me like a useless baby, because I'm not. I will not break, physically at least. Emotionally I'm a damn mess. I haven't cried this much in my entire life," I say as a tear escapes my eye. "Look, if you want to better understand what I'm going through, read that book with me. I think it will help you understand. Talon on the other hand just wants to protect me from all the physical dangers." I look over at him and Mills before looking back to Kyle. "You want to protect me from myself. So read it with me."

"Okay, panda. I will." He smiles, leans over and goes to kiss me on my cheek. I turn at the last minute, landing my lips on his and he groans. "We don't have time," he grumbles. "You're about to start something you can't finish."

I give him a wicked grin and kiss him again. "There's always time," I breathe.

Our heart to heart seems to have worked earlier. Kyle is far more affectionate toward me but I know that something is still bothering him. But now isn't exactly the time to discuss it. I have a show to get ready for.

"Angel?" Talon calls from the bedroom.

"In the bathroom."

"You alright?"

"Yeah, just getting ready," I say as he comes into the bathroom.

"Wow, angel, you look amazing."

I'm wearing the top and super wide leg pants that I thought was a skirt that he gave me back in Phoenix. I plan on wearing my replacement Louboutin too. "Thank you," I say and he kisses my cheek. I have my hair super curly and up in a banana clip. Giving my hair a cascading effect.

"I don't want you performing tonight," he says straight faced.

"What, why wouldn't I?" He looks pointedly at my stomach.

"Oh no, you don't."

"It's my call, and I say no, not tonight."

"Talon Carver, what the hell are you doing? You can't do that, unless..." The worst possible thing imaginable runs through my mind and rather than get emotionally upset, I get pissed. "You can't sing with me, can you? You don't want me up there on stage because you can't sing to me?"

"Jesus, god no, Addison."

"No, seriously, the only thing that would ever stop you from pleasing your fans is if you're afraid of something happening and I'm not talking about to me. You don't think you can sing with me because it doesn't mean the same thing to you anymore..."

"God, Addison, stop. If anything, I can't sing with you because every time I look at you, I love you even more. Every time I see you, I want to cry with tears of happiness because I love you so fucking much." He paces out into the bedroom. I follow him and find Kyle leaning against the doorjamb to the bedroom.

I turn to Kyle. "Did you know about this?"

"About what, baby girl?"

"That he wasn't going to let me sing tonight."

"What?" he says, as he stands up straighter, away from the door.

"He just told me that he doesn't want me on stage with him tonight."

"Damn it, Addison, I don't want you on stage because I don't want the added stress on you." That freezes me in my tracks. "You don't need to be put under that pressure right now. You should be relaxing, should be..."

"I won't sit around and do nothing, Talon," I say softly. "More questions will be raised if I'm not on that stage. Especially tomorrow night, because we don't know how many tickets were sold because of our duet."

"I know and I don't want you feeling that pressure."

"You don't want me feeling it, or you don't want the added worry about me while I'm up there? I swear to god, Talon, you're going to make yourself mental if you do this to yourself. We have a long way to go with this pregnancy and it's barely two days old for all of us," I tell him.

"I just don't want to..."

"Did it occur to you, Talon, that the rough estimate of the date of conception is Albuquerque, the first night I went on stage purposefully, and that I've been performing with you every performance since then, already pregnant?"

"Albuquerque?" Kyle whispers behind Talon.

"About that time, yes, give or take a day or two. So you see, Talon, my being pregnant has nothing to do with my ability to perform. You're just being selfish and it's unnecessary."

"Damn it Addison, I don't know if I can sing either song, looking into your eyes without completely breaking down."

"See that's different, Talon. God, you should have said that, said something like, 'I don't know if I can do this tonight.' That would have been different, Talon. We could have discussed that. That's a whole hell of a lot different than you being overly protective of me."

"Well, that's part of it."

"Don't, you can't do this. Do you have any idea how many singers perform while pregnant?"

"But you're not them. You're you. You're mine and Kyle's girlfriend." He sits down on the bed and I walk over to him. His legs automatically open for me to step between them, and he wraps his arms around my legs and puts his ear to my stomach. "I don't want anything to happen to you," he whispers and I can't tell whom he's talking to, the baby or me.

I run my fingers through his hair. "Do you honestly think that Kyle, Mills, Tori, Dex, any of the guys, will let anything happen to me? Whether they know I'm pregnant or not. Since I stepped onto this bus, I have been the cocoon that everyone has gravitated toward and surrounded with their love and protection. You and Kyle are in the center of that protective wall. I know you won't let anything happen to me. I won't let anything happen to me. Which is why I'm coming back here after the show. I won't be going to the after party."

His arms squeeze a little tighter around me. "I don't know what else to do," he whispers and Kyle comes over to sit next to him. He puts his hand on Talon's back, rubbing it.

"We're all in the same boat, but smothering Addison with overprotectiveness isn't exactly the best way to go about it. Believe me, I understand why you feel it's necessary to protect her like this. God, Talon, I want to wrap her in bubble wrap and put her in a padded room for the next nine months, but I can't do that to her. I won't do that to her because it's just going to make us all crazy. The best way we can protect her is to love her, cherish her, and be there for her."

Talon nods against my stomach.

I put my hand on Kyle's cheek and continue stroking Talon's hair. We stay like that for a couple more minutes. Kyle kisses my palm and then takes my hand in his. "Talon?"

"Yeah?"

"You okay, big man?"

"Yeah, I'm sorry, angel."

"Don't be sorry. I understand, honestly I do, but there is a time and place for me to not be on stage with you and this isn't it. When I'm nine months pregnant is a good time. But not now. No one will know."

"I know and that's scary enough."

I chuckle. "For you it is. For me, not so much. If you cry, you cry. The songs are beautiful and very romantic. So unless you completely lose your spot in the song, no one will know. And even if you lose it, I know the song. But I have faith in you, big man. I know that you're more than capable of keeping yourself in check. There will be time to cry later."

I smile down at him and his eyes finally meet mine. Then he kisses my stomach, just above my pubic bone and I damn near lose it.

chapter 13

Both Cincinnati performances go great. Talon cried the first time we sang together, but by the time we got to 'To Be Free', he had it under control. Though I could see the glossiness in his eyes, seeing him cry nearly made me cry.

Kyle continues to wait on me hand and foot and when he's not doing it, Talon is there. It's nice but after nine months, this is going to get old. I have three meals a day delivered to me; whether in the suite of the hotel or on the bus and I learned very quickly to eat before performances. After I was done with 'To Be Free' during the first concert, I felt oddly weak. I chalked it up to being tired, which is the new name of my game lately. But I was quickly brought chicken mac n' cheese from Noodles & Company which I devoured and instantly felt better.

On Sunday I started tracking in my pregnancy journal the things I ate, the things I did, it even has a sleep counter. The problem with that is the fact that I barely notice when I fall asleep and usually am running straight to the bathroom to either pee or vomit when I wake up.

Zoey Derrick

Morning sickness is something I don't think I will ever get used to. It sucks so badly. But it seems to be first thing in the morning and the most I've ever done it so far is twice in one day.

We left Monday afternoon for Philadelphia, putting us there around midnight, which of course I was asleep for. The show isn't until Thursday night. On Wednesday Talon is taking me to meet his mother. I can't say I'm jumping up and down about meeting her, but it's important to Talon. Who is also bringing Kyle along for the ride.

Today is Tuesday and I have a doctor's appointment. I spent a good portion of Sunday looking for doctors in the Philly area. I didn't want to wait until New York to get checked out; the idea scared me just a little too much. With my history, I'd rather be safe than sorry. When I couldn't find one that sounded like I could trust, I called my normal OB back in LA.

Needless to say she was ecstatic for me and wanted me in immediately, under the circumstances. I told her I wasn't in town, but that I could fly back. We have a couple of days, but she said no, and when I told her where we were headed she got really excited and called one of her best friends who is an OB in Philly. When she called me back, I am promised absolute confidentiality, and privacy. Dr. Paige (my LA doctor) also promises to send over digital copies of my medical file for Dr. Breckenridge to review before my appointment at three.

When I wake up on Tuesday morning, I have a double whammy going on. I have to pee and puke. Great, I'm on the damn bus. No privacy. But I throw on Talon's t-shirt and go into the bathroom. I manage to pee before vomiting.

When I go back into the room, both my guys are awake. "You okay, angel?"

I nod.

"Did you throw up?" Kyle asks and I nod again and pull the t-shirt back off. "Oh!" Kyle says, shocked.

"What?" I look around and then back at him. He's pointing toward my stomach. Talon's mouth is hanging open.

I look down and squeak. "Oh, oh my god…" I touch my stomach, "Not something I ate then," I mumble. "It's too early, way way way too early for…I'm skinny, I know I'm skinny, but nowhere does it say anything about this *this* early." I continue mumbling to myself and I put my hand against it. It's hard, though it's been gradually growing a little harder with each passing day. It's not huge, I think I'm making this out to seem bigger than it is, but there is a definite distention just above my pubic bone. "Jesus guys, say something." Panic wells inside me.

"You look fucking incredible," Talon says softly.

I've been eating like a damn horse for three days now, more than I think I've eaten in a normal week. I no doubt have gained some weight, but when I put my hand against it, it disappears, that's how tiny it is, but to me, it looks massive.

"Come here, baby girl," Kyle says softly and I look up. "Why are you panicking?" he asks.

"I…I'm not sure," I stutter.

"Well relax, we go to the doctor in," Kyle looks at the clock, "four hours. We will get all the answers we need."

I nod and climb up onto the bed and lay down. Neither one of them wastes any time in touching my belly. Which when I lay down disappears. "Sit up again," Talon says and I laugh.

"Why?"

"Because I want to see it," he says like a little boy and it makes me smile. I look to Kyle who shrugs.

"You realize there is going to come a day where it won't go away when I lay down, right?"

They both laugh. "We know," Kyle says, "but it's so cute." I roll my eyes.

"I know something else that's cute," I say with a salacious grin.

"Oh really?" Talon says. "What exactly would that be?"

"The two of you, entertaining me."

They look at each other and shrug, then Talon reaches over, grabs Kyle by the back of the neck and pulls him into a kiss. I let out a hot rush of air from my lungs and my legs automatically scissor together. "That's not what I had in mind," I moan. "But don't stop."

They don't. They both come up onto their knees and their cocks are hard as stone dangling just above my stomach as they continue to kiss. I put my hands behind my head and watch. "This is better than porn," I mumble as Talon takes Kyle's cock in his hand. "Fuck," I groan.

My nipples are way too sore to touch them so I let my hands slide down my body. My fingers seek my clit to play with. Kyle stops me. "Oh so not fair," I growl.

"Just watch, baby girl," Kyle says, breaking his kiss with a wicked smile on his face. He slides back on the bed and leans forward, licking and sucking Talon's cock into his mouth. Talon grunts and puts his hand in Kyle's hair, guiding him up and down on his cock. I can't stop my legs from scissoring together, desperate for relief.

I try in vain to touch my nipples and hiss through my teeth. Talon looks down at me and Kyle stops. "What's wrong?"

I want to cry. "They hurt so bad," I groan. "I want to touch them, but it hurts."

Kyle's hand dips down between my legs and immediately finds my clit. My nipples harden and I groan in pain and pleasure. Then I watch as Kyle takes Talon back into his mouth while continuing to flick my clit. I writhe in pleasure as they continue above me.

Kyle slides two fingers inside of me and I explode almost instantly. My pussy is sensitive and I shatter. Grinding my hips against his hand while he continues to suck Talon off. But once I have my orgasm Kyle stops, sitting up, and licking his fingers. Talon steals his hand and puts Kyle's fingers in his mouth. "That's so fucking hot," Kyle groans and I'm instantly ready for another. Kyle gets off of the bed and goes to the infamous drawer. Pulling out lube and the little silver bullet. I scowl at him as he clicks it on, handing it to Talon who promptly brushes it against my slit.

I tremble. Pleasure vibrates through my body once again. "Take it, angel," he says and I take the bullet from him. "Get yourself off." I continue working the vibrator against my clit, pleasure spiking again and again. But I am distracted when Talon lies down on his back and Kyle begins lubing himself up.

I watch as both my men stroke their cocks, Talon bends his legs, cutting off my view. "Are you sure you want to, like this?" Kyle asks and Talon nods.

I stop with the vibrator and reposition myself so that I can see down Talon's body from above his head and Kyle comes in between his legs, stroking his cock and massaging Talon's hole. "You ready, big man?" Kyle asks and Talon nods again, his hand stilling on his erection.

Kyle lifts Talon's legs up for easier access and Talon hangs on to them. I watch as his cock bobs up and down with the motion then I see Kyle pressing into Talon, who hisses through his teeth. His own pain and pleasure.

Kyle's thrusts are short and frequent as he lubes his way in. Talon's arms begin to shake as the pleasure is nearly too much for him to handle. Kyle thrusts inside and Talon groans.

I sit up. I have an idea. I straddle Talon's face. Putting my dripping pussy right on his mouth and he sucks me into him. Milking my clit. I see Kyle is looking down and I follow his eyes. My little pouch is back and Kyle begins thrusting into Talon whose moans are absorbed by my sex.

I reposition slightly but Talon never lets up his tongue stroking my clit. I lean forward, putting Talon's legs under my arms, helping Kyle to hold them up. Talon grunts and cries out when the position changes, but its pure pleasure, not pain. I lean my head down and Kyle takes Talon's cock, stroking it and then positioning it just right for me to suck it into my mouth.

"Argh, fuck, damn it." I am rewarded with a long sickly sweet shot of pre-cum and I swallow it down. My eyes are open as I watch Kyle's cock pumping in and out of Talon, spurring me on, and bringing my orgasm to the surface.

I continue sucking him like my life depends on it while Kyle pounds into him. Kyle doesn't stop stroking Talon's cock in time to my head bobbing. I'm so close, right there, my body locks down on me and Talon's mouth comes away as he screams out an orgasm unlike anything I've ever heard. I suck on him harder and faster as his cock erupts into my mouth. Kyle's motions slow down, but I notice he hasn't come yet.

I look to him. "Keep sucking him," he mouths and I do. With each pump down of my mouth, Kyle pumps up. Together we're working his cock and Talon is shattering beneath us. We both feel his cock twitch and then Kyle starts to move again. "Get her off, big man, and I'll get you off again," Kyle says and Talon's mouth immediately latches on. It doesn't take long for pleasure to take me once more as Kyle starts pounding out a feverish rhythm in Talon.

I suck harder and faster, pushing him closer to climax. Then suddenly I hear the bullet click back on and it's pressed up against my ass. "Come, baby girl. Let us have it," Kyle says above me. Talon stiffens, Kyle's movements falter slightly and I lock down hard. "Give it to her, Talon, make her come," Kyle orders and the bullet is pushed in just enough to send me flying over the edge at the same time as Talon erupts into my mouth with guttural cries as Kyle pours himself into Talon.

chapter 14

We all slowly untangle ourselves from one another. Talon, though, doesn't move a whole lot. I can tell that he's shattered and even more so because he's gone flaccid. A first for Talon after two orgasms. But I think that first one really got to him.

Once I unwind my arms from Talon's legs, his legs fall to the sides. He's spent. I lay down next to him. "How you doing, big man?"

"Mmmgmdmph."

"I'll take that as amazing," I say and he nods. Kyle disappeared into the bathroom to wash up. When he comes back he has a warm washcloth for Talon.

"Let me clean you up," Kyle says and Talon does a half ass job of lifting his hips, but Kyle cleans him up anyway before throwing the washcloth into the hamper. Then Kyle strips out of his boxers and lies on the bed. His cock is still hard and impossible to resist. Leaving Talon to recover, I roll over to take Kyle into my mouth. His hand slides gently into my hair and I look at him. His returning look is full of love and devotion.

After only a couple of minutes of sucking he whispers, "Take me. I want to watch you on top of me."

I can't say no to that and I straddle him. Positioning the head of his cock at my entrance, I slowly slide down, moaning my way to the base of his erection and he closes his eyes. When he opens them they're darker, hooded and full of lust. I tremble and begin to move on top of him. His hands begin sliding along my calves, up my hips to my pouch. I tremble again when he makes contact and it sends a ripple of happiness through me. I continue riding him as his hands explore my body. When he gets to my breasts he hesitates. "It's okay," I murmur as I grind against him. His hands are gentle, touching from the outside in. Fingertips rubbing along my nipples are the perfect mix of pain and pleasure. I cry out. My pace falters. I take his hands from my breasts.

"I'm sorry, baby."

"Shh. It's fine." I intertwine our fingers and then pin them above his head with my own hands, grinding and pumping on his cock. I brush my nipple over his lips and he opens but doesn't do anything. "Take it, please," I moan and his tongue comes out, feather light and I move my nipple against him. "It's okay, cowboy," I'm breathing heavily, "take it."

I watch as he takes it into his mouth. My orgasm erupts around his cock. I can see he's shocked by it because he didn't know it was coming. Neither did I, but he starts pumping up into me and I moan. "Kyle," I scream, "oh fuck." I am so wrapped up in what's happening between us that I didn't even notice that Talon got up. He's behind me, between Kyle's legs and I feel the cold wet glob against my ass. "Oh god. Yes. Fuck yes." It's been so long since they've taken me in tandem and I soak it up. Feeling Talon ready me to take him, I pound harder against Kyle.

"Easy, baby," Kyle says and I slow down just as Talon puts the head of his cock against me. I nearly explode once again, but I bite my lip and Kyle releases my breast. The cool air swirling around it causes it to harden even more, pain pulses through me as Talon breaks that barrier, pushing the fattest part of his cock past my tight ring, then he makes quick work of sliding home and I explode around both of them.

Neither one of them let up through my orgasm and another one is building hard and fast within me. "Gah, I can't, too much...Fuck!" I moan and I become suspended between the two of them. My mind floats off as I feel weight and life lifting from my shoulders. Their pounding doesn't stop, doesn't let up and I don't want them to stop. I cry out as the pleasure overcomes me and I explode around them in the most glorious, weightless orgasm I've ever felt in my entire life. Being claimed by them means I am theirs, wholly and completely.

I collapse onto Kyle's chest, panting. Talon withdraws first and Kyle, now soft, slides free of my slit. I don't even realize when Talon leaves and comes back. He has something in his hand and he rubs it onto my lips. I can smell it, it's sweet, I lick it and he teases me with it. Finally letting me have it. It's chocolate. "Eat it, baby girl, it will help."

"What happened?" I moan around the chocolate. God, it's fucking good.

"Not entirely sure, but whatever it was, it was amazing. You just let go, your body tuned to ours and you let go," Kyle says.

"Felt so free of everything, like I was floating."

"I think you found something referred to as subspace. It's a term used primarily in the BDSM community. It's usually a point the sub meets when everything gets let go and she gives herself over to her dominant. Though I don't know, as if I've never heard of it in a vanilla relationship," Talon ponders.

"This isn't exactly vanilla," Kyle chuckles.

Talon joins him. "You know what I mean," Talon says with a smile. "Let's get you cleaned up, angel."

"I need a shower," I groan. "But I don't want to move."

Kyle wraps his arms around me, holding me to him and I lay there for some time.

The next thing I know, I'm being woken up. "Hi angel."

I'm looking into Talon's eyes. "Oh god. Why didn't you move me?" I say to Kyle who's still under me.

"And miss the cuddle time? Never," he says with a smile. I'm stiff when I sit up and there is a sheen of sweat on my torso.

"What time is it?"

"It's time for you to shower while Kyle makes you lunch." I groan. "You didn't eat breakfast. I don't want to hear it." Talon smiles. "Come on, panda. I have a t-shirt ready for you."

I climb off of Kyle, kissing him before I dismount my man-pillow. My stomach rolls. "Quick," I say as I reach for the t-shirt. I head for the door, throwing it over my head. I don't care who sees me naked. I barely get myself covered when I round the corner. Shit, someone's in the bathroom. Damn it. I race past Mouse on the couch and down the steps. I barely make it off of the bus before I wretch.

"Addie," I hear someone shout. "Shit, get a blanket," Kyle yells back into the bus. He grabs my hair, pulling it out of the way and I puke again. Within seconds there is a blanket wrapped around me. My grip against the bus begins to slip as I continue retching. Someone wraps his arms around my shoulders, holding me up.

After what feels like forever I finally stop puking and switch to heaving. Then after three or four of those, it passes and I feel better. Weak, but better.

"Come on, baby girl, let's get you inside. Dex is out of the bathroom. It's all yours," Kyle says while helping me to stand up straighter and I lean into him as he escorts me onto the bus and into the bathroom. Talon is talking to the guys but I can't make out what they're saying. Kyle closes the door and removes the blanket from around me and then pulls the hem of my shirt over my head.

We switch places and he turns on the shower. "I can do this," I tell him. "I'm alright now."

"I know, but let me get you started, and then I'll go make you some food."

"Ugh..."

"Hey, I think food helps you stop from losing it. You don't puke after you've eaten. But you haven't eaten. I'll keep it light. Chicken soup?" I nod. He kisses my forehead and we switch places again so I can step into the shower. Once I'm situated, Kyle leaves me to it.

After my shower I return to the bedroom and chicken soup, saltines and toast. I sit down and eat it all. No wonder I have a pouch. "I feel like a pig," I grumble as I take the last bite.

"Do you want more?" I shake my head at Kyle. He kisses my forehead, collecting my paper dishes. "You're not a pig, you're just eating for two. Remember what the book said?" I smile at the memories of Kyle and I reading

'The Book' after the Cincy shows while Talon went out with the guys.

"I remember, but still, I'll be hungry again in an hour."

He chuckles softly. "Then I'll feed you again." He looks up at the clock. "We need to leave in about forty-five minutes." I groan at him. "Sorry, love, we didn't want to wake you, besides, it's just the doctor."

Forty minutes later I am dressed in a pair of flannel pants. My clothes have always been very form fitting, not a lot of extra room and if this pouch is here to stay, elastic waistbands or unbuttoned pants are going to be my friend for a while. I wasn't able to fully button up the jeans I was going to wear anyway and these just looked more comfortable. I put a cami on underneath my Nirvana t-shirt. Some things you just can't change. The outfit looks great, except I'm wearing tennis shoes instead of boots. I know it's all coming off when I get there.

The guys left me alone to dress, so I grab my purse and head up front to meet them. Within five minutes, we're in a car, on our way. We're actually in an SUV that they rented versus the car service like they usually get. But given the location, I imagine they want to keep this as discreet as possible. Mills and Tori are in the front seat.

My men are on either side of me and I can tell they're nervous, but I don't know how to comfort them because I'm nervous too.

When we arrive, it's a small office building and I know we're going to the second floor.

When we enter the office, it looks a lot like Dr. Paige's back in LA. There is no one in the waiting room except for the receptionist. "Hi Addison," the receptionist says.

"How'd you know?"

She smiles politely at me. "Dr. Paige told Dr. B to provide you with privacy and discretion. So there's no one here now and she is closing when you're done, so no one else will be here."

"She didn't have to do that."

"Nonsense." She smiles. "Can you fill this out for me?" She hands me a clipboard. I notice the majority of the paperwork is filled out already; I just need to fill in my insurance information. Which I have and do quickly. Verifying the information, I sign the papers and give them back to the nurse. "Perfect, thank you, Addison. Can you come back with me?"

Kyle and Talon stand up. "Breathe, boys. Please let me do this initial part alone. I will send the nurse to come and get you as soon as my initial exam is done."

"But..." Talon protests.

"I am not leaving you out of this. I just need to get my exam done without you guys there. I am nervous enough, I don't need you guys freaking me out more."

"I promise you guys that if Dr. B does an ultrasound, which is pretty likely, I will come and get you," the nurse says to them. They both relax.

"Thank you," I tell them, both kiss me on the cheeks and I go back with the nurse.

"I'm Becky, by the way," The nurse says.

"Hi Becky, Addison, but you knew that already." I smile at her.

"They're very protective of you." I smile at her.

"Yes, they are. We have a very unconventional relationship," I tell her very nonchalantly.

"As in, the three of you?" She gasps and I wink. "Wow. You go girl..." I laugh. "Okay, I'm going to take your height and weight, then I'm going to draw some blood so we can do a hormone test. That will confirm your pregnancy."

I chuckle. "I'm pretty sure I've got that nailed already."

She smiles, "Well, we will do it anyway, plus it will give us a base for where you're measuring and how far along you are." I want to roll my eyes. I already know, but that's alright.

chapter 15
kyle

I lean forward, putting my elbows on my knees and my face in my hands. The nurse just took Addison back for her exam and I can hardly breathe. Panic, fear, and anxiety...those are just some of the emotions running through me that I can name.

"How you doin', cowboy?"

I scrub my face and sit up. "I'm a fucking wreck. You?"

I feel his hand rub along my back. "The same." I hear him take a deep breath. "I'm so confused right now. I don't...I don't know what to think."

He puts his head against the wall behind our chairs. His eyes are closed and I can see the tension in his neck. "Will this ever get easier?"

"I'd imagine at some point it will," he says quietly. "Though the way I feel right now, I don't know that it will be anytime soon."

"You know, until this morning I think I was growing okay with it."

He brings his head up to look at me. "What changed this morning?"

"The bump," I say quietly. "I don't mean it's a bad thing, it's just, it's really fast, Talon."

He leans forward, much like I was a minute ago, scrubbing his face. "I know," he says in to his hands so it's muffled. "It's not normal. Is it?"

I shrug. "I don't think so, but what scares me the most is what the book says."

He looks back at me. "What?" he asks slightly exasperated, I don't blame him.

"I read in the book, it doesn't touch on the subject much, but it's there."

"Spill it, please, Ky, I can't..." He scrubs his face again.

"Twins, Talon. The book talks a little about carrying multiples." My heart starts racing as I watch the shock settle across his features. "It says that a sign of twins or," I swallow hard, "more, means increases in symptoms, earlier signs of pregnancy..." I stop when his eyes widen. I don't know what else to say but at this point it's all speculation. I lean forward, "Aw hell, who am I kidding, I think my mind is just running out of control."

"God, I hope so. I can't keep handling all of this unknown. It's driving me crazy."

"It's why we're here," I say.

chapter 16

addison

It only takes Dr. Breckenridge a minute to come in after I get seated on the table. "Hi Addison, I'm Dr. Breckenridge. It's nice to meet you. Paige and I had a nice chat about you this morning."

"Great to meet you too." Dr. B is young, like Paige is, she's a little heavier set, but not at all unattractive. I'm comforted immediately by her. "I hope it was all good things."

She laughs. "It was. So, tell me, Addison, how are you feeling?"

"Bloated, tired as hell, my boobs hurt like a bitch." She laughs. "But other than that, I feel great."

"Good. We ran your blood work, I'm a little concerned."

"Why?"

"Because your hormone level is higher than I'd expect. When did you say your last period was?"

"March fifth."

She does a twist of the circle in her hand. "That puts you due around December tenth. But that means you're only five weeks along. Give or take a day or two. But your blood HCg is running about double that." I slide down off of the table.

I lower the blanket, "Would that explain why I have this?" I show her my little pouch.

"That wasn't there before?" she asks.

"No, I just discovered it this morning."

She smiles at me. "I think it might. Let's do the exam and then we will run an ultrasound, how's that sound?"

I nod and climb back up and lay back. She brings the stirrup cups out and helps me guide my heels into them. "Scoot down just a little bit." I do as she asks and I can hear her stretching gloves. The room goes eerily quiet and all I can hear is the sound of my blood pumping through my ears.

She starts her exam and I squirm. I'm sensitive, compliments of Talon and Kyle. "Does that hurt?"

"No, just sensitive."

She laughs, "I'd imagine, keeping up with those two."

I blush as red as a cherry. "How'd…"

She chuckles, "Becky is a little too talkative sometimes."

"Does that bother you?" I ask.

"No, in fact, I think it's awesome. So long as you're happy, and I know Paige will understand too. She's a wild girl herself."

"Oh my god," I squeak. "I had no idea."

She laughs and continues. "Paige said your last pap was about nine months ago, I'm going to go ahead and run another one for you, if that's alright."

"As long as you call with the results and then make sure Dr. Paige gets them."

"Of course."

I can feel her moving around down there and I try to ignore it. After just a couple more minutes she's done. "This is going to be tender, but I will try and be gentle," she says as she slides two fingers inside of me and then pokes along my lower abdomen. I flinch. "I can feel your cysts that Paige talked about. I also feel the reason why you're here."

She pulls back, pulls off her gloves and throws them into the red container. Then I watch as she washes her hands and sanitizes them. The routine is so mundane; I realize that I'm over focusing on everything else to avoid the elephant in the room. Then she comes to stand at my side. "Paige said you had implants done about six or seven years ago."

I nod, "Is that going to be a problem for breastfeeding?"

"I doubt it. You had them go in under the muscle for one, and for two, if your boobs are hurting that means they're doing what they're supposed to be doing during pregnancy." She begins examining one breast, she's pushing and I flinch. "Sorry, sweetheart, I'm almost done." She moves onto the other one. "No, I think you'll do fine in the breastfeeding department, but the next few months might be really painful. You may start to notice your scars more. You have armpit incisions?" I nod and she pulls her hands back, covering me again. "I imagine that as you develop closer to delivery, you'll see them and feel them again."

I nod and sit up.

"What questions do you have?" she asks as she sits down to write down her exam notes.

"I'm on tour right now, living on a bus, up late at night, is that going to be a problem?"

"I don't see why not. I'm going to give you a prenatal vitamin prescription that you need to take every day. I recommend at night, after dinner. Stay away from pain relievers other than acetaminophen for aches. Though I can tell you it won't help much with the breast soreness. Stick to the recommended dosage and do it as a last resort. If you catch a cold or think you're getting sick, call Dr. Paige or me, one of us will call in a prescription for you or determine if you have to see someone. How much longer are you on the road?"

I do the mental math quickly. "Seven or eight weeks, can't remember for sure, but we have a break where I'll be going back to LA."

"When is that?"

"Um, four or five weeks from now."

"Good, make an appointment with Paige. With your history of PCOS, I can imagine she will want to keep you under supervision throughout your pregnancy. You're not exactly considered high risk at this point, but you'll need to pay attention to your body. If it tells you to sleep, sleep. If it tells you to eat, eat. If you feel pain or aches, pick up the phone and call one of us. Here..." she reaches over and pulls a couple of pamphlets off of the wall holders, "read these, they're shortened lists of good foods, bad foods and what to avoid, like caffeine. There's dozens of books out there, but I recommend the What to Expect books."

"I have one." She chuckles. "They're a little bit excited." I jerk my head toward the door and shrug.

"I can tell. They were chomping at the bit to come back here. Becky put them in their place." She laughs again. "That's good for them to be that way. Which is going to lead me into my theory."

"Your theory?"

"Based on your blood tests, my exam just now, your little pouch already and the high flush of hormones you seem to be experiencing, I think there is a good possibility that you've got twins in there."

"What?" I say in a rushed breath.

She smiles widely. "If it's twins, then things are going to be slightly different for you. For one, you will show much faster and given that you think you're about five weeks along, it won't take you long before you're buying new clothes. Two, your hormones will run higher for the next three or four months, which means, high emotional ups and downs. From laughing one minute, to crying the next…"

"Too late."

She smiles, "You may get snappy with your guys or anyone who steps on your toes. Your diet needs to increase. I'll confirm with the ultrasound before I go getting it stuck into your head and we find out there's one."

I nod. "Is it…" I can't get the question out. "If it's twins, is it possible for them to have two different fathers?" I ask quickly and mumbled.

"Try that again? Addison, you have nothing to be embarrassed about here."

I take a deep breath. "What are the odds that if it's twins, that they have two different fathers?"

She smiles. "They're low, but not impossible, but we won't know that without testing and that can't happen for a long time. If those guys are as feisty as I think they are, you may have a higher chance of having two babies at the same time with two dads."

"Oh my god, that sounds so bad."

She stands. "Hardly, it would be a miracle and you've got two men to take care of you throughout all this. I think they'd both be excited to know they each scored."

"Doctor B," I scold and she bursts out laughing.

"It's every man's dream, darlin'." She smirks. "Go ahead and put your top back on. Leave the bottoms off. Because you're not that far along, I'm going to do an internal ultrasound. I'll send them in."

"Please, and Dr. Breckenridge?"

"Yes, Addison?"

"Thank you, for everything."

She puts her hand on my shoulder and squeezes. "Paige is very fond of you. I know that your PCOS diagnosis tore her up."

"Really?" I raise an eyebrow at her. "You guys talk about me?"

She smiles. "Not like you think. We talked this morning when I was going over your records. She said that when she gave you that diagnosis you were so shell shocked, and that it broke her heart. But you've proved her wrong and gotten pregnant. I don't want to put a damper on your pregnancy, but you need to be careful. You're at a high risk of miscarriage because of your PCOS. So like I said, listen to your body."

"What about sex?"

She smirks. "Enjoy yourself. What happens from here on out is up to you and your body. So far, your body is working in your favor. Now get dressed, I'm surprised they're not breaking down the door."

I laugh and she leaves. I take a big deep breath and slide off of the table. As if worrying about one baby was bad enough, now possibly two. I want to faint. But I ditch the gown, throw my cami back on, then my t-shirt and lay back down. I'm barely putting my head down when the door opens. Talon first, followed by Kyle.

"Relax, guys, please?" I say to them both. Talon comes around the table to stand by my right and Kyle on my left.

"How you doin?" Talon asks.

"Well, I'm pregnant."

They both laugh. "We kind of already knew that," Kyle teases.

"Yeah, I know."

There is a knock on the door and Becky comes in with a cart that has a computer on it. She sets it up, plugs it in. "What's that?" Talon asks.

"This is an ultrasound machine. Dr. B is going to have a look at the baby. She'll check size to make sure Addison is measuring correctly and maybe even snap a few pictures for you too." Becky smiles sweetly and takes her leave, but doesn't close the door. The guys squeeze my hands and I can tell they're nervous but excited.

"Easy, guys. It's alright."

Dr. B comes back in. "Hi guys," she says, "you're not giving her a hard time are you?"

"No ma'am." Talon is quick to answer. I roll my eyes.

"Alright, Addison," she reaches down and pulls out the stirrups again and guides my feet into them. "Scoot down for me until you feel the edge of the bed." I do. "Okay, here's what I am going to do. I'm going to use this." She holds up a wand, "and take a look from the inside. You're not far enough along to guarantee I can see from the outside."

She sets out getting the device ready, I've had an internal before so I know what she's doing and Talon blushes when she pulls out a condom and squirts the gel inside. I chuckle silently. "Breathe, Talon," I say and he takes a deep breath.

chapter 17

Dr. B does her thing. "Ready?" she asks me and I nod. The monitor is turned away from the guys and me so none of us can see anything. I feel her pushing the wand inside of me and it's not uncomfortable until she starts moving it around. Then I can feel it and I flinch. "Sorry, Addison," she says and I settle down. I can feel Kyle's thumb caressing the back of my hand and they're both looking at me for reassurance.

I smile and nod to both of them and squeeze their hands.

"Addison?" Dr. B says. I look at her and she has a wide smile on her face. "I was right."

"No way." My head gets light headed.

"Right about what?" I hear Talon ask.

She looks at me for reassurance. I nod my head. "Talon, Kyle, I'd like to introduce you to Baby A." She turns the monitor so that they can see. There isn't much to see, just a black space among the static, inside the black spot is a white dot.

"Baby A? Why Baby A?" Kyle asks, panic rising in his voice.

"Because..." she clicks a couple buttons, "this is Baby B."

I close my eyes and start crying. I hear a click. "See?" Dr. B says and I blink through the tears and on the screen one is a little higher than the other one. "You're having twins," Dr. B says.

"Twins?" they both breathe out together.

I nod, tears streaming down my cheeks. "How?" Talon says and Dr. B chuckles. "Well, you know what I mean...don't you?" He says so child-like, it's kinda cute.

"Well, they're fraternal twins, which means Addison dropped two eggs that were fertilized and implanted. Which is why she's already showing. That little pouch she has. I'm sure she's eating a lot and sleeping more than you like. And Addison, it plays into your other question. That possibility has just gone up."

"Wait, what possibility?" Kyle asks.

I nod to Dr. B. "Addison asked me that if it was twins, if there was a chance that there could be two fathers, one for each twin."

"No way," Talon says shocked. "That can happen?"

"It can, though we can't confirm it until much later in the pregnancy or once the twins are born." My heart is pounding and I think for the first time, I'm truly starting to freak out.

I don't hear much of the conversation between the guys and the doctor. My eyes are locked on the monitor. "Addison?"

"What?"

"You checked out on us, you okay?"

I nod to Dr. B. "Just freaking out, that's all."

She smiles. "It's really going to be okay. Let me show you." I feel the wand move again and she points to the screen. "Here are your cysts." She points to a cluster of white on the screen. "They're perfectly fine and they're on the opposite side from where the twins are. As the pregnancy progresses, Dr. Paige will keep a closer eye on them, but I don't see them being an issue right now."

I nod my understanding and take a deep breath. I look up at my boys who are in awe, Talon has a smile on his face and Kyle looks shocked. "What else do I need to know about twins?" I ask. Trying to get as much information as I can.

She pulls the wand from me, and wipes down there. "Here." She hands me a few small pictures. Ultrasound pictures. I smile at them. "Why don't you get dressed and we can talk out in the reception area where you'll be more comfortable."

"Okay," I say and she leaves the room. The guys haven't let go of my hands since they came into the room. "Guys, I need my hands." I giggle.

They slowly let go, as I hop down I notice Kyle is swaying. I rush over to him and take his arm, wrapping it over my shoulders. "I got you, cowboy. Breathe for me. Come on, cowboy. I can't have you passing out on me." Talon skirts the table quickly, taking his other hand and he swings it over his shoulder.

"Come on, Kyle, look at her. Look at Addison." Kyle's eyes meet mine. Panic. "I got him, Addie." Talon tells me and I slide out from under his arm and stand in front of him. His eyes follow me.

"Hi cowboy. I need you to breathe with me, okay?" He nods, sort of. I take a deep breath in and he follows me. "Good, now let it out." I blow out and he does the same. "Let's do it again." We repeat the process a few times and

115

the color is coming back into his face. "Much better, cowboy, now, can you talk to me?" He shakes his head. "We're okay, cowboy, it's okay. I know it's shocking, I know it's twice as scary, but we got this. The three of us can handle this. We will do this and we will be damn good at it."

I look to Talon for some help. "Hey big guy, she's right. We're gonna be dads to two of the best kids in the world. We got this, we can do this, *you* can do this. Your dad, your brother, your mom? They're not you, they're not who you are. You're better than them, better than that. Our girl needs us now more than ever. So come on, buddy, talk to us."

"I...it's so much, too much, too fast, can't process..." His words are clipped and I can see confusion in his eyes, which haven't left mine.

"We're all processing this, cowboy, even me. Imagine my surprise, I go from being told I have very little chance of children to being pregnant, to being pregnant with twins. I need you, cowboy. I need my rock, can you be my rock?"

He pulls his arm off of Talon's shoulder and wraps them around me, holding me to him. "I'm sorry, baby girl, god, I'm so sorry." I want to cry at the anguish in his voice.

"Don't be sorry, you have nothing to apologize for. It's scary, I'm scared, Talon's scared, we're all freaking out a little, but I need you." I pull back to look at him, "I love you."

His lips land on mine. "I love you."

I smile and reach my hand out to take Talon's. I look over at him. He's on the verge of tears. "I need to hug him now, okay?" I say to Kyle and he nods, letting me go and Talon pulls me into his arms.

"I love you, angel," he says as he kisses my forehead.

"You okay, big man?"

"I will be." He kisses my forehead again.

"Why don't the two of you go to the waiting room? I will put my pants on and be right behind you."

"Okay," Talon says, taking Kyle's hand and leading him out of the room.

I take a huge breath. I honestly thought he was going to pass out on me. I don't know if I could have handled that, on top of the fact that I'm pregnant with not one, but two babies. My head spins and I sit down in the chair with my purse. I put my head into my hands and cry.

"Addison?"

Doctor B comes into the room. "I'm sorry," I say.

"Oh don't be sorry. It's a lot to take in, a lot to handle. But let's go chat some more, okay? Can you get dressed?"

I nod and she leaves the room. I slide my pants on and slip into my tennis shoes. I grab my purse and walk out into the reception hall. Talon and Kyle are sitting a chair apart, but their hands are linked together. "Got room for one more?" I ask sweetly, trying to hide my own distress. They let their hands go and I sit down. They quickly take my hands in theirs and Doctor B comes to sit across from us. She has a large envelope stuffed with something.

"Okay guys, here's the deal. Addison is pregnant with twins, which means a few things. One, she's going to be more emotional. Things will upset her easier; she can go from happy to crying in a matter of seconds. Two, she needs to eat more, and it needs to be healthy food. I'm not pulling her from the bus, but she needs to have healthy food to eat. High fiber and folic acid." She holds up the envelope, "In here you will find a lot of information on pregnancy, foods, activities, and what's going on with her body. I've included three copies of some things. Those are the things that the two of you," she points to Kyle and

Talon, "need to read with her. Thirdly, be gentle with her. Sex is not off of the menu, so don't deny her that, but just remember to be a little more gentle than normal." She smirks. "Lastly, let her sleep. If she's tired, let her be."

Both Talon and Kyle nod their agreement with her. "I have a question," I say.

"Go ahead…"

"I'm subject to migraines, I've already had one on this trip, prior to conception, what can I do if I get another one?"

"Do you know what triggers them?" She asks me.

"Stress can, but sometimes they just come on."

"How often?"

"It depends. Sometimes it's once or twice a month, other times I go three months without one."

"Okay, you have medicine prescribed?" I nod. "Don't take that. I can write you a script for an approved medicine, but I strongly suggest you do anything you can to avoid taking it."

"That's hard."

"Oh I know, but ice can help. But I think you'll find you'll tolerate things differently when you know you can't do anything about it. Like colds and things like that." I nod.

"I don't want a script for medicine. I can handle them without it, if I get one."

She smiles. "A few things for you, missy…" she stares pointedly at me, "you're now a high risk pregnancy, but please don't panic on me, twins are usually upgraded to that because of the toll it can take on your body. No lifting more than five pounds." The guys snort.

"They don't let me do that now."

She smiles, "Good. Limit stressful situations when possible. Keep some food in your purse, crackers or granola bars, if you start to feel faint, eat. If they bring you food, eat it, but guys, don't over feed her. Last, but not least," she hands me her card, "here's my card, with office number, cell phone and emergency number. If it's outside of office hours, call my cell, if I don't answer, go to the emergency number, tell them who you are and I will call you back immediately." She hands me another small piece of paper, "per Dr. Paige's request, her office, cell and emergency number. Program them and use them, even if you just have a question."

"Do you do this for all your patients?" I ask her.

She smiles sweetly, "No, just the ones that are carrying celebrity babies."

"You've known the whole time?"

She laughs, "Oh honey, I knew who you were because Paige pointed it out. I knew who they were because I love 69 Bottles. I'm less than two years older than you are, darlin'."

"Oh my god," Talon says, "thank you for being discreet."

"It's my job. Though I have to tell you, I can't keep this from Paige, she's a huge fan."

"Oh my god." I burst out laughing. I even hear Kyle laughing, which is great, all the tension lifts and I take a deep breath.

"Thank you, Doctor Breckenridge."

"Call me Sara," she says.

"Thank you, Sara," I say and stand. The guys follow me. "I think we're okay, for now."

"Thank you Doctor." Talon and Kyle both say, shaking her hand and we leave. Mills and Tori have been standing by outside this whole time. I look at my watch, it's only four-thirty but it felt like we were in there forever. Talon and Kyle both take my hands as we leave the building.

chapter 18

The guys don't let me go the entire car ride home. "How did it go?" Tori turns back looking at me. I look to both of the guys.

"Can I show her?" Talon nods excitedly and Kyle just nods. He's still in shock, but doing better. I pull the pictures out of my purse. I flip through them to see what we have. I could kiss Sara. There is a picture that has both babies and they're labeled Baby A and Baby B. I hand it to Tori.

"No way?" she smiles back at me. "Twins? Seriously?" Her excitement is infectious and I nod excitedly. "Congratulations, guys," she says and Kyle softens a little bit.

"Thanks," Talon says.

"Thank you," Kyle adds and for the first time since leaving the doctor's office, he smiles.

Tori hands me back the pictures. "Where to?" Mills asks.

"Cheesesteak," I say and Talon bounces in his seat like a little boy.

"Alright," Mills says and he turns at the next light. I'm assuming he knows the place to go. "The band wants them too."

"Awesome."

Kyle looks at me, "We need to fill your script." And my rock is back. I nod toward Mills. 'Tell him' I mouth and Kyle looks panicked again. I squeeze his hand. "Mills, we need to stop by a pharmacy, Addison has a script to fill."

"Let's do that first, then we can swing back and pick it up." Mills looks at Kyle in the mirror and smiles.

"Okay," Kyle says. "I'll run it in." He adds.

"You don't have to do that," Talon interjects. "We can all do it."

"No, not if we want to keep this a secret longer. Let me do it," Kyle says.

"Thank you, cowboy," I tell him and he smiles at me.

A couple minutes later we pull into a CVS and Kyle goes in with my prescription and insurance card. Mills and Tori step out of the car, giving Talon and I some privacy. "When we get back, can I have the bedroom to talk with Kyle?"

"Of course. He's really freaking out about this."

"He is, but I think he just needs some time with me. He needs to see that this really is okay. When I'm done, I want you to talk to him."

"What more can I say to him?" he pleads sadly. "I'm not very good at all this."

"You're better at it than you think. But I think this is going to take some time to settle in. I think it's going to take some time for all of us. Yes, it's exciting, but I am scared shitless. Not just about the twins but life in general. This really changes everything. It's going to affect my career, regardless of what I choose to do. It's going to affect a lot of things going forward."

"You say that like you're going to be doing this alone. You're not, I'm not going anywhere and despite Kyle's reaction, he won't either. He just needs to let it soak in."

"I know I'm not alone, and I'm not saying I'll be doing it alone, but the bottom line is that this changes everything, but in a good way."

"You're right it does change everything, but it changes nothing about how I feel about you and it certainly shouldn't change how Kyle feels about you."

"I don't think it does. I think he is positively freaked out because of the fact that he's going to be a dad; maybe it has a lot to do with his mother, his brother and his father. Think about it, Talon. He's on his own in this world, that's scary. I have my mom, you have yours, Kyle has one who is alive and hates him because it's convenient for her to do so," I say, emotions filling me to the point of crying.

"Oh baby, don't cry, please."

"I don't mean to."

He chuckles, "I know you don't. But he'll be coming back in a minute. How about I take Tori and Mills into the restaurant for our food, you and him stay in the car."

"Oh god, don't do that. Let Mills do it."

"No, I am capable of getting my two favorite people in the world cheesesteaks. You try talking to him. We'll be in there for a bit, but why don't you guys eat in the bedroom, I'll sit with the guys."

"Are you sure?"

He holds me close and kisses my forehead. "Of course."

Kyle comes back and I lean into him, wrapping my hands around his arm, holding on for dear life. Kyle kisses the top of my head and my heart swells. No matter how bad he's feeling, he doesn't forget about me.

We arrive at the restaurant and Talon argues with Mills about getting dinner, but Talon wins the argument and Mills escorts him inside.

"I imagine social media is blowing up."

Kyle laughs, "He grew up close to here, it might not be that bad."

"I hope so." I turn in my seat to look at him. "Are you feeling better?"

He snorts. "No."

"You're hiding it well."

"Good." He leans over and kisses my forehead.

"What's freaking you out?" I ask bluntly.

"Is this really the place for this?"

I shrug. "You and I are eating in the bedroom. We're going to talk, so we can either wait until then, or you can give me an indication so that I can figure out how to handle this with you. I don't expect you to be all butterflies and roses when we're done, but this, the way you are, it's hurting me. I don't like it, but I can't let it go."

"What if I asked you to tell me what's on your mind first?"

I shrug, "If that's what you think it will take to help you talk..." I let the thought trail off.

"I guess I just need to know whether or not we're sharing some of the same feelings and it might make it easier for me to tell you what I'm afraid of," he says quietly, I can tell he's afraid that he's alone in his fears and that is far from the truth in this situation.

"I'm scared because..." I take a deep breath, "because it's all so fast, too fast. We're barely beginning this journey together and now," I can't hold back the emotions anymore, "now we're becoming a family. I'm terrified that you and Talon are going to realize that and bolt." He shakes his head, sadness in his eyes. He opens his mouth to speak and I quiet him with my finger. "Please, I've started, don't let me stop." He nods his agreement. "I'm terrified that we're testing the boundaries of our new relationship beyond what we're ready for, what we're capable of. That this is going to destroy whatever we have building between us. That it's all too much for even me to handle, or process." I wipe tears from my cheeks, "If you and Talon hadn't been there or if I'd managed to do this on my own, finding out without you, I'm afraid I would have run away or that something is going to drive you both away from me."

I pause, taking in the sight of Kyle's tears in his eyes. "I've always wanted kids, but I've lived my life knowing that having them was nearly impossible and now, five weeks into all of this, here we are and I'm still scared shitless you're going to run. You should run, you both should, and I don't know that I would blame you if you did. We didn't plan this, we didn't spend days, weeks, months or even years trying for a baby, planning it, making this time an enjoyable time. Instead we didn't try to stop it either." I look down at my lap, fidgeting with my hands.

"I should have told you guys to wrap it back up after our first night in Phoenix, but I didn't. I relied on too many things and every one of them failed me. I mean, hell Kyle, we never even talked about it. Neither of you asked me about birth control, we never discussed my problems, we never did anything to stop this from happening and I want to believe that we all knew the risks and we didn't care."

"Panda, I don't want to interrupt you, but what do you mean everything failed you?" He asks me quietly. I can tell he's looking at me, but I can't look back at him.

"My PCOS, my birth control - I should have been checking for it all along. I shouldn't have waited until that Sunday to try and pull it out. I should have stopped you both from unwrapping, then I shouldn't have told you. I should have..."

"Don't. Don't say that. I'm glad we know, I'm glad we were there for you." I finally look at him. I don't know what else to say so I don't say anything. He continues, "I have no doubt that at some point I will find true happiness in all this, but right now it's hard because it's all so new and I'm scared. I need it to sink in, but it certainly doesn't change how I feel about you, or about where I see this relationship going."

I wipe the tears again.

"What if they're not mine?" he says bluntly.

"Is that really what's bothering you?"

"It's part of it."

chapter 19

"Kyle, look at me." He does. "It doesn't matter to me if they're yours or Talon's or both. Both you and Talon have equal rights when it comes to these little ones. I will not ever deny you or Talon paternity rights. Regardless of who is the biological father. In all honesty, I don't want to find out. I don't want to know who they belong to because to me it doesn't matter. If you're honestly in this relationship wholeheartedly, it won't matter to you either."

"I'm afraid that if I find out they're Talon's that I won't be able to love them the way they deserve to be loved. I want to be the father; I think that's why it bothers me. I want one or both of them to be mine."

Tears flow down my cheeks at his confession and I press my forehead against his. "I will do a paternity test if it matters to you when the time comes. I won't hesitate to do it. But fretting over it right now is pointless. We can't find out for months and I don't want that between us during this time. This is a time that we should be happy. I realize the risks involved over the next several weeks, but at this point, we shouldn't be worrying about nine months from now. I need you as my rock; I need you to love me, to love Talon, and to love these babies. Because what you're telling me right now is that you don't think you can love them unless they're yours."

He doesn't say anything for a few heartbeats and I start to go mental. Finally he moves, reaching his arm across his body and places his hand on my pouch. "I... god, baby girl, I love you so fucking much, it hurts. It's killing me to know that I'm hurting you and I don't mean to. I, fuck..." his hand comes away from my belly and into his hair. He starts to cry.

I unbuckle my seatbelt and I climb on top of him, he wraps his arms around me and cries into my neck. My heart breaks and I cry silently too.

"I love you so much it hurts, Addison. It hurts so much that it scares me. This scares me. It kills me to see you in pain because of what we've done to your body, what we're doing to your body. I fear a miscarriage. I'm afraid that I'll fall in love with the twins and something will happen to them before I get to meet them."

His speech encourages me, gives me hope I haven't felt since this all came crashing down. "I think you're already in love with them. I don't think you could fear miscarriage if you didn't already feel for them. I think that what's happening to my body hurts you because you love me so much you want to take it all away." I reach into my purse for the pictures. I grab the one I showed Tori. "This, these two little blips on the screen, make every ounce of pain I feel worth it. They make everything that's going to happen to my body worth it. You and Talon loving me, makes all of this worth it. That's how I can throw up every morning and still be okay afterward. These two little blips that will soon be babies in my arms, make it all worth it."

He holds me tighter to him. "I do love them, I love them so much I'm scared shitless. I love you so much that I feel like I'm going to suffocate you and push you away. Every person I've ever loved has left me. I can't let that happen with you."

I run my fingers through his hair. "Kyle Black, I love you with all of my heart and every ounce of my soul. I am not going anywhere I refuse. You and Talon are who I am; you're who I am meant to be with. I'm pregnant for a reason, not just because we didn't have protection. I'm pregnant because I'm supposed to be, it's meant to be. That's what I have to believe. I've been told for too long that it wouldn't happen without a great deal of medical assistance, that I would face long struggles to get pregnant and possibly face disappointment again and again. I have to believe it's happened for a reason."

He doesn't say anything and I know Talon is going to be back soon. I really don't want to be a mess when he comes back.

Finally he lifts his head and his eyes are red with tears. "I don't understand how Talon can be so carefree about this."

I laugh silently for a second. "I don't think he understands the gravity of what's ahead of him. I think it will be some time before it finally sets in, but that's what makes you two so amazingly perfect. You're the grounded one. Talon is the carefree one. You are my rock; he brings out my wild side. You'd rather be lying in bed with me reading pregnancy books than out partying with the guys. But I know Talon would rather be home with us too sometimes, but he goes, and frankly doesn't put up much of a fight. You'd go if I forced you to, which I'm likely to do soon. I think you need to get drunk and let it all go for a little while. Maybe it might give you some clarity."

"I do let it all go, you're my alcohol, my drug, my sobriety all rolled into one, Addison. When I'm with you, everything else goes away. When I look into your eyes I forget that you're pregnant. I forget that it hurts, I forget my fears and worries. I get lost in you." His eyes are a brighter blue than normal. I could stare into his eyes for hours.

"I know what you mean," I breathe. I blink, breaking our contact and he chuckles.

"See."

"And that, Kyle Black, is how I know that all of this is meant to be. I can get lost in your eyes; I find comfort in them that I've never had before. I find it that much easier to love you because I can see into your soul and know that you love me as much as I love you."

"No, baby girl, I love you more." His hand rests on my belly, "Because there is more of you to love."

I start to cry again. This time happy tears. We made a breakthrough and I rest my head on his shoulder, crying into his neck and he just holds me close. Rubbing my back, loving me.

kyle

Jesus, I had no idea that's what she was feeling with all of this. It makes everything I'm feeling seem completely stupid and unnecessary. I've been so wrapped up in my own emotions that I haven't stopped to consider what she might be going through.

God, the fact that she thinks she should have run away. I've given her that impression, I know I have. "Is it because of me that you think you should have run away?" I ask her softly as I hold her in my arms.

She pulls back, looking at me. "No, Kyle, I don't. I think I feel that way because in all honesty I feel responsible for this, for what we're facing."

"No, baby girl, we all played a role in this. It's not your fault."

She sniffles, "Yeah, it kind of is. I should have paid more attention."

"Panda, you couldn't have known this would happen. After the appointment, I feel I understand better the odds that we faced."

"It was supposed to be next to impossible," she says quietly.

"But impossible is what we're good at. We've defied the odds already. Look at how well we work as a threesome," I tell her.

"I know, but sometimes I feel like it's superficial. After Minneapolis and Talon getting upset, it reminded me how everything we have can be shattered so quickly."

"No, baby girl. Not at all. You didn't see him like I did that morning. He was so shattered that you were gone, at what he'd done. He honestly hadn't realized what we had going until it was stripped away from us when you used your safe word. My one and only goal was to talk sense into Talon and make him see, but I didn't have to. He already knew. I knew then that nothing else mattered if I couldn't figure out how to keep us together. Which is why I told him then that I love him. I didn't expect his reaction," god, I certainly did not expect that, "but I knew that he needed to see it wasn't just about you, that it was about the three of us." I take a deep breath.

"I didn't know that." She gives me a small smile.

"That was even before all this. But no matter what, I know that those hours were the longest in my life and I will do anything I can to avoid that again in the future."

She snuggles into me, wrapping her arms around me, hugging me tightly. She doesn't say anything, she doesn't have to, just having her close to me like this is all I need. I bury my face in her hair, breathing in her beautiful vanilla scent, knowing that she's here, she's real.

She's pregnant, and I am scared to death of what the future holds. Not just with the twins in general, but with the three of us. I know I am not ready for this and I haven't even been able to process how to get ready for this when the twins were thrown at me by the doctor. I can't even process this, I don't know how, or even where to begin.

chapter 20

addison

A few minutes later Talon returned to the car. He and Mills put enough food in the back to feed an army and I snuggled into Kyle on the way back to the pharmacy for my prescription.

Once he was inside I turned to Talon. "How'd it go?" he asks before I can say a word.

"Really well. He's scared, like you and I are. But I think he realized that there is more to be scared about than just being scared of the future."

"What do you mean, angel?"

"What I mean is the fact that he wouldn't have anything to be scared about if he didn't love me, you, or the babies. It's one of the same reasons I'm scared. He's afraid of the fact that he can't take away the pain, vomiting and everything else I'm feeling. He feels like I'm burdening it all alone." He scowls at me, confused. "I'm not alone because I have you and him. You're both here, you're not pushing me away or running away from me. Not yet anyway."

"Angel, if anything, you being pregnant has brought us closer together."

I smile. "I know that, big man, but Kyle needed to see that, to feel that and I hope I showed it to him. It's going to take him some time to adjust and based on what Sara told me, that adjustment isn't going to have much time. But I want him to do something for me when we get back."

"What's that, angel?"

I smile, "I want him to take a picture of me and my pouch. I want him to be able to see the chronological events, see the progress. He thinks that being pregnant is a burden and I need to show him that it's not. You and he think differently, which is why you both work so well together. You're my bad boy and he's my thinker. You lift me up and make me wild and carefree, while he grounds me and keeps reality in check. It's the perfect balance."

"Good, I'm glad." He kisses my forehead.

"Good, now answer me something..."

"Anything, angel."

"Do you love him?"

"Yes, I do," he says without hesitation.

"Are you in love with him?"

He smiles. "Nearly as much as I am with you."

"Then tell him that. He needs to know, he needs to hear it and he needs to feel it. Sometimes I think that he's thinking he's the third wheel and he's not."

"No, he's not, he's far from it. He's the frame that holds us all together."

I smile. "Don't tell me that, tell him that." I encourage.

"I will."

"When?" I ask.

"Tonight."

"Good."

We finish our brief chat just as Kyle leaves the store. He comes out with not just my prescription but two bags full of stuff.

When he gets into the car I look at him with what I am sure is a confused look and ask, "What on earth did you buy?"

He smirks, then from one of the bags he pulls out a big bottle of apple juice and I moan with delight. That's become my favorite this last week or so. Then he pulls out a box of saltines. I giggle. Then out comes heaven on earth, a box of Lindt Chocolate Truffles, then a container of- "Oh my god!" I squeal when I see the label. Ben and Jerry's Salted Caramel. I throw my arms around his neck. "You're the best ever." I kiss his cheek.

"That's not all, but I'll show you the last thing when we get back."

"It isn't condoms is it, because it's a little late for that," Talon teases him and Kyle and I burst out laughing. Mills and Tori join in.

And like so many other times, the weight is gone. Lifted from the air with a single sentence.

"I'm still going to eat with the guys," Talon tells me as I get out of the car.

"Okay. If something happens between Kyle and I, that would be okay, wouldn't it?"

He kisses my forehead. "I hope it does. I think you both need the time to connect, alone. I'll steal mine another time." He smiles widely.

"And that is why I love you, Talon Carver."

"That's all?" he teases and I laugh.

"No, that's only the beginning."

Talon and Kyle help Mills and Tori bring the hoard of food onto the bus. The guys immediately attack the bags and I can see Talon digging around. He breaks free of the group, bringing me my sandwich. "No onions." He smiles, proud of himself.

"I'm not sure it would matter. I've been nauseous since you brought it to the car. But thank you." He kisses me.

"Now go, be with our boy."

"You're still going to talk to him?"

"Absolutely. Unless you wear him out and he falls asleep." He laughs.

"Alright." I kiss him on the cheek. "Love you, big man."

"Love you, angel."

I slide past the hoard of men in the galley and duck into the bedroom with my cheesesteak and french fries. I set it down on the nightstand and ditch my pants and the Nirvana shirt I'm wearing. Leaving the cami on, I throw on one of Kyle's soft t-shirts. I grab a towel out of the closet for under me so I don't slop food all over the place and I climb up, crossing my legs. I dive in with gusto.

My mouth waters as I chew. So good. I moan with my food-gasm and eat a french fry. "I could watch you eat for hours," Kyle says leaning against the wall in the doorway. "It's one of the most erotic things I've ever seen. Even before we started feeding you regularly." He smirks.

"Where's yours?"

"In the galley. I was waiting for everyone to get theirs before I had to fight them all off. That smells amazing. The guys came over from the other bus. Apparently they bought cheesesteaks for the guards, the roadies and the band."

"Jeez. No wonder there was so much and it's like heaven on a bun. I miss these."

"Oh, did you use to live in Philly?"

"No, from when I lived in NYC. I'd drive down here once every three months or so, spend the night and eat two while I was here."

"You're a food whore."

I burst out laughing. "Yes, yes I am." He laughs and it's a beautiful sight to see. "Go get your food, so you can come back here and watch me eat."

He laughs and comes to the side of the bed. "I saw this in CVS and it made me think of you." He pulls something out of the bag I didn't get to see. It's a purple and black panda bear and it's got the cutest face I think I've ever seen. It says Philly on it and I love it even more. I reach out for it, and he gives it to me. I hug it. Then I set him in my lap. "Lucky bear," he mumbles with a smirk and goes to leave.

"Can you bring me some juice when you come back?"

"Of course, anything else?"

"Mmm ice cream," I moan.

"After you eat your dinner." He smiles wickedly at me.

"Why do I get the impression you might be eating more than me?"

He laughs again and leaves the room.

When he comes back I'm moaning around another bite of cheesesteak and he chuckles again, handing me a bottle of apple juice. "Where's the stuff from the doctor's office?" he asks as he sits down.

I swallow my mouthful and set my food down. "It's in my purse, want me to get it?"

"No, eat, panda girl. We can get it when we're done." I smile and open my apple juice. Drinking down half of it before putting the cap back on it. "I stuck one of the big bottles in the freezer for you so it would get colder faster."

I lean over and kiss his cheek. I leave a greasy imprint. "Crap," I say, reaching for a napkin.

He laughs. "Leave it."

I giggle and go back to my food.

I burp. "Oh my god. I'm so sorry," I blurt.

Kyle starts laughing so hard he almost falls over. I can't help but join in, until I get the hiccups, which only makes him laugh harder. "So not co..." hiccup "...ol."

That only adds fuel to the fire and I try to get rid of them and fail. I end up drinking the rest of my apple juice and finally they disappear. "You okay, panda girl?"

I laugh, "Yes. God, that's embarrassing."

"I think it's hilarious," he says with a smile. "Compliments to the chef," he says with a smirk, and then takes a bite of his sandwich. I laugh a little more. "Are you done?" he asks and I look down at the Styrofoam carton my food was in. Then I look at his. Half his fries are gone and there is still a good quarter of his cheesesteak left.

"Jesus, I ate that whole thing." I fight back another burp.

"Hungry?"

"Not anymore. God, that was good." I lean back against the headboard, holding the bear to my stomach.

"Let me see him," he says and I hand over my new bear. "Hmm, baby girl?" I look at him. "Look," he says nodding toward my stomach and I look down.

"Dear god. I look like I swallowed a softball whole." My stomach is distended enough that it's pushing out the t-shirt I'm wearing, though it's tucked in to where my thighs come together and pulled tight, it's very obviously visible.

"As long as you're full, you can eat whatever you want." He rubs his hand along my stomach.

"You like that, don't you? My belly?"

He smiles. "It's sexy as hell and I love it even more knowing that you're full, feeding the panda cubs." I giggle at his nickname for the twins. He smiles, "It's still not easy to say that."

I put my hand on top of his. "It isn't easy to hear sometimes, but it's reality, so I suspect it will sink in over time. Listen, I want you to do something, um, starting tomorrow. I was gonna have you do it tonight, but I think I've blown it with that cheesesteak."

"Do what?"

"Well, since tomorrow is Wednesday and officially five weeks, I want you to take a belly picture of me every week on Wednesdays documenting my growth."

"Why?" His voice is more curious then skeptical.

"Two reasons. One, I want to be able to see it from a different point of view. All I get is the looking down and mirror shot and two, I think it's important for me and for you to document this journey. Like right now, I'm going to pull out my journal and write down that god awful cheesesteak and french fries, and document that today, here, in Philadelphia, we found out that we're having twins."

He smiles. "I think that's a great idea on both counts and I'd be honored to take your pictures for you." He smiles. "So why don't you grab the stuff from the doctor's office, your journal and The Book, and I'll go throw this stuff out. What else do you need?" He gets off of the bed, handing me back my bear.

"More juice." I smile.

"Ice cream?"

"Mmmm, ice cream," I look back at my belly, "maybe later." I smile.

He disappears and I get my purse and grab The Book from where we left it on the nightstand.

chapter 21

kyle

"Hey Kyle," Talon says as I walk into the kitchen. "How is she?" I notice that Talon is sitting alone.

I snort. Then flip open her container. "I'd say she's full."

"Good god. She really ate all that?" He looks down at his in front of him and it looks like mine, three quarters gone. He makes a bloated face.

"Yeah, she did, plus a bottle of apple juice, she wants more, then I'm going to give her her vitamin."

"Okay good."

"Why are you in here alone? I thought you were eating with the guys?"

"Oh I did. They're outside, starting a fire. We were going to jam a little bit."

"Oh, nice. Want us to come outside? I'm sure she'd love that."

"That'd be great. But don't force her. Let her relax. She's had a trying day," he says quietly.

"Yeah, and I feel awful about it too."

"Hey, don't. We're all dealing with this in our own way."

"Not you, you're, I don't know, man, I never expected you to be like this, so calm and collected."

"It's the duck on the pond theory, in reality. On the surface, everything is calm and normal, underneath my legs are moving a million miles a minute," he says hoarsely.

"So, why the front?"

"Ah, she doesn't need that man. She's being so strong for both of us. You saw her today, she'd just found out she's pregnant with twins and she was there holding you up." I hang my head. "Don't. It's alright. In fact I think it's good for her, it takes her mind away from herself and what she's feeling. Don't make a habit of it. But she really loves you and she wants you to be good, to be okay with all of this. Are you?"

I shrug. "I'm better than I was before we talked. She aired some of her own fears."

"What do you mean?"

I give him a half smile, "Everything we think we're feeling, she's feeling times ten. Did you know she might have run away if we hadn't been there?"

He looks at me, fear in his eyes, "why?" he breathes.

"She feels like it's all too much for both of us, that it's too fast, she's scared of what it means for the three of us," I tell him, though I can't hide the sadness in my voice.

"Jesus, she's right though, it's all too fast. It's insanely fast. But...but I don't think I'd change it. In fact, I can't change it." he says softly.

I watch as he puts his head in his hands. "Talon, I think we need to show her she has no reason to want to run away. After talking to her I understand better that I can't change it, that I can't bear the burden of it for her and I know that she's found her happy place. She looks at that picture, the one with both babies in it, and she says that's what makes it worth it, and she's right. In the end, that's all that matters."

He smiles at me. "You're absolutely right. I can't even begin to imagine what she's thinking about all of this."

"She's scared, just like you and I are. She just hides it better than we do."

"Which is why I'll continue being a duck for a while. I just need to love her, you know?" He stands up and comes toward me where I'm leaning against the counter. He sets his container down and takes my cheeks in his hands. "Just like I need to love you."

My breathing stops, my cock grows hard instantly and I stare into his eyes. "I've realized something in the midst of all of this madness. I've realized that not only do I love her more than life itself, but I'm in love with you too."

"Jesus, Tal, talk about knocking a guy on his ass. Do you mean it?"

"I wouldn't say it if I didn't. You know that. I love you, cowboy."

I love that he uses Addison's nickname for me. "I love you too."

Then his lips meet mine in a warm dance of lips and tongues, I can't help the moan that escapes before he pulls away. "Now go take care of our girl. Come out if you want. But bundle her up, it's chilly out tonight," he says as his thumb rubs along my cheek before releasing me.

"Hey Tal?"

"Yeah."

"I needed to hear that tonight. Thank you."

He winks at me and hops down the steps of the bus, pushing open the door and I can hear the guys jamming outside. I readjust my cock and go back toward the bedroom. I get halfway there before I remember her apple juice and I turn around.

Going back into the kitchen, I pull the bottle from the freezer and pour her a big plastic cup full. As I head back, Peacock steps out of the bathroom. "Hey man, you alright?"

"Yeah, why?"

"You look upset?" I cock my head. "Wanna talk about it?"

"I honestly just have a question."

"Shoot."

"Are you and Talon and Addison together?"

I smile, "Yeah man, we are. Does that bother you?"

He chuckles. "God, no. It's nice to know though. Makes things easier."

"Easier, how?"

"I'm not ready to talk about it."

"Eric? Seriously, it's alright. We already know, dude."

He looks at me, shocked. "How?"

I shrug. "You've never been into the ladies. You put on a front, which is good for you, but that's not who you are. We don't talk about you or anything, but Talon and I figured it out a long time ago. Whether Mouse or Dex know, I have no clue, but you saw Dex the other day, he doesn't give a shit and Mouse is your best friend. I'd be surprised if he doesn't know."

"He knows."

"So that leaves who, Dex? Man, open that can of worms with caution though. He won't be mean about it, but you know it will give him ammo, you know how he gets."

"Yeah, I know. Does Addison know?"

I raise an eyebrow at him, "I don't think so."

"Good, don't tell her. I've been promising her a talk for a long time, about what really happened between Jess and I back in San Diego. Let me tell her, okay?"

"Absolutely." I smile and take his hand, we bump chests like we always have. "Now get out there. I'll go see if Addie wants to join you."

"I didn't intend to eavesdrop from the bathroom, but, is she pregnant?"

"Shh." I smirk.

"Congrats, man." He smiles wide.

"Thank you, Eric, that means a lot."

"Anytime. You guys need anything, holler."

"Will do." We slide past each other and I finally make it back to the bedroom. I expected to see Addison asleep on the bed when I return, but she's not. She's writing in her journal.

"Hey baby girl."

She looks up at me with her bright, beautiful green eyes and the warmest smile spreads across her lips. "Hey cowboy. What took you so long?"

I smile, truly happy for the first time in a long time. I set her drink on the bedside table and slide onto the bed. "Talon and I just talked."

"Oh, about what?"

"He confessed to loving and being in love with me."

She covers her mouth with her hands. Then pulling them away she asks, "How does that make you feel?"

"Fucking amazing."

chapter 22
addison

"I'm so happy for you," I tell Kyle. I knew it was coming and I doubt that Talon would ever lie to me, but sometimes I think he doesn't understand his own emotions.

"You knew, didn't you? That he was going to tell me that?"

I sigh. "Yeah, we talked about it in the car; I just didn't think he'd do it so soon."

"Why did you talk about it?"

"Because he's so worried about you and I needed some reassurance. All of this is so overwhelming that..." I pause and take a deep breath before continuing, "I needed to know that it's real."

"Oh panda girl, it's always been real, whether we admitted it to each other or not." He lifts his hand and strokes it gently along my cheek, I lean into his touch. "I knew I loved him and I've told him I love him before, it's just... I don't know. I know it's hard for him," he says sadly.

"Does that bother you?"

"What? That it's hard for him?" I nod. "No, actually it makes me happier because I know he doesn't just say it to placate me, or even you. I know that when he says it, he truly means it. So yeah, it makes me happy and I'm glad he confided in you. You bring out parts of him I never knew existed and I love you all the more for it."

He leans in and kisses me on the lips. It's not charged, but it's sweet and I melt into him. That's when I hear music playing. I pull back from him, listening. "What are they doing?"

Kyle smiles, "They're doing what they do best."

"Where?"

"Outside, around a fire. You want to go out there?"

I hesitate. "I wanted to spend some time with you tonight."

"Oh baby girl, we can do that and still go out and watch them for a while, it's..." he looks at the clock, "just after seven. Come on, let's get you bundled up"

I'm back in my flannel pants, still wearing Kyle's t-shirt and I have my hoodie and wool pea coat on. Kyle grabs a spare blanket from the closet and brings it with us. When I step off of the bus, I am greeted with the biggest smile from Talon I've ever seen. He literally lights up the night. The smile grows bigger when Kyle steps off of the bus behind me.

They're jamming, playing a new song I don't recognize and I instantly fall in love with it. Talon, Peacock and Mouse have their guitars and Dex is hitting what looks like an electronic drum set.

I turn to Kyle. "I have an idea, do you mind grabbing my phone?"

He kisses my forehead. "Not at all, I'll be right back." He hands me the blanket and I fold it over my hands and Talon nods for me to come sit next to him.

I walk carefully over to him and lay the blanket out on the ground for me to sit in front of the log he's on, but off to the side. I want to make room for Kyle too. I watch and listen as they continue with just music, no lyrics, but it doesn't matter, it takes everything I have not to get up and dance.

Kyle returns and sees me sitting next to Talon and smiles. He comes around the fire and sits behind me and I settle in between his legs. "Here you go," he whispers in my ear as he hands me my phone. I put it in my pocket and then put my hands on his knees, lifting myself onto his lap. He gently wraps his arms around me, holding me to him. The guys finish out the song.

"Okay, that was awesome. Do it again," I say with a big grin on my face.

Talon laughs. "With lyrics this time?"

I look at him and smile wide. "Yes, please."

He laughs, "You got it, angel."

Dex whacks his sticks together to count them off and then beats his drums. Peacock picks up next on the bass and the sound is booming, but beautiful. Then Mouse and Talon join in. They play a couple of bars before Talon starts to sing and I'm transfixed. Forgetting my plan all together as I listen to the words. The song is upbeat and I want to dance.

His voice is sultry, but yet has his hard gravel to it that makes my panties wet and I shiver.

Kyle misinterprets my shiver and picks the blanket back up off of the ground. He wraps it around my legs and I smile at him, lean in and kiss him sweetly as he sways me back and forth to the music.

"Wow!" is all I can say for a minute. "I have an idea, if you're interested…"

"What's that, angel?"

"A sound bite."

"The label would be pissed," Dex says from across the fire.

"I wouldn't release it without their approval, Dex. Believe me. But I think it would be awesome. Something raw and unplugged from 69 Bottles."

"Go for it," Talon says with a smirk. "Guys, let's do the other one."

"Which?" Peacock asks.

"The one right before they came out. 'Sunshine and Roses'."

"Got it."

I get my phone ready to record and nod at Dex, who counts it off. I push record as Dex and Peacock set the tone, they're quickly followed by Mouse, then Talon steps in with a separate guitar part.

When I look at you, you're all I see
The love in your eyes is all I need
There isn't any love greater than yours
You're perfect, like sunshine and roses…

I stop the sound bite but the guys keep going and I start crying. It's one of their softer pieces, like 'Your Eyes' is, but it has a harder edge to it…

I need your look, your touch, your laugh,
I need your eyes like I need
Sunshine and roses

Talon is looking at me as he finishes off the song.

I'm crying, of course. "You didn't?" I ask him.

He laughs. "Yeah, angel, I did."

"What the hell are you doing to him?" Dex takes his stab. "He's gone all love crazy over you. It's sad really. He used to be a great songwriter." Dex is laughing so I know he's joking.

"He still is, dickweed."

"Ah hell, for you he's amazing, but I'm pretty sure you're biased. But no matter, it's a great fucking song."

I roll my eyes at him and he laughs.

Kyle and I stay out for another song that I pull a sound bite from, the song is good, but I like the first one better. Then of course 'Sunshine and Roses' just might replace 'Your Eyes' as my top played song.

Kyle and I say good night. I lean down and kiss Talon on the lips. "Love you," he whispers.

"Ditto, big man," I whisper back and he smiles wide.

Once we're inside, Kyle helps me undress, taking my coat and hanging it up. "Thank you."

"For what, baby girl?"

"Taking me out there. That was fun. I've never seen them so raw before. It was awesome."

"Anything for you, panda. How you feeling?"

"Tired, but good."

"You ready for ice cream?" I smile huge and nod with excitement. "Good. I'll get that, plus your pill."

"Okay, love." I climb up onto the bed and open my journal. I reread what I wrote earlier…

Today, everything shifted, turned real and became ten times better than I could have ever imagined. I feel so loved. We're having twins!

I add the date and then add ice cream to my list of foods for today.

When Kyle returns, I close the journal and set it back on the nightstand. "Are you done with that for tonight?"

I nod, "As long as I don't eat anything other than ice cream, yes."

He laughs as he sits, or rather lays on the bed, propping himself up on one elbow holding the container. "Take this and then I want to feed you," he says. I smirk at him. I take my vitamin from him and swallow it down with my apple juice from earlier and then open my mouth to him for ice cream. He chuckles at my eagerness and then he puts the spoonful in my mouth and my tongue dances with delight, causing me to moan.

The salted caramel is sweet with the barest hint of salt. Giving me my beloved salty and sweet in one spoonful. I watch as Kyle takes a bite. "Not bad," he says as he digs out another spoonful for me. I open like a baby bird and he feeds me another bite.

This goes on for about ten minutes before we've managed to drain the carton between the two of us. Though toward the end it was mostly me. "I'm so glad I have an excuse to eat," I say as I lean back against the headboard with my hand on my stomach.

"No, you have two," he retorts with a smile.

"See a little easier with each pass, isn't it?"

"It is." He wraps his arm around my thighs and slides closer to me. His head comes to rest on my stomach. I start to play with his hair. "You keep that up and you'll put me to sleep," he says with a grin.

He tilts his head up to look at me, though all he really gets is an eyeful of breasts. "Make love to me," I whisper, as I get lost in his eyes.

Zoey Derrick

He adjusts once again so that he is resting back on his elbow. His hand glides over my thighs and across my sex. Then slowly up my shirt and under the cami I'm wearing. "We need to get you more of these," he says as he slides his fingers underneath.

"Tomorrow," I whisper hotly as his hand slides further up my stomach to just under my breast.

"Does it hurt?"

"No," I breathe and he continues. Slowly sliding his hand along the underside of both breasts then gently working his way toward my nipples. When his hand comes in contact with it I hiss as that delicious pain and pleasure course through my veins. "Don't stop," I moan and he doesn't. Gently he caresses my left nipple, and then moves across my chest to the other one. I arch my back and close my eyes. Feeling the sensations radiating through me.

He keeps going, gently massaging my breasts and nipples until his hand slides back down my belly to find my wet slit.

chapter 23

Kyle wastes no time as his hand eagerly finds my clit with a flick of his finger and I tremble with excitement. I look into his eyes and everything heightens. I can feel the blood rushing to my skin, making my nipples harden and the pleasure flare. I touch his cheek and urge him to my lips. He takes them with his own sense of urgency. His finger pace and pressure increase and I moan into his mouth.

His tongue does a dance with mine, licking and stroking and my head begins to spin from dizziness, thanks to his glorious kiss. I feel his fingers sliding and exploring my dripping sex. I shiver with anticipation as he rims the entrance of my pussy. But he doesn't stop kissing me; I begin to tremble more. The anticipation is too much. "Relax, baby girl. I got you." I smile against his lips and kiss him again, but he doesn't linger. He sits back and I sit up. Pulling on both my cami and t-shirt. Tossing them off to the floor. He moans at the sight of my body and it sends goose bumps dancing across my skin.

He slides a finger inside and I'm immediately panting with desire as my back arches, pushing my pussy down onto his finger. "Fuck!" he growls and then he shifts so he is looming over me, his hand still sliding in and out of me, making me hotter and more wanton than before. His mouth comes to my right nipple and his eyes silently beg for permission.

"Please," I beg him and his wide flat tongue licks long and slow across my nipple. The sight is sexier than you'd imagine and I nearly explode. I bite my lip. He continues his licking but it doesn't take him long before his lips are wrapped around my nipple, bringing gentle sucking pulls with long soft strokes of his tongue. I arch again, moaning and panting with an urgency to come.

"Don't hold out on me, baby girl. Give it to me."

My breathing spikes at his command and I feel powerless to stop the onslaught of sensations blossoming deep in my core. My eyes roll up, my moaning increases, my body locks down and I explode around his fingers. His motions inside of me speed up and his sucking intensifies, magnifying my orgasm by five. "Kyle!" I scream out and I reach my peak and start to fall back down.

His hand slows, and releasing his mouth from my breast he rears up. I watch him rip off his t-shirt in a lust filled craze, he gloriously rips open his button fly jeans, springing his cock free. My mouth waters. I want to taste him. When I move so that I can, he stops me. "I want to make love to you here." His hand lightly strokes along the seam of my pussy. "Not your mouth, baby girl." I pout prettily at him and he laughs, "There is plenty of time for that, I promise, but tonight is all about you." He sheds his jeans, kicking them off of the bed and then he takes his cock in his hands.

My veins are instantly on fire with desire and I spread my legs for him. Opening for him, inviting him inside of me.

He brings his knees up under my legs, lifting them higher. Then I feel him stroke his cock along my sex and I shiver in anticipation of what I know is coming. "I'm so eager to be inside of you. I don't want to hurt you."

I reach out to place my hand on his stomach. "You won't hurt me." I let my hand slip south, taking hold of his cock and I watch as his eyes roll up into his head. I shiver. Knowing I caused that look is heady for a woman, especially me. I line the head of his erection up with my entrance. "It's your turn, cowboy," I say and our eyes meet. Blue to green, and he slips inside of me. My pussy is hungry for him, clenching and releasing along his shaft as he slides inside. But I can't take my eyes off of him. The rush of breath he lets out the moment he slides home sends shivers of love and affection across my body.

Our bodies are joined as one, and through each other's eyes, our souls meld and change and I fall deeper in love with him with each little thrust inside of me. His pace is slow, but deliberate. Each little thrust sending fireworks of pleasure across my skin. He's in no hurry and neither am I.

When his strength fades and pleasure overcomes him, he falls forward, hands on either side of my head; I wrap my fingers around his wrists, holding him. We never lose eye contact and it's hard to keep track of all the sensations, but each little burst of pleasure intensifies, making me moan and fight to keep my eyelids open. I feel him tremble and my orgasm starts to overtake me. "Come with me," I beg and he moans, his lips crushing mine. My orgasm erupts from within. Everything clamps down around him and his pleasure is heard in our mutual cries of release as I feel him pouring inside of me.

When he's conscious enough, he falls onto one elbow, he hasn't pulled out of me yet, but I can feel he's softening inside of me. His hand comes to cup my face. "I love you, baby girl," he says with such sweet joy that I start to cry. Feeling the very depth of his love and emotion.

"I love you, cowboy," I finally manage to squeak out between gentle sobs.

"So why are you crying?" he asks me gently as he wipes away a tear from my eye.

"Because I feel it. I see it, I feel every ounce of love you have for me and it's too much, it's overpowering and ah hell," I snort, "I'm a friggin' basket case. But I know, without a doubt that you love me, and I love you too."

"Without a doubt," he agrees.

About an hour after we've finished making love, I am curled up on Kyle and he's got one arm wrapped around my back, my cami and t-shirt pulled up in the back so that his hand can be skin to skin. With my head resting in the crook of his shoulder. I can still hear the band outside jamming. Kyle found a couple of e-books that are about twins and a lot like The Book, as we lovingly call it. He starts reading one of the books about twins and what to expect. He's reading to me and bookmarking and highlighting certain passages as he goes along. I don't question some of them, but realize this is his form of studying. It makes me smile. When I start to doze off he shifts, putting the book down. "Don't stop because I'm falling asleep," I mumble.

"I want to hold you," he says as he wraps his other arm around me. I settle into his chest and he fixes the covers. I doze off to the sounds of 69 Bottles jamming outside in the dark.

chapter 24

I wake up a little bit when Talon comes to bed. He snuggles in behind me and I can feel him wrap his arms around me and Kyle.

"How's she doing?" Talon asks Kyle, who must still be awake.

"She's better. She fell asleep about an hour ago."

"Did you guys have a nice time?"

"We did. Thank you."

"For?"

"Giving me time with her tonight. I needed it and I think she did too."

"You're welcome. How are you doing?"

"I'm much better now. Still scared shitless, but in the end, we have nine months to worry about it. Worrying to the point of hurting her, now, isn't worth it."

"You're right, it's not. We just need to love her and take care of her."

"You're right." I hear Kyle say then I feel gentle kisses on my head.

"I'm sorry that I sprung on you what I did earlier," I hear Talon whisper.

"Don't apologize unless you're taking back what you said. I needed to hear it and tonight was the perfect night for it."

"I'm not taking it back. I meant every word of it. I love you, Kyle."

My heart swells and I fight the tears. I don't want them to know that I'm awake.

"I love you, Talon."

I can't fight the tears anymore.

"Angel". "Baby girl," they say at the same time.

"I'm sorry, I woke up when Talon came to bed, I didn't mean to eavesdrop, I thought I'd fall right back to sleep, then you guys started talking and...." I lose steam on my confession and both sets of arms wrap tighter around me.

"Don't be sorry, angel. I didn't mean to wake you."

"No, it's okay, it's just...hearing you two talk, it makes me so happy," I sob.

"So why are you crying?" Kyle says with a small laugh.

"Because..." I whine. "I can't seem to do anything else."

They both laugh a little. "Aww baby girl, it's alright."

Both of them comfort me until I fall back to sleep, ending any chance of hearing more of their sweet confessions.

"Come on, angel, time to get up."

"Go away," I grumble.

"Nope, you need to wake up, take a shower, get dressed and eat breakfast."

"Why?" I moan.

"Because I'm going to see my mom. You and Kyle are coming with me."

"What time is it?"

"Eight."

"Too early."

He laughs, "I know, but if we go now, you can sleep before the show…"

Confused, I ask, "What show?"

"We have that added show tonight. Remember?"

"Oh my god, I completely forgot," I grumble and start to wake up. I roll over and that's when the nausea hits. "Oh god." I cover my mouth, fly out of bed and down the hall to the bathroom.

"Addie?" I hear Kyle from in front of me and I shut the door, barely making it to the toilet.

The door opens and Kyle slides in. He shuts the door again so he can reach me and pulls my hair back.

It takes a little longer to move past my morning sickness, but once it passes and I regain my strength I feel so much better. "How you doin', baby girl?"

I nod, "Better. You know you don't have to watch this."

"I know, but I want to be here for you," he tells me softly.

I don't get into the fact that it makes me feel guilty, like I'm rubbing all my ailments of pregnancy in his face, making him wish he could take it away that much more.

"Better?" he asks.

"Much."

"Let me go grab you some clothes. What do you want to wear today?"

"Something comfortable. My grey pants would be great."

"Bra?" I put my hands to my chest to feel how my nipples are doing and hiss. "I'll take that as a no. Though, it might actually help."

I look at him. "I read some more after you fell asleep." He smiles, proud of himself, and he should be. "It said that support can help."

"I don't have anything soft. Just lacy stuff," I tell him.

"Then maybe we need to go shopping?" he says with a smile.

"Tomorrow," I reply.

"Promise?" I cock my head at him.

"Why is that important to you?"

"I want you comfortable, panda, that's all."

I can't help but smile at his tone. "Alright, I promise."

He kisses my forehead and slides out of the bathroom. I turn on the shower and brush my teeth then climb in.

Instead of Kyle, it's Talon who brings me clothes. He strips and slides into the shower with me. "Hi angel."

"Hey big man." I smile. He's hard as a rock. "Thought you'd try shower sex too?" I tease.

He gives me a wicked grin and then pushes me against the wall gently. I feel his cock between us, rubbing dangerously close to my clit. His lips take mine in a warm passionate kiss. "It won't take long. I'm horny as hell because you fell asleep on me last night," he teases and thrusts his hips at me.

"Then take me big man. Show me how much you miss me." He releases me, takes my hand and turns me around. I spread my legs as wide as the shower will allow and his hand and cock are playing with the entrance of my pussy. I moan and he lines up, sliding in and sliding home quickly but not hard.

He growls and the animalistic nature of it sends a chill through me, I shiver and moan as he begins rocking in and out of me from behind. "Jesus, Addison, you're so fucking gorgeous." He continues thrusting up and into me, hitting that sweet spot without much effort and my legs tremble.

REDEEMING KYLE

His hand comes around me, sliding down my stomach and over my pouch. Warmth and love spread throughout my body and then I feel his fingers flick against my clit. My orgasm burns hot and ready. Being taken by him in such an animalistic way turns me on. "Don't. Hold. Back," he growls into my ear and I explode around him. His orgasm sends those beautiful grunts of pleasure straight to my core, milking my orgasm and my body soaks up his.

"I love it when you take me like that," I groan. "So primal," I tell him and he shivers, wrapping his arms gently around my chest, under my breasts.

"I love that you let me be myself," he says softly.

"It's the perfect balance. Kyle is sweet and you're an animal," I tease and he laughs as he slips out of me. I sigh at the loss and he helps me wash my hair and body before washing his own. He helps me dry off when we're done and I have a new cami, one of Kyle's t-shirts and a pair of wide legged sweatpants to slip into.

"You look..."

"Frumpy?"

He laughs. "No, actually, you look comfortable and still sexy as hell. I love that you're wearing his t-shirt."

I smile. "I can change."

"For my mother, no." He shakes his head. "I want you comfortable. Have you seen yourself today?"

"No, why?" He lifts up my shirt and slides my pants down.

"Because you look amazing." He sits down on the toilet and kisses my belly. It isn't any bigger than it was yesterday, at least not noticeably bigger, but his gentle kisses make me want to cry.

"I'm gonna cry if you keep that up, big man."

He looks up at me and smiles. "Not my intention."

I run my hand through his hair. "I know it wasn't. It's just...when you guys touch me down there, it's impossible to describe. It's sweet and it's a massive comfort to me. Right now it makes me cry because I'm an emotional roller coaster, but you loving on me, loving on our babies, it...it makes me love you so much more."

I watch as Talon's eyes well with tears. "I'm so scared."

"Aww, there's nothing to be afraid of, Talon. This happened for a reason, it happened because it was meant to be and what happens from here on out is how it's supposed to be. Being scared means you love me and you love them. I'm scared too," I reassure him softly.

"I know, I'm trying to be strong. It's hard."

I give him a small smile. "It is hard, believe me, I know. It's hard because I'm trying to stay strong for you and for Kyle and for the babies."

"That sounds like a lot."

"It is, but it's all worth it. In the end, when I can hold them and kiss them and love them more than I already do, it makes it all worth it."

He kisses my pouch one more time and then lifts my pants back into place and lowers my t-shirt. "I will try to remember that," he says softly. "Now, it's time to feed you." He smiles and we leave the bathroom.

chapter 25

When we step out of the bathroom, my nose is assaulted with the delicious smell of bacon and eggs and syrup. I go into the kitchen and Kyle is standing at the little tiny two-burner stove. Pans on both, one with sizzling bacon, eggs in the other and on a hot plate are pancakes. My mouth waters.

I walk up behind him, wrapping my arms around his waist. "Hey baby girl. How you feeling?"

"Starving."

He laughs. "You amaze me. Half an hour ago you were puking and now you're ready to eat."

I laugh with him. "I can't help it. I had no idea you could cook," I tease him.

"Oh, don't get your hopes too high. I'm not that good."

"Well, I appreciate it." Talon joins us after taking our towels back to the bedroom.

"Ky?"

"Yeah?"

"Why don't you go take Addison's picture, before she eats."

"Oh," I perk up, "good idea. Come on, cowboy."

"Go, I got this."

"You don't want to see?" I ask Talon.

He shakes his head, "That's going to be your guys' deal. I'll see the pictures when you're done." He smiles, takes the spatula from Kyle, kisses him on the cheek and Kyle and I go back to the bedroom.

"Where, baby girl?"

"The back of the door?"

"Sure," he says as he pulls his phone from his pocket. "Want me to send it to you?"

I shake my head, "No, take one with mine. I'd rather not send them out just yet." I wink.

With my right shoulder to the door, I lift my shirts to just below my breasts and lower my pants like Talon did in the bathroom. Kyle snaps a couple pictures with his phone, then mine. I can't stop smiling because he's smiling. "Face me," He says and I do, he takes another picture with my phone. Then he comes over, kneels before me and kisses my pouch.

I run my hands through his hair; I'm trying not to cry. He pulls back before it becomes too intense for me, then stands and kisses me. "Breakfast should be ready."

I smile, "Good, I'm starving. I'm going to pull my hair up and I'll be right out."

"Okay, baby girl."

He leaves the bedroom and I find a scrunchy. My hair is still wet, but I don't feel like drying it right now.

When I get back to the galley, Talon is sitting down and Kyle is dishing up plates. Mouse has joined us and I can hear someone in the shower. Judging from the bunks, it's not Dex.

162

Tori comes out a few minutes later, just as Kyle is setting a heaping plate in front of me. "Hi Tori," I say with a smile.

"Good morning." She's already dressed. I'm impressed, god only knows what time she gets up. "There enough for me?" she asks Kyle.

"Absolutely," Kyle says as he sets buttered toast down in front of me.

"I'll bet you a hundred dollars you can't eat all that." Mouse says to me with a laugh, and he's right, the plate is heaping with eggs, bacon and pancakes.

Talon and Kyle both laugh. "You're on," I tease him and dive into my food. I devour the pancakes first. "Jeez Kyle, these are really good." I keep going, plowing through three pancakes, then onto my eggs and bacon, which I break up mixing it into egg scramble. "Do we have any cheese?"

Kyle is watching me eat, a look of awe on his face. "Not shredded. I'll add it to the grocery list."

I nod and dive into my concoction and eat some toast to go along with it. With only a couple of bites left to go, I feel ridiculously full, and I don't need the money, it's a matter of principle now. I down my glass of apple juice before I take the last couple of bites. "Fuck me." Mouse says with a laugh. "Where the hell does it all go?"

I laugh. "It used to go to the gym with me, but not so much anymore..." I leave it hanging in the air.

"Dude," Talon says to Mouse, "did you finish your cheesesteak last night?"

"Hell no, I had like half of it left, plus a good chunk of fries."

"Me and Kyle too." He thrusts his thumb at me. "She ate it all, including the fries."

"I'm never betting on you again." Mouse looks at me and laughs. "You've certainly proved me wrong." He reaches into his back pocket, pulls out a hundred dollar bill from his wallet and slides it over to me.

I slide it back, "I don't want your money, Mouse." He looks sad. "I would have eaten it all anyway for starters and it's not entirely fair when you're eating for three."

He raises an eyebrow to me and Talon stiffens slightly. "What do you mean 'three'?"

I laugh. "Talon hasn't told you yet? Or you haven't figured out why I puke every morning."

"Well yeah, I figured that part out a while ago, but three?"

"Twins, Mouse, I'm having twins."

"No fucking shit!" he says with a big ass smile on his face. "That's fucking awesome." He covers his mouth. "Sorry." The entire room erupts into laughter.

Dex peeks his head out from behind his curtain. "What the hell, guys?"

"Dude, Addison's pregnant."

"No way." Dex laughs. "Way to go, guys."

"Oh, there's more, Dex," Mouse says. "She's having twins."

Dex damn near falls out of his bunk. "Well, I guess if you're gonna do it, might as well do it right. Congrats guys!" I see Dex sniff the air..."How the hell did I miss bacon?" And just like that ADD Dex shows up and is off onto something else.

"Where's Peacock? Might as well tell him too."

He steps out of the bathroom. "I'm right here, Addison. Congrats you guys. That's fucking awesome." Peacock slaps hands with Kyle then with Talon.

"Dude, I lost a bet to her," Mouse chimes in.

Peacock looks at him, "What was the bet?"

Mouse laughs, "I bet her a hundred bucks that she couldn't eat three pancakes, four strips of bacon, a mountain of eggs and two pieces of toast. She fucking devoured it, dude. She won't take my money though," he says dejected.

"Why not?" Peacock raises an eyebrow.

"She said it wasn't fair, which is why the entire bus now knows she's pregnant and with twins."

"Well, then buy her something nice," Peacock says.

"Like what?"

"Hell if I know, ask her boyfriends," Peacock says with a laugh.

The banter continues for a little while longer and my heart swells with pride that these guys are family, my family, our family, and regardless of the fact that we've only been together a few short weeks, the band thinks that our news is amazing. No one asks who the dad is; they all just congratulate Kyle and Talon together. Throughout the entire conversation, I see Talon and Kyle smiling, interacting with their friends and I can visibly see weight lifting from their shoulders. It doesn't matter to the band who the father is, so why should it matter to both of them.

"We better go," Kyle says. "Dex, there's still some bacon."

"Thanks, man." he calls from his bunk.

"I'll get coats," I volunteer and stand. My head spins hard, my stomach whirls. I sit back down.

"Addison?" Kyle kneels before me.

"I'm alright, stood up too fast."

"Relax a minute, angel. I'll get our stuff."

I put my forehead in my hands and breathe through the nausea. I really don't want to vomit, I haven't done it after a meal yet and I really don't want to insult Kyle. But something isn't agreeing with me. "I'm sorry, cowboy, but I need you to move."

He's stunned for a moment then moves. I skirt past him straight for the bathroom and throw up. Kyle is by my side in a moment. "Baby girl, I'm so sorry..."

"Stop," I say between heaves. "Apparently they don't like bacon," I say quietly.

"How can you tell?"

I heave again, sending more chunks up. After a couple of dry heaves it passes. "Look," I point to the toilet. "Its just bacon."

He laughs. "I've never seen that before."

I laugh too, "Me either." There is other stuff there too, but the primary content is bacon.

"So I guess we have to take bacon off your menu, huh?" I pout and he laughs. "For now at least." I smile and flush.

"Let me brush my teeth and I'll be out."

"You sure you're okay?"

"I'm great now."

He shakes his head, smiles, and then leaves me to brush my teeth.

When I come out, "Bets off, you ralphed," Mouse says with a laugh.

"Whatever, it stayed down for more than twenty minutes." I cross my arms over my chest and tap my converse covered foot on the floor.

"Yeah, okay, fine," Mouse pouts.

I laugh and lean over the table. "I don't want your money, Mouse. It's all good. Challenge me in a year when I'm not pregnant, double or nothing."

He bursts out laughing. "You're on, Red."

"You okay, angel?" Talon asks.

"Perfect. We ready?" He nods and holds my coat out for me. I slide my arms in and I go to take my purse.

"Nope, I got it," Talon says, serious.

"I can carry my own..." He just shakes his head. I roll my eyes.

"It weighs more than five pounds."

"Oh for Pete's sake." I laugh and walk down the steps and off of the bus and climb right into the center of the back seat of the SUV. Talon slides in on one side and Kyle on the other.

"I threw this in here for you, thought you'd want to catalog your breakfast. Though, I don't know if it counts anymore." He raises an eyebrow.

I smile at him. "It still counts, they apparently don't like bacon." He cocks his head so I explain to him.

"Okay, that's funny."

"No, it's not," I pout, "I love bacon." Everyone laughs and I take my journal from him and pull my phone from my pocket and I flip through the pictures Kyle took showing them to Talon as we drive toward his mother's house.

chapter 26

We got to her house around eleven, and she has this beautiful one story house and is the lone building in a cul-de-sac. She's a petite woman, about five four or five and round around the middle. She dotes on Talon and I'm surprised when Talon introduces me as his girlfriend and Kyle as his boyfriend, though she already knows Kyle. I imagine a phone call or two from her in the coming days, wanting more information about the relationship, but for now she brushes it off. She doesn't take to me right away but when I step into the kitchen to help her with lunch, she warms up to me a little bit. I eat, despite not being very hungry after breakfast but the guys give me that look.

We don't stay very long once the boys notice that I'm starting to fade. She becomes disappointed when Talon tells her that during the tour break he needs to be in LA to take care of business. I know that's not the case, but he's going to be there because I have another appointment. He doesn't tell her about the twins or even that I'm pregnant, which is okay with me. I understand immediately why they've grown closer over the years. She is very loving and affectionate toward him and her pride in his success is palpable.

It's about one when we return to the bus, but I'm so tired that I fall asleep on the way back and the guys take me to bed. "How long do you need to get ready?" Talon asks as he lays me down.

I shrug, "ninety minutes?" He looks at the clock.

"So wake you up about five thirty?"

"I don't need to sleep…"

"Nonsense angel. Sleep as long as you like, if you're up before then great, if not, we'll wake you."

"What about sound?"

He smiles, "we got this. You sleep." He kisses my forehead. Kyle follows suit and they both leave me to sleep.

"Baby girl…"

"No," I groan.

"Yes love, time to wake."

I wrap my arms around his neck, throwing him off balance and he falls onto the bed next to me. I snuggle into him and fall back to sleep.

"Come on, baby girl. It's time to get ready and you need to eat. I made you mac n' cheese," he taunts me to wake up and he knows that will do it.

"Fine. I'll get up, only because you have mac n' cheese for me."

He laughs and I crawl out of bed to pee.

When I come back he's sitting on the bed with a big bowl for me and I climb up, he gives it to me and I start eating. "I'm going to be an elephant by the time this pregnancy is over if you keep feeding me like this."

He laughs, "I doubt that. You've hardly gained any weight so far and you've been eating like this for over a week."

"I just wish I wasn't so tired all the time."

"It will pass. Pretty soon we won't be able to keep up with you."

I finish eating and I drink my apple juice. When I'm done, I start to get ready for the show. I decide to just pull my hair up tonight, not wanting to mess with it, and I do my make up while still in the clothes I slept in.

I put on the red dress Kyle gave me, accent it with my thigh high fishnets and a garter that's now sitting a little higher on my waist and rather than the big heels, I go for my calf high Doc Martins. I sweep my hair off to the side into a messy bun and add a small red flower over my ear. I need to dye it again, but I don't have time today.

When Talon comes in he stops dead in his tracks. "What?" I say.

"You look amazing." He comes over and wraps his arms around me. "I love that dress on you." He leans down and kisses my shoulder.

"Thanks, big man."

"Listen, the guys want to go out after the show. I want to take Kyle, will you come too?"

I shake my head. "No, I don't have the energy for something like that, but I want you to take him out. Spend some time with him."

"I don't want to leave you here alone," he says.

"I won't be alone, Tori and probably Rusty will be here. I have some work to catch up on and it will be great for you and Kyle to spend some time together, the two of you, without me."

"Alright, angel. As long as you're okay, but if you're not, you better call us."

I tap his nose with my finger. "I promise."

The show goes amazing, as always. The ritual tonight doesn't change, though Dex has taken to calling me preggo, quietly of course, whenever he's near me. I smacked him the first time he did it. Then laughed the second. My visual of Kyle's arms wrapped around me sort of came true tonight when he put his hands on my pouch while Talon kissed me. It made my heart swell.

Our duets went great, again he got a little glossy eyed, but he contained himself. When we were done, he hugged me, kissed my cheek and whispered I love you in my ear and I walked off stage, right into Kyle's arms and a big Talon smile when he looked at both of us.

The greenroom was packed and I was the center of attention, much to my dismay. But this is the added show, again after our duet went viral. Pictures were taken and autographs signed and I retired to the bus after some argument with Kyle about him going out tonight. He didn't want to go, but I reminded him about what I said yesterday and he reluctantly agreed.

When I got back to the bus, I ate two bananas and drank an entire glass of apple juice with my vitamin before taking up residence in my bedroom. I change into pajama pants, a cami and one of Kyle's t-shirts and make myself comfortable.

I work for a while and when I leave the bedroom to pee, Peacock is sitting at one of the tables.

"Hey."

"Hey," he says back.

"Give me a minute, I'll be right back." He nods and I step into the bathroom.

When I come out he hasn't moved. I sit down next to him. "I think it's time we talk," I tell him and he nods. "Why aren't you with the guys?"

"I was for a little while, but I decided to come back."

"What's on your mind, Eric?"

"Thank you, for introducing me to Jess."

I smile. "I didn't do that, you guys did it on your own, I just provided them with the passes."

He chuckles. "True, but she's become like a best friend to me."

"That's great, are you guys...?"

He shakes his head. "No, it's not like that."

"Then tell me," I say with a smile.

"I'm gay, Addison."

"For some reason, that doesn't surprise me." I say with a smile.

"Why does everyone seem to know?"

"Why do you say that?" I ask him.

"The other night, Tuesday night, I was in the bathroom when I overheard Talon and Kyle and what Talon said to him." Oh... "When I came out of the bathroom, Kyle and I talked for a couple minutes."

"He didn't tell me that."

"I didn't think he would. He's pretty discreet about stuff. But I asked him about the three of you and then it came up. He said he already knew, and that most of the band does, just that no one will say anything about it."

I smile, "That's because they're waiting for you. I had an idea, just because of the way you were around the women at the clubs. You weren't exactly gung-ho about them. Not in the way Dex or Mouse or even Talon and Kyle are. You always had this quiet reserve about you, but the girls naturally love a bass player so you played the part, not the stereotype. Are you ready to come out of the closet?"

"Sometimes I think I am, but then Dex will say something and I think twice about it."

"To you?"

"No, just, well you know the way he is. He'll stick his dick into anything with a receptacle for it. Mouse is that way too, but not quite as intense as Dex."

"Do you have feelings for Mouse? You guys are always together..."

"Yeah, I do, and Mouse knows. He knows how I feel about him and while sometimes I like to wish that he's just unsure of who he is, I'm usually reminded that he likes the chicks and I just kind of let it go."

"Are you worried about the public perception if you come out?"

He snorts. "No, I couldn't care less. I've been out to my parents since high school and I've had my fair share of guys since then, and even now. I usually manage to pick up a guy or two here and there and it works for me. I just don't see myself settling down any time soon."

"Well I'm glad you've come out to your parents and Mouse, maybe now it's time to come out to Dex, and officially to Talon. Everyone on this bus is family Eric. No one will judge you. Even Dex, with all his crazy antics, I think you might be surprised with him. Shit, sometimes I think Dex hides behind his own sexuality. I mean, come on, how many straight guys do you know actually talk the way he does? But the openness of this band is what I love most about all of you. I mean, look at me, Kyle and Talon. We have a highly unconventional relationship and Dex still teases me about sleeping with him, or me turning to him when I tire, which will never happen by the way, of T & K. It's a dynamic that works and it's a dynamic that has kept you guys together for so long. You never fight, you all keep your shit pretty clean, and you have a great time. Hell, last night was amazing. Watching you guys raw like that is an experience I will cherish forever."

"I understand why they love you so much," he says with a smile. "You're so sweet and your views are inspiring. I will work on coming out to Talon and then figure out how best to tell Dex. Though that's not something I'm looking forward to."

"Dex loves you, just like he loves everyone else. He won't care one way or another. But do it when you're ready and when you do, you'll see that fretting about it is not worth the effort." I smile sweetly at him.

"Thanks, Addison."

"Anything, Eric, anytime. If you need a hand to hold when you tell Dex, let me know. I'll be there."

I leave Peacock to his musing at the table and retire back to the bedroom

chapter 27

Our second show in Philly goes just as well as the first. The attention in the greenroom shifts back to the band, though they still want autographs and pictures of me too.

Immediately following the show, we're on the bus, packing up to head to Boston where we will play Saturday night. Kyle and I never made it shopping on Thursday in Philly, so we spend our Friday afternoon, in Boston, shopping at one of the malls. I find a couple bras that are cotton based and they feel pretty good when I put them on, so Kyle buys them for me. I argued, and lost. Then we found my camis and bought one in every color. I also found some slip on flats that are ridiculously cute. One of the things we'd read about is balance being an issue, after that, Kyle got paranoid about my heels.

Boston's concert goes off with a couple of minor glitches, but a true testament to their performance ability comes when Talon's microphone goes out, he encourages the crowd to sing until someone tells him it's back up. I think I panicked more than he did, though I wasn't on stage.

Immediately after the Boston show, we head back south for New York. When we arrive we check into the Marriott right on Time Square, which is where we're staying for the next two weeks.

Morning sickness is my worst enemy, but so far bacon is the only thing I've found that doesn't agree with me. Salads are becoming a best friend of mine and grapes are like m&m's. Each passing day makes me feel a little fuller and a little rounder, but my pouch is still that, a pouch.

After arriving in NYC, the guys drew me a bath and I soaked in it for over an hour before they finally dragged me out. We spent the rest of the afternoon eating popcorn and watching movies in bed. I have to say, I love those times with them.

We have three shows here in NYC- Thursday, Friday and Saturday. Which, come to find out, are going to be recorded and videotaped for live and future promotion shots. We have Sunday off, then Monday starts three days of press including a concert for one of the morning shows. But tomorrow Talon and I are in the studio. We're set to lay down 'Your Eyes', the duet version on Monday. Talon reassures me that it will be easy because there is no music to lay down first. It's already done. It's just my vocals that are missing. Tuesday, Wednesday and Thursday are blocked off for 'To Be Free', which Talon is going to be working on the music tracks while I'm doing 'Your Eyes'. I'm nervous as hell, but my guys remind me that I'm amazing and that helps.

Somewhere in all this is a photo shoot with the band that I am looking forward to. At least until I get an email from Cami telling me that once the band is done, it's my turn and it's scheduled for Friday, during the day, before the show.

Raine, Cami's assistant and now mine I suppose, arrives around seven Sunday evening. Once she settles into her room she stops by our suite and we talk about the schedule for the upcoming two weeks. She meets Talon and Kyle, does a little fangirl jig for Talon and it warms my heart to see him respond to her in such a warm way. We all chat for about an hour before she heads off to get started on some business.

Cami has put her in charge of my social media outlets while she's here, both for the band and me. Cami really wants more updates from me and I just don't have time over the next couple of weeks.

Around nine, pizza arrives, real New York Pizza. "If you eat all of that, I think I will go ballistic," Kyle teases me as he hands me my pie. We ended up ordering three because I have a craving for black olives and green peppers. The black olives turn Kyle off and then I could probably chase Talon with green peppers. Ironic? Definitely.

"I think I will go ballistic or end up puking it back up if I eat it all," I tease him back.

We all dive into our pizzas and three pieces later, I'm stuffed. Though I still ate more than the guys, I didn't devour the whole thing, not this time anyway. We have a full kitchenette in our suite, so Kyle puts away the pizzas and when he comes back, I have my feet on the coffee table, my shirt pulled up and my pants pushed down. I feel huge and while I can tell it's grown a little over the last couple of days just by how my pants fit, it's really not bigger, except after I eat. Talon lays his head on my lap, looking up at me and Kyle joins him.

They tease me and rub my stomach, then for some unknown reason, they both start tickling me. My laughter and protests only spur them on even more. They're laughing and having fun. Reminding me of two little boys and it is positively cute. That is until I start tickling them back. "Uh huh, I know all your ticklish spots," I say as they lay back down, defeated.

That's when I go for the kill that will make them putty in my hands. They're both wearing gym shorts, so it's not difficult for me to tell they're already hard, they have been most of the night. So I reach out with both hands and run them along their cocks and they both groan. Then I work my hands under their shorts and take them both into my hands, skin to skin and they begin thrusting with my motions. I tease them both for a while and then shift my legs, pushing the coffee table out of the way.

I stroke them both until they are to the point of pleasurable bliss, then I get up, letting their heads fall to the cushion. "Hey." They both say together then watch me as I strip out of my t-shirt and pajamas, letting it all fall to the floor. Pushing the coffee table a little more, giving myself more room, I drop to my knees, putting my hands in my lap, tucked against my pouch, I lift my chin and open my mouth and count to myself...one...Sit up...two...stand up...three... shorts down..four...shirts off...five..."That took you five seconds..." I tease and grab both of their cocks in my hands, pulling them toward me. I stand up on my knees and I first suck Kyle, then switch to Talon, then back to Kyle. Just teasing sucks and audible pops.

I feel like a fucking porn star. Then I take Kyle's cock into my mouth as far as it will go, pumping my hand and mouth in a rhythm that makes his knees shake. Once I have him good and wet, I switch to Talon, licking and sucking him in as far as my mouth will allow. My hands never stop moving, never stop stroking their lengths, keeping them close but not too close. My pussy is dripping down the inside of my thighs and I am desperate to touch it, to flick it and to make myself come, but this isn't about me. No, this is about my men.

I switch back to Kyle, sucking and stroking, my hand getting wetter with my own saliva and an idea pops into my head. I continue sucking him until I know my fingers are wet enough, then I release my hand, seeking my second favorite part of his body. The tight ring of his ass, and I push inside at the same time I release his cock. "Fuck Addison!" He growls out.

"Stroke yourself. Fuck your hand while I fuck your ass." His hand comes to grip his cock, he strokes and his knees get weak. "Don't you dare stop," I tell him through hooded eyes as he stares down at me. I stick my tongue out for the dribble of pre-cum and he wipes it on my tongue and shudders.

I turn my attention to Talon. Sucking him into my mouth deep and hard. I fight the gag I feel when I take him in too far. I keep stroking him and sucking his cock until my fingers are wet enough for his ass and when I pull my hand away I watch him shiver in anticipation. "What do you want, big guy? You want my fingers in your ass too?"

"Fuck yes," he growls and I slide my hand to his hole and suck his cock deep into my mouth, holding him there I wiggle my tongue. He moans and I push my finger inside, stroking his prostate, causing his head to fall back and his knees to shake.

I free his cock from my mouth. "Fuck yourself, Talon. Hard."

He grips his cock and strokes. Like Kyle, there is undiluted pleasure wracking through his entire body.

179

I sit back and watch, stroking my fingers along their most sensitive spots. Pre-cum treasures await me and I lick them off, teasing each of them with my tongue before sitting back again. "Do you want to come?"

"Yes!" They both growl together. I scoot closer and sit down on my feet.

Lifting my chin again I watch as the two of them move in just a little closer. "Where do you want to come?"

"Your mouth," Talon growls. I increase the pace of my fingers in their holes and they both groan.

"God, Addison, I...agh! I can't hold it!" Kyle growls.

"Yes, you can." I urge with force and I watch as he melts.

"Fuck, it hurts," Talon says as he strokes his cock. I massage his hole just a little longer, then lift my chin, opening my mouth to them.

"I want it, now," I growl and they both erupt above me, showering me with their cum. Their grunts and growls nearly make me explode without even touching myself. I lick my lips and open again for those last little drops of cum. They missed on more than a few strokes and I have drops of cum on my cheeks, my chin and down my chest. What happens next is a testament to how much they both love me and love each other. I extract my fingers from both of them and Kyle falls to his knees first. Taking my face in his hand and he kisses me. Tasting him, Talon and myself. He moans into my mouth as the taste assaults him.

Talon is next, but he starts licking the drops from my chest. Taking a moment to tease my nipples into hard peaks in the process. I moan into Kyle's kiss. He pulls back. "Let's clean you up." Talon continues licking up drops along my neck then onto my chin then finally taking my mouth. I can taste both of them and I moan again.

Kyle stands up and goes into the kitchen. I hear the water running and he comes back with a warm washcloth. Talon pulls back and I take the cloth from Kyle and start wiping off my face just as Talon takes Kyle into a deeply passionate kiss.

chapter 28

I moan watching them kiss. They're both still hard as rocks and my pussy is so wet that rubbing it will be an impossible task because I won't find any purchase.

They break from their kiss and I groan in frustration. "What's the matter, baby girl?"

"I want to come," I whine.

"You do, do you?" Talon turns toward me. "How badly do you want to come?"

"So bad..." I whine again as I try to play with my pussy but fail. "I'm so fucking wet..." I mewl, "I can't..."

"What do you think, Kyle, should we help her come?"

"I don't know, she's been a pretty bad girl... Tickling us, fucking our asses, thinking she has control..."

I whimper.

"Look at that," Talon says, pointing to my breasts, "her nipples are hard. I bet they're aching to be licked. To be sucked..."

"Oh god, please," I beg. Talon reaches down and pulls my hand from my pussy, taking my fingers into his mouth. I immediately dive in with my other hand and Kyle snatches that one up too.

"No!" I cry out as he starts sucking on my fingers.

Talon reaches over and grabs Kyle's cock, stroking it. Kyle follows his lead and begins stroking Talon's cock and I shiver and shatter into a thousand pieces without even being touched. "Oh fuck!" I hear Talon say with amusement as gentle hands lay me down on the floor.

When I come back around a couple minutes later they are both looming over me. "If the two of you needed any proof of what you do to me, I think I just gave it to you," I tease them both.

"That was amazing," Kyle says. "I had no idea that what we do, when we're together, affected you so intensely."

"Me either," I tease with a smile.

"That was, fuck, angel, that was fucking amazing." They help me sit up.

"I didn't even know... it was so spontaneous and I was so turned on, it was, fuck... I can't even describe it."

"Now that we're all even with orgasms for tonight," Talon teases.

"Oh no, you don't, big guy. I'm so not done yet. I gave the two of you yours, you haven't even touched me. Get on the couch," I tell Talon. I give him a hard look and he scurries into action. I know he knows I'm playing but he sits down on the couch, sliding his ass to the edge and laying back. I climb up and straddle him, but I don't let him inside. "Come here, cowboy," I say and he comes over, stands up and lets his cock rub against my ass. "Get yourself wet," I tell him and I wiggle my hips. I hear Talon's pouty sigh so I kiss him as Kyle slides inside of me. Sliding in and out gently. I am so wet that it only takes him a couple of thrusts and he's coated.

Kyle withdraws and begins pressing into my ass and I take Talon's cock in my hand. Kyle pushes in and I cry out. "Relax, baby girl." His hand slides down my back and I arch into his touch as he slides in all the way, sliding back out and back in again and again. My eyes roll up and Talon takes hold of his cock, lines himself up with my entrance and he starts pushing himself in.

"Oh fuck," I groan as I take both of them. I feel Kyle add additional lube by using his own saliva. I didn't want to wait for lube. "Fuck fuck fuck!" I moan as they begin their perfect assault against both my sensitive spots and Talon gently cups my breasts. He's careful not to hurt me intentionally and the pain mixed with pleasure is enough to send me over the edge. My orgasm rocks through me and like fireworks in my veins, sensations explode everywhere.

As I come back down, neither has slowed their pace and I can feel another orgasm building already. Talon's mouth moves from one breast to the other and back again. Licking and sucking, moaning around my nipple in his mouth. I feel Kyle's hand come between me and Talon. He quickly finds my clit. "Oh god!" I scream. "Oh Fuck, fuck, fuck!"

It's too much for my body to take all at once and I shatter around them, my entire body trembling and shaking. My pussy tightening and relaxing and after three more thrusts, they both pour themselves into me, filling me, loving me.

The next thing I remember is being carried to the bathroom and brought into the warm tub. "Let's clean you up, baby girl and then you can go to bed." I rest my head against Kyle's shoulder. His front to my back, he's still hard, but I know he came. I feel hands moving gently around my body, washcloths sliding up my sex, cleaning me. I settle into the massaging rhythm of their bathing me and I know I fall asleep a couple of times, but they keep me afloat.

When they're done, the water is drained and I am lifted out and immediately wrapped into a huge warm towel and dried gently. They don't put any clothes on me, which is fine, before they lay me down in bed. Tonight they start a ritual that I will come to expect and miss terribly when it doesn't happen anymore. First Talon, who caresses my stomach and kisses my belly. "Good night, little ones," he whispers softly.

Then Kyle, gentle touches and caresses and then two kisses, one on each side, "Sweet dreams, little panda cubs," he says and I start to cry.

Talon takes my face in his hands, kissing me on the lips, soft and sweet. "Good night, angel. I love you," he whispers and kisses me again. When he's done he settles in behind me, wrapping his arms around me.

Kyle comes up, first he kisses my forehead, then my nose, then finally my lips. "I love you more than life itself," he says and the tears don't stop. He lies down in front of me and I take my spot in the crook of his shoulder. My hand slides across his stomach, holding him to me and I hitch my leg over his.

Wrapped up in them and their love, I fall asleep with tears gently sliding down my cheeks.

chapter 29

"Addison?" Kyle and Talon call for me as I run into the bathroom. My morning ritual of puking is growing really old.

"Hey, baby girl... You okay?" I shake my head. I can barely hold my eyes open, I'm surprised I made it to the toilet. I continue puking up everything I ate last night. All the pizza is coming back up. Weird.

"What time is it?" I say between heaves.

"Just after midnight."

I groan as I throw up again. Not good. Kyle comes over to me. "Baby, you're burning up, what's wrong?" I can't stop heaving long enough to answer him. I really don't feel good at all. I shake my head. "Talon?" Kyle shouts.

"Yeah," he says right behind us.

"Oh sorry, can you get her a cool washcloth, she's burning up." I heave again, this time it's mostly liquid and it burns. My knees give out on me and I slump to the floor. "Whoa, easy, baby. Talk to me...what's wrong?"

"Don't feel good."

I hear Talon's knee snap as he bends down in front of me. He holds the washcloth out in his hand and I just push my head into it. I jump because it feels so cold. "Grab the thermometer out of the kit," Talon says.

"Kit? What kit?" I ask

"We put together a kit. It's nothing huge, just, well, being on the road, we wanted to make sure we had some things with us for you," Talon says sheepishly.

"Oh."

Kyle comes back into the room and crouches down next to me. "It goes in your ear," he says and he does it, pushes a button and it beeps.

"Grab my phone," Talon says and Kyle goes after his phone.

"What's wrong?" I say.

"You have a hundred and two fever, angel. We're gonna call Dr. Paige. See if we need to take you in."

My stomach rolls again and I heave, but nothing comes up.

"Try her cell," I hear Talon tell Kyle and then I hear the speaker click on. The phone rings a couple times.

"Dr. Paige."

"Hi Dr. Paige, this is Talon Carver, Addison's boyfriend."

"Hi Talon, what's going on?"

"Addison just woke up, throwing up and she's running a fever of a hundred and two. Do we need to take her in?"

"Did she eat something tonight?" Dr. Paige asks.

"We had pizza, we're in New York. She had pepperoni, sausage, black olives and green peppers. And it all just came back up."

"When did she eat?"

"About three hours ago," Talon replies, and he's surprisingly calm.

"Does she have any other symptoms?"

"She clammy, sitting here shivering…"

"My whole body hurts," I add.

"Hi Addison," Dr. Paige says. "My primary concern is the fever. Addison, would you take some Tylenol?"

"No," I say determined, I don't want to risk it.

"I thought not. Okay guys, I'm going to put you to work." Dr. Paige gives them instructions. I zone out. I'm feeling worse the longer I sit here. My whole body aches, like I'm getting the flu or something. Though I haven't a clue what it is that's doing this. I don't move from Talon's hand holding my head up. The washcloth feels nice even though it's warming up.

I'm pulled back into the conversation when I hear Talon ask, "What would Tylenol do?"

"Reduce the fever, but it is a pain reliever and she is pregnant, so there are some risks to taking it. Which is why most pregnant women don't," Dr. Paige tells Talon. "Don't force her to take it though, it is her choice. Just keep an eye on her for the next couple of hours, if it gets worse, take her in."

"You got it. Thanks Doctor."

"Anytime. Addison, call me tomorrow, let me know how you're doing."

"Okay, thank you Doctor Paige."

"Good night," she says and Talon disconnects the phone. Kyle goes to work with the bath. And Talon adjusts my washcloth.

"Thank you," I say to him.

"For what?"

"Keeping a cool head, calling Doctor Paige."

"Kyle started it," he says.

"I know, I'll thank him too."

He smiles. "Are you feeling any better?" I shake my head. "Let's try this one more time, shall we?" He holds up the thermometer. I nod and he sticks it into my ear. It beeps and he shows it to me. One oh one point six. "It's coming down already."

I nod and give him a small smile. "At least I don't feel like throwing up anymore." I try and tease and fail when I see his sad face. "Aww, I'm sorry."

"It's okay. I'm just worried about you."

I smile. "I'm okay."

"Your bath is ready," Kyle says and I look at him. He's terrified.

I reach out for his hand and he helps me stand. Talon takes the washcloth away from my head but doesn't move. I stand up and Kyle wraps his arm around my waist. "Hi cowboy."

"Hi baby girl."

"You okay?"

"You're the one who's sick and you're asking me if I'm okay?"

"Yup, because you look a little green."

"I just hate seeing you like this," he admits softly.

"I know, but I promise you, I'm alright. The fever is already coming down. I'm still achy, but I'm starting to feel better."

He nods somberly. I touch my finger to his nose and he kisses the pad of my finger as I bring it down. "Love you, baby girl."

I smile. "There's my cowboy. Love you too."

He helps me into the tub. I shiver and pull back my foot when I go to step in. "Is it too cold?" Kyle asks.

"No, I'm just too warm," I say and then step back in, lowering myself. I shiver a couple of times but then settle in. They both loom by the side of the tub for a few minutes, just to make sure I'm alright. I can tell they want in with me, but they don't ask and I don't give the okay. Kyle sits down on the edge near my head and Talon near my feet. I put my head back and close my eyes. I'm so tired.

"Let's check and see where you're at," Kyle says and I hear the beep of the thermometer. I turn my head so that he has access and he gently presses it into my ear and after a moment it beeps. I see him smile. He shows it to me and it's down to ninety-nine.

"How are you feeling, angel?"

"Really tired."

"Okay, can you drink this for me?" I didn't even hear him leave the bathroom. I sit up and he hands be a glass with a light orange color liquid in it. "Gatorade, watered down. It's gonna taste awful."

"No, it's okay." I drink down the whole glass without even really tasting it. "More, please," I say.

"Let's give it a couple minutes, see how your stomach reacts."

"I feel better, my body still aches, but I think I'm just really tired," I tell them both.

"Okay, let's get you out of the tub," Kyle says and I nod, standing slowly with the help of his hand. Talon put the glass down and is ready with a towel to wrap around me. I shiver because I'm cold.

"I'm cold," I say through chattering teeth. Talon wraps the towel around me quickly and Kyle grabs another one to get me dried off faster. They've brought in one of my camis and a pair of boy shorts.

Once I'm dry, Talon slips on my top and Kyle helps me step into my panties then they both escort me back to the bed. My skin on the cool sheets causes me to shiver. They cover me up with the flat sheet and nothing else. I shiver again and settle in.

I don't know whether or not they join me because I fall asleep quickly.

chapter 30

Waking up a few hours later, Talon is on the bed, but he's some distance away, Kyle however isn't. I actually feel normal, no nausea this morning, so maybe with any luck I got it out of my system early this morning. I look at the clock and it's seven-thirty. Talon and I are supposed to be at the studio at eleven.

I need to find Kyle. I look around the room and he isn't anywhere to be found. Odd. I go to the bathroom and again when I come out, I don't see him. Talon is snoring softly on the bed. I check the floor on his side, just to be sure and nothing. I leave the room, still in my cami and boy shorts. When I step into the living room, I see him asleep on the couch and my heart breaks. Why is he out here?

I go to the kitchen and get some more Gatorade, I fill the rest of the bottle with a new bottle of water. I shake it up and drink it down. Finishing the bottle quickly, I throw it away. I look over at the couch and decide that he needs a cuddle buddy. I go over to the couch and he's lying with his head back and his feet on the floor.

I get onto the couch and snuggle into the crook of his arm, sliding my hand under his back and then over his stomach and hug him.

"Baby girl?"

"Hi cowboy," I say quietly.

"What are you doing up?"

"I woke up."

"Are you sick?"

"No, I didn't even throw up. Or feel like throwing up. I even just drank a bottle of mixed water and Gatorade and you'll be happy to know, I'm starving." I turn and kiss his chest.

"We can't have that," he says but there is no teasing or playfulness in his voice.

I sit up and look at him. "Why are you out here?"

"I couldn't sleep."

"Why?" I ask.

"I just couldn't," he says a little harsher than I like with him.

"Don't...damn it, don't shut down on me."

"Why not? Isn't easier than hearing the same argument from me over and over again?"

"Kyle Black!" I unwrap my arms from around him. "Do you honestly think that I don't care that you're scared or that you wish you could take it all away for me, carry the sickness and the soreness? Because Kyle, I do care. I fucking care so much that it hurts like hell when you're like this. You can't take it away from me. You can't shoulder this. This is for me and for my body to do what it was designed to do. I was built and designed to carry a baby or babies as is the case." I take a deep breath, desperate to settle some but it doesn't work, "Did you know that morning sickness is a sign that everything is healthy, that the babies are healthy?" He shakes his head. "It's also a sign that I am healthy. This could be so much worse. I throw up once a day, at most twice, some woman are puking non-stop all day and night. Some can hardly keep anything down because they're throwing up all the time. I throw up once and being pregnant with twins, I'll say that's pretty damn good."

He starts to say something and I stop him...

"No, let me finish. Do you know that my breasts and nipples hurt so much because my body is working and changing so that it can produce milk to feed these two when they're born? That a lot of the pain I'm feeling is actually because of a choice I made to get implants years ago? I chose to get them because I was all nipple, nothing else. I got them for me. So being naturally very small chested my body is going to go through a lot of pains as it adjusts. I know that these two will be fed from what my body is going through up here," I gently put my hands to my chest, "I tolerate the pain. Did you also know that when you and Talon are sucking on them, you're both so gentle that it actually turns the pain into the most exquisite pleasure?" he shakes his head. "So yes, I know it hurts you to see me sick, to see me uncomfortable, but I am not suffering. It is worth every minute. But this... with you, is getting harder to handle sometimes. One minute you're touching and kissing the twins, then the next you're sleeping on the couch because you're freaked out. That's hardly fair to me. It hurts me to see you so upset over something you can't change. If you keep freaking out like this, you're going to go insane. We're not even at six weeks yet. We have thirty-four more to go. If there is something truly wrong with me or with the babies, then you need to freak out. But it's not, nothing is wrong, everything is fine. So please, take a deep breath."

I stop talking. I'm still upset, but I feel better having said my piece. Now if it sets in with him. I watch as his eyes fill with tears and spill over. I lean up over him, taking his head in my hands, wiping away his tears. "I'm so sorry. I'm sorry that I keep freaking out, that I keep bringing it back to this. It's never my intention, it's never what I want. You've got so much on your shoulders, you don't need to worry about me."

"But I'm going to when you freak out like this on me." As much as what I'm about to say kills me, I need to say it and I pray I can make it through without crying. "Are you ready for this? For what's to come? Is that what's freaking you out? You're not ready to be tied down with a family?" I'm mumbling and my eyes are watering, but I force myself to stop. "And don't tell me that you love me, because for this, loving me is not enough."

He doesn't answer me. I pull back from him, his silence is deafening. I can't stop the tears as I look at him. As I see him sitting there, not looking at me, not saying a word to me. "If you're not ready for this, I need to know."

"Bottle cap."

I hiss through my teeth, the ache in my chest explodes, sending shockwaves of pain and heartache through my body. This is too much for me right now, I can't take it. I turn, leaving the room, going to the bedroom I slam the door shut and I scream at the top of my lungs then everything goes black.

talon

"Addison?" I watch as she slumps onto the floor. "Jesus." I jump out of bed and race to her side. "Addie, come on, angel. Talk to me. What's wrong? Are you alright? Come on Addie, look at me." She just stares off, she looks completely shattered. "Kyle!" I shout. "Addie, what do I do, what happened? Come on, angel, look at me."

"Kyle!" I shout again and nothing. I pick her up, taking her to the bed and I lay her out. She curls into a fetal position so I know that she's at least moving. "Kyle!"

"Bottle cap," she whispers. "He called bottle cap."

"What? Why?" I ask her. "Addie, come on, what happened?"

"He's not ready. He's not ready for all this- the babies, the pregnancy, the family, the life, he's not ready," she whispers.

"I'm going to fucking kill him." I pull off of the bed and go straight for the door.

"Talon! Don't!" she shouts toward me.

When I step into the sitting room, he's sitting there with his head in his hands. I charge at him, pushing him over. "What the fuck do you think you're doing?" I shout at him. "What the fuck, Kyle? She's fucking catatonic in there. What the fuck did you say to her?"

"Get off me," he growls.

"Fuck you! What the fuck did you do, what the fuck are you doing? She doesn't need this shit right now."

He doesn't say anything to me. He locks his lips.

"Don't you fucking ignore me. Goddammit, Kyle, what the fuck?" I push off of him and sit with my back against the couch. "I will honor your safe word, but I'll be goddamned if I'm going to let you go peacefully. This is hard, for all of us, what do you want her to do? Get an abortion?" I hiss through my teeth and he flinches, but doesn't answer. "I'll take that as a no. But goddammit, Kyle, if you can't fucking do this, if you're not in this for her, for me, then" I pause, "… you know where the fucking door is." I tell him as I get up. "She needs us. Stay or go, but if you fucking stay, be here, be here for her, be here for me, be here for the babies. Goddammit, Kyle."

I leave the living room and go back into the bedroom. Addison is full on sobbing on the bed and I climb in behind her, wrapping her in my arms, holding her, stroking her hair, touching her arms. When I go to touch her stomach, "don't," she says with finality. "I don't need the reminder right now," she sobs out.

"Okay angel, I'm sorry." She sobs harder after that.

What the fuck is he thinking? God, I know he's not ready for this, I'm not ready for this, but the reality is that it's fucking happening. Fuck, maybe… Jesus, I can't even finish the thought. The idea of sending her home to LA, no, damn it, I won't do it. I need her, I need her here with me. I already go fucking crazy enough as it is when I'm not near her, I can't imagine sending her across the fucking country.

I'm gonna kill him if he fucking leaves.

chapter 31
addison

Talon left me to go order room service for me. When he comes back he's completely crushed. "Food's on its way."

"What's wrong?" I ask him.

He sighs. "He's gone."

"That mother fucker!" I am so unbelievably pissed off that it energizes me to get moving. After my shower, I get dressed in a pair of comfy pants, a cami and my favorite Nirvana t-shirt.

I manage to sit down and eat some oatmeal with brown sugar and strawberries, toast and I drink two glasses of apple juice. Talon ignores his breakfast and I know I would have but I have two babies inside that need substance. Talon continues to decline. I don't have the strength for him right now. "He called bottle cap. He has twenty-four hours," I tell him as I grab my purse and messenger bag. Talon steps up, taking them from me. I hand them over without a second thought.

"When I went out there, I told him to stay or go, if he stayed he had to be here and be ready for this."

"And he left," I whisper.

He nods.

"I will give him his twenty-four hours, if he doesn't return, I will call him once, if he does not answer, then I don't know what I'm going to do. But he bottle capped on me, not you."

"I will leave him alone for twenty-four hours, out of respect for the rules, but after that, I make no promises. You deserve answers. He didn't just walk out on you, he walked out on me and on us."

"It's my fault."

"Stop. It is not," he says in his demanding tone.

"Really? Because I'm the fucking pregnant one. I'm the one who got pregnant in the first place, I'm the one that didn't pay attention to her birth control. You don't think he blames me for this? Talon, we've been together all of what, a month and a half? That's hardly enough time to classify a lifelong commitment. I'm not surprised he left, and frankly, I wouldn't be surprised if you left too."

"I'm not going anywhere," he snaps.

"You should."

"No, damn it, this isn't your fault, my fault or his fault. It fucking happened. I can't change it, you can't change it and he sure as hell can't change it. It's not ideal circumstances. I'm not going to lie, but Jesus, I have never felt something so right as when I'm with you and him. I know six or seven weeks is hardly enough time to know how you honestly feel about someone, but god," he says exasperated. "It's been the best time of my life. For the first time I actually feel like I belong somewhere, that everything is going right in my life. Whether you got pregnant now or four years from now, I'd still be freaked out. I'd still be worried every day that something was going to happen, and I'd sure as hell be worried about the future and what it holds for being a dad. But I wouldn't change it, not for anything."

I don't know what to say. It is probably the longest emotional speech Talon has ever given and I'll be dammed if I know what to say to him. He doesn't say anything else. He just stands there. He's looking at me, but there is no expectation in his eyes. He's just looking at me with love.

"I know," I finally say softly, "I just, I expected this out of you, not him. Not after all the time we spent together reading the books, looking stuff up." Tears threaten, "We spent a lot of time together, he seemed okay after our car talk. Things shifted, now not even a week later it's all in the fucking toilet. It's too much for any one person to handle, Talon, let alone three of us. The three of us have had a life altering event happen and we're all shouldering that in our own way. I know you are for yourself, I know I'm not ready for this, but I have to be. I have no choice. You and Kyle, you both have a choice. If you tell me you can't do it either, I will be beyond devastated, but I have two babies growing inside of me who need me right now more than anything. If you want out, now is the time to tell me, Talon, because staying and changing your mind three months, four months, eight months from now will not work for me. So you need to decide what you want."

"Angel," he growls.

"Don't. Think about it. Think long and hard before you make that choice. Either way, we will talk about it later. We've got to go."

I walk out of the suite and into the hallway where our entourage is waiting. I try in vain to take my bags from Talon, but he keeps them. We don't talk in the car on the way to the studio, and once we're there, he drops me off where I'm supposed to be and goes to where he's needed.

Three takes later and we've put down the 'Your Eyes' duet and it's just after one. I walk toward Talon's studio and I can see him through the glass. He's playing but my heart is breaking watching him. He's so torn up, it's in his eyes. I watch him for a few minutes before he sees me, puts down his guitar and comes out to me. "You okay?"

"No, but physically I'm fine. I'm done. Will you guys be ready for me today?"

"No, I keep screwing up."

"Do you want me to stay?"

"No, go back to the hotel, rest. I'll be back as soon as I'm done here today. They also want to drop a drum on it, so Dex is coming in tomorrow to work on that. We likely won't need you until Wednesday, but I will know more tonight."

I nod. He leans down and as he goes to kiss my cheek, I turn my head and capture his lips. Oh god, that was a mistake, if he's leaving me... Oh fuck it, I throw everything I feel for him into the kiss and I don't care. When he pulls back he looks a little mesmerized. "Wow," he breathes.

"Go get 'em, tiger."

He gives me a smile and ducks back into the studio.

"Ready?" Tori asks me.

I nod and leave the studio. "Has anyone seen him?"

"No, but we've got Beck and Casey working on trying to track him down. He's a member of this group and our responsibility."

I nod. "Keep me posted, please?"

"Absolutely, and if you don't mind, what happened?"

"Long story short, he's not ready for all this. Talon gave him a choice, to stay or to go. He left."

"That doesn't mean he's gone for good." Tori is very optimistic.

"No, it doesn't, but if he's gone more than twenty-four hours, I don't know if I can take him back."

"Why twenty-four hours?"

"It's our rule. If someone invokes the safe word, the other two are required to leave that person alone until they're ready to talk, or twenty-four hours, whichever comes first."

"Great rule."

"Stupid fucking rule," I grumble as we duck out of the studio and into the SUV.

We drive back to the hotel, Rusty is behind the wheel and he stops at a deli for lunch. I get soup and a turkey sandwich which I will force myself to eat when I get upstairs.

Once upstairs I eat my soup and the majority of my sandwich, then change and climb into bed. I'm exhausted, but yet I don't sleep. Every time I close my eyes, all I can see is his beautiful blue green eyes and his marvelous smile. Both of which bring tears to my eyes and uncontrollable crying. At one point I switch to the other bedroom, hoping that the new scenery will make it easier to fall asleep. It doesn't at first, but eventually I nod off.

chapter 32

I vaguely remember Talon coming back to the suite. I barely remember eating the mac n cheese he brought for me, I just remember being awake long enough to eat and go back to sleep.

Tuesday arrives and Talon is sleeping in the chair in the guest bedroom. He looks miserable, but the fact that he's here warms my frozen heart just a little bit. I look at the clock and it's eight in the morning. His twenty-four hours are up. But I won't be calling him, not this early in the day. No point in wasting my phone call when I'm pretty confident he's passed out. I roll over and like clockwork, my stomach rolls and I dart into the bathroom.

Talon comes to my aid, holding my hair and rubbing my back, reminding me of Kyle and my heaves quickly turn into gut twisting sobs. "I can't do this," I breathe out between heaves. When I finish, I flush the toilet. "I have to pee," I say and he dutifully stands up and leaves the bathroom, closing the door.

After I flush again he comes back in. "Talon, I can't do this…I can't be strong anymore. I can't…"

"Angel, look at me." I look at him with tear streaked cheeks and eyes. "You don't have to be strong. You don't have to hide everything you're feeling, you should have never been doing that in the first place. We all agreed to talk and be open and honest with one another. You've been a champion of that from the beginning and now… now you're hiding and holding out on me, on Kyle…"

"Kyle's not here. It's been twenty-four hours. He's not back, he's not coming back. This is all my fault. I've lost one of the two men I love more than anything in this world because I fucked up, this, all of this, is my fault. I was so naive to believe that I was still protected, I should have been checking for my birth control, but I was so wrapped up in you and in him and I relied on what I've been told for years, that I can't get pregnant now here I am, six weeks pregnant with twins. Twins who I can't even tell you who the father is. I can't… I can't do this," I sob harder.

"Angel, I need you to look at me. I need to look into your eyes when I tell you this." My eyes meet his. I don't get lost in his eyes like I do with Kyle's, but there is still a depth to his eyes that allows me to see into his soul. "Addison Lynae Beltrand, this is not your fault. It takes two to make a baby, Addison. It still only takes two to make two babies. Do not blame yourself for this. This is absolutely not your fault. The three of us made a choice. Once we broke that barrier and went skin to skin, neither Kyle nor I looked back or thought twice about what we were doing. We didn't think about what could happen and I don't think we thought about it because we honestly didn't care. God, I was so in love with you. I fell in love with you the moment I laid eyes on you. I knew then that I would spend the rest of my life with you. I loved you so much that I couldn't make you choose between him and me. Then I fell in love with him, I fell in love with us and I fell so hard.

"I can honestly tell you that no, I am not ready to be a father, I am not ready to settle down, but that is not going to stop me from trying, from fighting, from making myself ready for it. I'm the wild one, I'm your wild one, you called me that before and it's true, but just because I'm wild, doesn't mean that I love you any less, doesn't mean that I don't love these babies growing inside of you, and damn it, it doesn't mean I won't grow and change over the course of the next nine months.

"Right now, you are so unbelievably important to me, but so is this tour, so is the band and right now I can't grow and be ready for this." He brings his hand to my pouch, "until I can give you all of my attention. I want this, Addison. I want you, I want to be a dad, I want to settle down with you and damn it, despite being hurt and scared that he won't return, I want Kyle, I need you and I need him. So I need your patience with me."

"Talon, I am not trying to tie you to my hip. I'm not trying to make you give up your career, and I am most certainly not asking you to give up your social life. The only reason I'm not out there with you after shows is because I don't have the energy. I barely have enough to sit here right now, but I want you working with the band, I want you to hang with the band, and I want you to live your life. Even after the babies are born. I would never, ever consider holding you back from your career and the band. I am far from housewife material, but you're not the first rock star to have a baby, you're certainly not going to be the last. You and even Kyle have this vision that I'm trapping you into full time daddy while I run off to work, and I'm not. I need you to lean on right now because I am emotionally a mess, I feel like shit and damn it, I just need to feel loved because I'm scared about my life post baby, I'm scared about telling my boss that I'm pregnant, I'm scared about the next time I throw up. I'm terrified that one time I'm going to wipe after peeing and it's going to be covered in blood. But I am just trying to get through one day at a time. One hour, one minute, one second. That's all I can do, that's all you can do, and damn it, that's all Kyle can do too. But if it's too much and you don't think you will be ready in nine months or less to welcome your babies into the world, I need to know. I need to know so that I can prepare myself for that. So that I can prepare for doing it on my own. That's all I need. That's all I needed from him. I understand if you and him don't feel ready right now, I don't feel ready, but it's coming and I will spend the next nine months making babies in my body. By the time they're born, I will be ready, just like I have confidence that you and Kyle would be ready.

"If it would be easier for you, and for Kyle, if he comes back to do his job, not having me around might be the best way to do this right now."

"No, it's not. I'm a mess when you're not around. I'm a mess, you saw it yesterday, I couldn't get the track down because I couldn't stop thinking about you, and him and how much I love both of you. It destroyed me. Without doing anything, you ground me. You make me feel love I never knew I was capable of. If you leave, I will lose that. I will lose it all and I can't do that. I can't do this without you, so please dear god, do not leave. I will be ready, I know I will. I know I will because the idea of losing you, and losing them kills me. That's how I know that I will be ready to meet them when they're ready to meet me."

I don't say anything, I don't know what to say to him right now.

"Please, Addison, please tell me you won't leave."

I take a deep breath, trying to calm myself down. "I can't promise not to leave the tour. But I can promise that I won't leave you. If he comes back to work, and nothing else, that is stress that I won't be able to handle. It will be unhealthy for me and for the babies, because I can't look at him and not love him. I can't look at him and not have him in my arms or by my side. It will kill me."

He runs his hand through my hair. "I understand because I don't know if I can do it either. I feel so lost and broken since he walked out that door. I feel like my life has gone more upside down than it did the moment we thought you might be pregnant, then finding out you were, then to top that off, it's twins. Kyle walking out that door has ripped out half of my heart. Someone that I've finally given my love to takes it and runs away, like it's trash, like it means nothing to him. Addison, I have to have him back. I can't do this," his hand rubs along my belly, "without him."

I stand up, my legs shaky from sitting so long and I grab his hand. "I can't either," I say through tears. I reach out for his hand and he wraps his arms around my thighs, pressing his head against my pouch.

Eventually we move onto the bed and I snuggle into his chest. Holding him while he holds me, I fall asleep.

Talon wakes me only briefly to tell me he's leaving for the studio. I fall back to sleep. Sleep is my safe haven right now. Nothing hurts me there...

chapter 33

Tuesday, after Talon left for the studio, I woke up long enough to eat and go back to sleep, only to wake up again, to eat and go back to sleep or to pee and drink. Sometimes I wonder if I was actually sleeping or just lying there with my eyes closed.

I kept my phone close, just in case Kyle decided to call, but I never hear from him. Talon comes home, exhausted, but the music is down and I will go in with him tomorrow to lay down the vocals. Doing that gives me something to look forward to because right now, I have very little, or at least feel like I do.

When Wednesday morning rolls around, I wake up and I actually feel rested and even a little bit better, that is until morning sickness kicks in and I spend five minutes over the toilet, alone. I try my hardest to not let it get to me and fail. Talon is off doing something; he wasn't in the guest room with me when I woke up. I jump into the shower and am getting dressed when Talon comes in. "Hi angel," he says. "How are you feeling?"

"I feel rested, for once, physically I feel good. Emotionally I'm still a mess. What about you, big man?"

He gives me a half smile. "I miss him. I miss you. I miss being with you and him."

"Have you heard..." He doesn't let me finish before he shakes his head. I nod and go back to putting on some light waterproof make-up.

"I brought my phone, it's Wednesday." I see him in the mirror and he has a slight smile on his lips.

"I can't, it hurts too much." His face falls.

"I know, I..."

"Hey, I'm not saying we won't do it, just, not right now."

His eyes are heavy with emotion. "Can I see and say hi?"

My eyes fill with tears and I nod. He reaches out for my hand and I put my stuff down and take his. He pulls me into the bedroom and over to the chair he was sleeping in the other day. "Sit, angel," he says and I move to stand in front of it. I lift my shirt and lower my pants, though they're dipping rather than sitting flat.

Talon slides to his knees and he looks up at me asking for permission. I nod and he places his hands onto my belly, I shiver under his touch. My heart races for the first time in what feels like an eternity as he brings his lips to my pouch, which is rounded further today than it was last week. "You're growing so big," Talon whispers and moves his lips to the other side and kisses there too. One for each baby. "I hope you're being nice to mommy. She's under a lot of stress right now, she misses one of your dads like crazy, so do I, but soon, we'll get him back soon." He kisses again and then kisses the other side again. "Be good in there, panda cubs."

I press his hands to my pouch and I sit down in the chair, tears weakening me. I take his head into my hands, staring into is eyes. "I love you, Talon Carver." I lean forward and press my lips to his, kissing him through our tears. He too is crying.

"I love you so fucking much, Addison." He brings his head to rest gently on my tummy and I stroke his hair.

"I think it's time to call him," I breathe.

He reaches into his pocket and pulls his phone out, handing it to me. I slide to open it, click the phone and the call history. There are no calls to or from Kyle since last week. I find his number and I press the call button then the speaker button.

With each shrill of the ring, Talon flinches. Finally his generic voicemail greeting comes on. We don't even get to hear his voice.

I feel drops of tears falling against my bump. I stroke his hair. "Give him some time."

"It's been two days."

"I know. Come on, big man, we have to get going."

"Wait..." he says, holding me in place. He lifts his head. "I miss you too, you know. I miss making love to you, I miss movies and popcorn and ice cream."

I cup his cheek. "I miss you too. Believe me, I miss you so much, but I'm not ready. I either need him back or I need closure from him. Until I have one or the other, I don't know if I can..."

"I understand, but please, don't be mad at me if I try."

I tap his nose and give him a small smile. "Never. Now let us up so I can get dressed." He smiles at the word 'us', I do too. And he leans back and he catches the first glimpse from the side.

"They're growing," he says, "I can see it."

"My pants are feeling it. Look." I show him how I can't pull them up and have them fit. They rest along the lower swell.

"Do I need to take you shopping?"

"No, not yet. This is okay, for now. I think it depends on what I'm wearing. I can't button my jeans anymore. But if I leave them unbuttoned, I can wear them." I give him a small smile. "I have a lot of pants that I can wear for some time before I'll need new ones."

He nods. "Go get ready."

chapter 34

We make it to the studio on time and sit in the mixing room. We listen to the music tracks that have been mastered and the drums added to Talon's guitar. I have to agree, it adds a little something extra to it.

My head is a bit dizzy so I sit in the chair a little crooked with my head in my hand. "Addison, are you alright?"

"Hmm, yeah." I tell Talon.

I don't need him worrying more. I try and rack my brain for why I could be feeling like this, but nothing is coming to me.

"You ready to give it a go?" Talon asks.

"Absolutely."

I get up and try to catch my balance but my head is spinning so bad, the next thing I know I'm falling, Talon's arms come around me hard and fast as I black out.

talon

"Call nine one one," I tell the sound guys. "Addison? Addison?" I lay her down on the floor and I vaguely hear Marc calling for an ambulance. She's breathing, she has a pulse, I think she's just passed out, but I can't wake her up. "Addison? Come on angel, come back to me. Come on, Addison." I smack her on her cheek lightly, and she doesn't come around.

"They're coming," Marc tells me.

"Mills!" I shout.

"I'll get him," Marc says as he opens the door. "Mills!" Marc calls out.

I hear footsteps. "Shit, Talon, what happened?" Mills comes to the other side of her, shoving the chair out of the way.

"I...I don't know. She was sitting here one minute, she didn't look right but said she was alright, then she stood up and went over."

"When was the last time she ate?"

I try to think, I know she ate last night. "Damn it! Last night." God, I need Kyle so much. Fuck, he was so damn good at making sure she ate.

"I called nine one one," Marc tells Mills.

"Okay, we'll give them a minute, then I'm taking her. Talon?" I look at him. "Breathe buddy, let's lay her down." I nod and he helps me lay her on the floor. He checks her pulse. "It's weak, but it's there. Addison?" he says, trying to bring her around but nothing happens.

"Damn it." A buzzer sounds.

"They're here," Marc says. Fuck, that was fast. Then again, maybe not.

The paramedics come in and I'm too shaken up to say anything. Thank god for Mills. "She's six weeks pregnant with twins and she just passed out," he tells them and they lay down a backboard and go about their work. I stand up and start pacing.

"Wha…" Oh god.

"Addison?" I try to squeeze in.

"Hey, let us do our job, okay?" the paramedic says. "Addison? Hi Addison, my name is Sam," he says to her. "Do you know where you are?"

"Uh, the studio?"

"Okay good, do you know what day of the week it is?"

Hell, I don't even know that. "Wednesday, I think."

"Okay good. Listen, can you tell me how you're feeling?" the paramedic Sam asks her.

"I'm dizzy. I was dizzy, then everything went black. Talon? Where's?"

"I'm right here, angel," I say with a tight throat.

"Addison, when was the last time you ate anything?"

"Last night."

"Okay Addison, we're going to take you to the hospital, okay? Let's get you checked out. Are you in any pain?"

"My rib." I watch as she tries to move to point.

Sam turns to me. "Did she hit anything?"

I shake my head, " I caught her when she went down. I…"

"Hey it's alright. We're gonna take her to Bellvue."

"I want to ride with you."

I can see Mills shake his head. "No, we'll drive over. Tori?"

"Yes?"

"Go get the car, please."

"On it, I'll pull up behind the ambulance."

"Okay great, let's get her on the stretcher," Sam says to his partner.

There is some shifting and then Addison is lifted off of the floor. "Talon?" she calls and my heart breaks.

"Right here, angel."

"Are they okay?"

I step up beside the stretcher. "We're gonna go find out," I tell her. "You're gonna be alright. I'll see you at the hospital."

"Call him," she says as they push the stretcher out through the security door.

"Come on, Talon, let's go," Mills says and I follow him out. Tori and the SUV are sitting behind the ambulance and Mills escorts me to the door that's open and waiting for me. "We'll follow you," I hear him shout to someone as he closes my door.

With shaking hands I pull out my phone, flipping to the call log, I pull up his number. It rings once, twice, then dumps into voicemail.

"I don't give a flying fuck how you think you feel about me, but she is in trouble. She is on her way to Bellvue in an ambulance." That's all I say and I hang up.

chapter 35
kyle

My phone starts to ring. I look at it. It's Talon. I'm incapable of dealing with him, I can't talk to him and no, it's not the first time he's called today. I push the button, sending it to voicemail and I down, wait what number am I on? Fuck it, I down another glass of scotch.

I walked out. I knew it the moment I did it that I'd fucked up, but I didn't know how to fix it. I didn't know what to do. I've spent two days drinking, bingeing and finding numbness.

The bartender pours me another round.

I did this to myself. *So why the fuck do I feel so fucking miserable?*

Because you're fucking stupid, that's why.

You thought that leaving and being on your own would be easier than dealing with everything that's been thrown at you.

Fuck that.

When my father was killed, that was pain like nothing I've ever experienced before. When Dan died, I knew I needed to make myself better, to be there for a mother who didn't want me around. But that was all a fucking picnic compared to this. This is pure agony.

My phone chimes. Voicemail… I let it sit. I don't think I can handle anything he has to say right now… It sits… *oh, what the fuck is wrong with me? Fucking listen to the message, you idiot.*

Picking up my phone, pressing necessary buttons to pull up my voicemail takes me a few minutes. I'm shaking and I'm so drunk my eyeballs are floating in my head.

"I don't give a flying fuck how you think you feel about me, but she is in trouble. She is on her way to Bellvue in an ambulance." I sober quickly.

"I don't give a flying fuck how you think you feel about me, but she is in trouble. She is on her way to Bellvue in an ambulance."

I play Talon's message again, and again, and again…I've been playing it for the last hour….

I fucked up, I know I fucked up, I know that leaving her, leaving him, was the biggest fucking mistake of my life, but I can't go to the hospital, not like this…

"Want another?"

I gesture with my fingers for the bartender to give me another…

It's eleven in the morning and… wow, I'm impressed I know what time it is…

She's in trouble, my baby girl's in trouble, the babies, my babies, fuck!!

I slam back the scotch and stand up, throw two hundred dollars on the bar and stumble my way to the door. Once on the street, I turn left. Walking aimlessly, to where, who the fuck knows. "Hey man, want some snow?"

I stop in my tracks, turn, look at the guy and walk over to him. "Whatcha got?"

dex

"Aww, you don't even know me and you turn me down."

"Dex Harris, I know you well enough to turn you down," Raine tells me.

"Give a guy a chance, would you?"

"For you, Dex, never."

"You're breaking my heart." No need to tell her that she really is breaking my heart. Fuck, she's god damn gorgeous. I met her yesterday while at the studio, and come to find out she's Addison's temporary assistant. "I'll make you change your mind."

"You say that today, but what about tomorrow, Dex-ster when you're done with your show and you've got bimbos hanging off of both arms."

"Oh ouch, you wound me, gorgeous."

My phone vibrates in my pocket, I pull it out. "What's up, T-man?"

"Dex, Addison's in the hospital."

"Shit! What happened?"

"All the shit with Kyle, she hasn't been eating and I've been shit at making sure she does. They're keeping her overnight, giving her fluids and all that good stuff."

"Damn man, what about the babies?"

"They're fine from what we can tell, nothing indicates otherwise."

'Okay good, want us to come down?"

"No, no. Stay put, I don't want to draw a bigger crowd. Listen, can you let the rest of the guys know? Mills, Tori and Rusty are taking shifts at the hospital, so if you go out, you'll need to work with what you got. And…have you heard from Kyle?"

"No T-man, I'm sorry I haven't."

"I called him around ten, when they were taking her to the hospital, but I haven't heard back. He wouldn't do this to her. I'm worried that something's happened. Or about to happen."

"I'll try calling him. We have a show tomorrow anyway. I'll find out what the hell."

"Thanks, D. Call my cell if you need me, I won't leave her."

"Right."

He hangs up. "Sorry cutie, I got some business to attend to."

"What's going on, Dex?" she asks me.

"Uh…" Shit, does she know? Fuck. "Just some stuff with Talon, no biggy."

"Doesn't sound like something that's not a big deal, Dex. What's going on?"

Fuck…I can't deny this woman anything. "Addison's being kept overnight at the hospital."

"Babies?"

"Uh, you might want to talk to them about that…Cheers," I say and walk out of the hotel bar.

I flip through my phone, find K's number and hit send. It rings once, twice, then finally he answers…

"Dex, I need help…"

"Did you do it?" I point to the baggie of coke on the table in front of him.

"No, I… I can't bring myself to open it."

"Good. Come on, let's get you cleaned up. Your girl needs you."

"I failed her."

"You screw someone else?"

"Fuck no!"

"So you fucking got drunk."

"For like, three fucking days. I've failed her so bad. She's in the fucking hospital because of me and instead of going to her, I fucking bought coke."

"You haven't failed her. Not yet, you haven't. Come on. Shower, now." Fuck, this hotel is the shittiest of the shitty. I know he can afford better, but I get why he came here.

I go into the bathroom and start the shower. I'm going to have to fucking undress him. Ugh. "I'm going to strip you out of your clothes, fuck, do you have more clothes?"

"No."

"Alright…"

"Take that shit off."

I pull my phone out. "Beck."

"Such a jack ass as always…I need your discretion and more than anything, this stays between us."

"What do you need, Dex?"

"I've got K."

"Shit, where?"

"Relax, brotha. He's drunk, he's been essentially homeless for three days and he bought a teenie."

"Fuck."

"Relax, he's clean. He chickened out, but listen, he smells like ass, I need clothes. Can you get some and bring them?"

"Of course."

"And, Beck?"

"Yeah?"

"You call anyone, I'll have your balls for breakfast."

"No one."

"Alright…" I fill him in on where we're at and he hangs up.

I turn around and Kyle is fucking naked as a jaybird. "Alright, let's go."

I drag him into the bathroom and throw him into the shower. "Oh FUCK!" he shouts. "THAT'S FUCKING COLD!"

I slap his chest. "Sober up, big man!"

chapter 36

talon

There is a knock followed by three quick knocks. I stand up. "What's wrong?" Addison says.

"Nothing, angel, Mills needs me." I bend down and kiss her forehead. "I'll be right outside. Go back to sleep."

"Okay," she says sleepily and before I clear her bed, she's back to sleep. I open the door quietly and Tori is standing in front of it.

"What's up?" I whisper and she steps out of my way right as the door clicks quietly closed.

"You mother fucker." I charge at Kyle, slamming him up against the wall opposite the door. "A little late, aren't we?"

"Come on, Talon. Fuck, I fucked up, I was fucked up."

"Where the fuck have you been?" I'm still pinning him to the wall, it's the only thing stopping me from punching his face in.

"I fucked up, I left, I regretted it the moment I did it but I didn't know how to go back...I, I got wasted, was wasted when you left that fucking message. I didn't know how to sober up, then, fuck, I knew she was in fucking trouble and the opportunity presented itself..."

"Are you fucking high right now?"

"No, god no, I bought it yes, but I chickened out. Dex fucking called me. I told him I needed help. He showed up, flushed it, threw my fucking ass in the shower so I could get here. I didn't know what else to do, I wouldn't show up drunk, I fucking couldn't."

I push on him and let him go. Then I haul off and give him one nasty ass fucking right hook. He grabs his face as Mills grabs me. "Easy, T. I know you're pissed but this isn't good, not for you, not for him, not for her. Back off."

Tori assesses Kyle. "You alright?"

"Yeah, I deserved that and more."

"If you're gonna fucking be here, be here for her, be here to fucking stay. If you're here because you fucking feel guilty for walking out and plan on doing it again, get the fuck out of this hospital. I won't watch her destroy herself again. She's fucking here because she didn't eat enough. She couldn't fucking get out of bed. She can't fucking deal with this shit without you, without us. I can't fucking do this without you." Mills finally lets me go. "It never fucking occurred to me to make sure she ate more than she was. I didn't realize until it was too late what kind of danger she was putting herself in because you fucking left her, Kyle, you fucking left me."

"I got scared. I'm not ready for all this."

"Do you think I am? Do you fucking think she is? Because I'm certainly not, and neither is she, but you know what she taught me while you've been gone? First, that she's selfless. Everything she does is for you, for me, for those babies. Second of all, that we're so fucking scared of the unknown that we can't see past our own fucking noses and look at what's coming in the long run and third, she'd

223

fucking leave me if you didn't come back to us. If you fucking came back to do your job, and not love her, she was gonna fucking leave me because she couldn't take it, looking at you, knowing how much she loves you and not being able to have you, to hold you, to tell you she fucking loves you. You walked out on us. You were fucking selfish and walked out on our family, all because you think you can't do this. Because you're trying so hard to take it all away from her, to shoulder it for her. She loves being pregnant, despite the morning sickness, despite the pain, despite everything else, she loves it, and she loves it because we showed her that we loved it too.

"It's Wednesday, Kyle. Today is the first day since you left that I could touch her stomach. That I could kiss our kids and that's because I begged her to let me. She wouldn't let me take her picture today. Said it hurt too much, it hurt because it was your damn job to do it, not mine. She made that pact with you because you were having the hardest time dealing with all this. She wanted to show you that it was alright, that it would be okay and more than anything, she wanted you to see what was happening to her. She hasn't journaled, she hasn't picked up her book and she's been throwing up alone because she wouldn't let me in bed with her. By the time I knew she was up, it was too late.

"Despite all of that, despite what's happened, she still loves the fact that she throws up because it means that everything is healthy, or so they say. She loves the fact that her breasts hurt because it means she's working to feed those twins. She will take everything this pregnancy has to throw at her with everything she has. She's taught me that when they're born and she can hold them in her arms that it will all be worth it."

By the time I'm done, I'm speaking softly and Kyle is wiping tears from his eyes. "And me, I gave you my love, the one thing you knew was nearly impossible for me to give up. I gave it to you and to her, and you left. You walked out the door, Kyle. Just like everyone else in my life."

"Stop..." he breathes. "I will spend the rest of my life making up for my mistakes this week. I've already paid a heavy price for it. I damn near broke eight years of sobriety because of what I did. But I didn't, because someone was watching out for me. Someone was pulling me back. That someone was you and it was her, and it was those babies. I left because I thought I wasn't ready, but I know now that I am more than ready. I know now that without you, without her, and without them, that I will be a worthless nothing roaming the streets. I can't breathe without you, without her." He stands up and I slam into him again. This time I take his face in my hands and I kiss him long and hard. I move my hands but not my lips. I intertwine them in his and hold them over his head.

"Say it," I demand against his lips.

"I love you."

"Say it again."

"I love you with all my fucking heart, Talon Carver!" I slam my lips against his again, kissing him like my life depends on it.

"I love you too," I say back to him and he nuzzles his nose against mine.

"How is she?" he asks quietly and I slowly let him go.

"She's dehydrated, but that's getting better. Her blood sugar dropped to way below normal levels, which is what caused her to pass out. Low blood sugar is from lack of food. She was eating, but barely enough for her, let alone the twins. I've never not seen her clean her plate and she left at least a quarter of a big bowl of mac n' cheese last night and because I was too caught up in showing her that I still love her and the twins, I forgot to feed her this morning. Which is one of the many reasons why we need you."

"How are the babies?"

I smile for the first time in three days. "They're good, from what they can tell. Everything seems to be intact. She's right on the cusp of them being able to get a visual on their heartbeats. They're going to do another one tomorrow and then give us instructions on when to come back for another one to make sure everything is alright."

He nods. "I want to see her," he says.

"She was sleeping when I left to come out here."

"I'm right here," she says from behind us. I whirl around.

"You're supposed to be in bed," I chastise her.

"I had to pee," she retorts with a smirk. She looks past me to Kyle. "If you cross this threshold, it's because you're here to stay. It's because you're here for me, you're here for Talon and you are here for our babies. It means no more guilt about my symptoms. I heard what he told you and he's right. I know it will all be worth it, in the end. Kyle, I love you more than anything, besides Talon and these little ones in here." She runs her hand over her stomach. "I cannot handle this again. I am still upset that you left, but I hope it gave you a chance to clear your mind of your fears and your doubts. I cannot promise that I won't freak out, say something that upsets you, or remain hurt over the fact that you left. I need time to heal and time to believe you're really here with me, with us."

She pulls herself away from the door jamb and turns, pushing her IV pole back into the room, disappearing behind the curtain. "The choice is yours, cowboy. Get on the horse and ride it, or stay behind and watch it leave." I give him a small smile and step into the room. She's crying, leaning against the bed. I take a step toward her and a hand on my shoulder stops me.

"You've seen this enough in the last few days. It's my turn to bear this one." He gives me a smile and goes to her. Kneeling down, he looks up at her. "Addison?"

"Oh god," she wails, falling forward and he catches her and scoops her up in his arms. I lean against the wall and watch as he holds her tightly to him and I know that today is the beginning of everything we've ever wanted.

chapter 37
addison

"Addison..." I put my finger to his lips.

"Shh..." I give him a smile. "What I heard out there is enough for right now."

"But baby girl, please, let me say what I need to say."

He lays me down on the very uncomfortable hospital bed and covers me back up. His hands brush along my pouch and I tremble. He notices and slides the covers back down just a little bit. He doesn't touch me skin to skin, but gently places his hands on my gown covered pouch. He starts crying and more tears drip from my eyes. His eyes meet mine. The emotions in his eyes show themselves to me immediately and I'm lost in them. "I'm not ready for this..." I fight to keep looking at him, and he doesn't stop talking, "but I will be ready. I know that now because for three days, all I could think about was you, the babies, and Talon. I made some very shitty choices over the last three days, choices that I don't want to take back because without those choices, I wouldn't realize what I would honestly be without you," his thumbs stroke along my stomach and warmth spreads through my veins, "the babies," he head cocks in Talon's direction, "and Talon. I realize that this is where I'm supposed to be, this is the path I'm supposed to take. I bought coke, did you hear that part?" I nod, "I bought it, but sat there staring at it for hours. Trying to build up the nerve to do it. That's when I realized that there are far more important things in my life than drugs. I know now what it would mean for you to lose me. The sacrifice you would make without me in your life and I realize that I can't let that happen because that would kill me a thousand times over. I love you more than life itself. I need you and I need Talon and I need these panda cubs." I sob at his use of the nickname for the twins. "I will be here every day, I will love you every day and I will show you how much I love you. I can't promise not to worry when you're sick, I cannot promise not to worry when you're hurting, and I cannot promise that I won't panic from time to time. But I can promise to remind myself that this is all worth it, this is all," his hands move from my stomach down, tugging on my hospital gown, lifting it to beneath my breasts. He leans down and kisses me. I sob harder. "Worth," he kisses the other side, "every minute, every hour and every day."

I see Talon from the corner of my eye. His eyes are red with tears. I hold my hand out for him to come and take it and he comes over, hesitantly. "The next time either one of you feel panicked about what's happening to me? Ask me, I will tell you. Read about it. Know about what's happening to my body, you both want to shoulder what's happening to me because you think it's a burden, it's not. It is an absolute blessing. Read the books, follow along with the growth, the progression, so that when something new happens with me, you don't panic on me. I've fought so hard to be strong for both of you, to be strong for the babies and I can't do it anymore. I'm exhausted and I feel like someone has stuffed a softball in my stomach." They both snort a laugh.

"That would be us, we did that part," Talon says with a wide smile and Kyle chuckles.

The tears that I'd finally managed to stop come back, but now they are happy tears. "We will do our best. But give us a little slack if we screw up," Talon says with a smile. "Because you know damn well we will."

Kyle pulls my gown back down, adjusts the blankets and covers me back up. He sits back down on the side of the bed. Talon releases my hand and walks around the bed to the other side where he sits. I'm looking at both of my men. The tears haven't stopped flowing but at least now, they're happy tears.

"What can we do, baby girl?" Kyle says sweetly.

"Get me out of here." My voice is choked with the happiness I'm feeling now that my family is back together again.

"Aww angel, I want to, I really do, but you heard them."

"I know, but I feel fine and I'm starving and..." I lose steam.

"They haven't fed her?" Kyle asks, looking sideways at Talon.

Talon laughs. "No, they did, but it was hardly enough."

"And it was awful," I pout.

"Will they let us bring something in?" Kyle asks again looking to Talon.

He shrugs, "Don't know, but it wouldn't hurt to ask. What do you want, angel?"

"Soup, chicken noodle, crackers, bread." They both smile at me. "What?"

"Nothing, it's just great to see you hungry again," Talon says with a half-smile.

"Let me go ask the nurses and let's see what we can do," Kyle says as he stands.

"I'll go, you stay with her." Talon stands up, squeezes my hand, then reaches across me to cup Kyle's cheek. "I'm glad you're home."

Kyle leans into his touch. "I'm sorry I left." Kyle kisses his palm and Talon leaves the room. He sits back down on the bed beside me. "Please, no matter what happens between us, eat. Always eat. Dr. Breckenridge told you that, it wasn't just me."

"I never stopped eating or drinking. I always did it, I just didn't eat enough. I ate enough to satisfy my grumbling tummy but that was all. I didn't realize just how much the amount of food I was eating mattered. But I went from eating enough for at least two people to eating barely enough for me."

"I'm so sorry that I put you in that position, to make you so upset you couldn't function."

I put my hand to his cheek. "I functioned when I needed to, like for the studio, until today, and everything in between is a blur. Talon suffered because of my being upset only to realize how much your being gone was hurting him too. He loves you, Kyle, he loves you as much as he loves me. You need to remember that. We both love you, and neither one of us wants to see you fail. I asked you about being ready, not because you needed to leave, or that you had to be ready right that moment. I asked because I needed to know so that I could figure out how best to help you." I put my hand down and he scoops it up into his, holding it to his chest. "Despite what you thought at the time, you safe worded on me. You're more ready than you think. You wouldn't lie in bed with me for hours when you could be out at the bar. Instead you laid around reading pregnancy books. You wouldn't feed me as well as you did, and you wouldn't be there to hold my hair when I threw up in the morning. It's a lot and more because we've only been at this a few weeks."

"A few weeks that have meant more for me than ten years could. Addison, I feel like we've been together forever. We have no secrets, we have no lies. Everything between the three of us is real and it's raw. We've done in six weeks what couples strive for over years and we're three people, which makes it harder. You're selfless, you fight so hard for Talon and I, you fight so hard for them," he nods his head toward my belly, "now it's time to let us take care of you."

"I don't know how to do that," I say through a wave of tears and sadness. "I don't know how to be taken care of."

"I think you do. I think you have. You let us be here for you, you let us feed you, wash you, dress you, pack and take care of everything for you. You just don't see it because we don't give you a choice. If we asked if we could dry you off, you wouldn't let us, but we do it without giving you a choice because we know what you want, you just don't know how to ask for it. Remember what Dr. B said? Don't down play anything. If you're hurting, we need to know. If you don't feel good, we need to know, and if you just want to be held and cuddled, we need to know. Just like you need to know when something is bothering us."

I nod, wiping tears with my free hand. "I will try harder to let go. It's not easy."

He leans forward, kissing my forehead. "We never said it would be." He cups my cheek and wipes the tears.

"Now, you're exhausted. I've put you through an emotional ringer. Sleep, my sweet girl. I will be here when you wake up."

I kiss his palm and he pulls back. I lay my head back and for the first time in three days, I fall into a deep sleep.

I'm awoken a little while later by the smell of chicken noodle soup and it brings me around. I devour the soup, crackers and two rolls before falling back to sleep.

chapter 38

When I wake up on Thursday, Kyle is in the hospital room with me, "Where's Talon?" I ask through sleep.

Kyle sits up from his chair, and lays his iPad on the bed. "Good morning, sweet girl." I smile at him. "There was a problem with one of the buses. He had to go take care of it."

"What happened?"

"It was the other bus. It was in an accident."

"Oh god, was anyone hurt?"

"No, everyone is fine. Though it was t-boned and the undercarriage was pretty tore up. Talon had to go assess the equipment and when I talked to him a little while ago, Dex was on his way to buy a new set of drums."

"Oh crap. Is he going to be able to?"

"Most likely. Talon, Mouse and Peacock all bring their guitars with them into the hotels. It's harder for Dex for obvious reasons, but any little dent in the drum alters the sound. They're assessing for more damaged equipment, the amps are down there along with microphones and things like that. He hated leaving you, but he said that he knew you'd understand."

"Oh my god, of course I understand, but shouldn't you be there too?"

"I should, but..."

"Then go, Kyle, I'm alright. I promise. You sitting here is doing nothing."

"Baby girl, I don't want to leave."

"Listen, cowboy, and listen good. Until this tour is over, your priority is 69 Bottles and your job. My job is to grow babies and sit on a computer keeping the band's reputation in line and get on stage and sing once in a while. I think one of the things that has caused some of this angst and what happened, is because you and Talon have devoted so much time and energy to me. When things go wrong you have no outlets. When things like this happen with the bus, there is panic and chaos because you're both so unsure of yourselves. So today, I am going to sit here, grow some babies, do some work and then get discharged, hopefully, and go back to the hotel. I have Tori and Rusty and I am sure that Raine is around here somewhere. They will take care of me. You go take care of our boy and the band."

"I don't know what to say..."

"That's easy, tell me you love me, give me a kiss and then go." I give him a big genuine smile. "Okay, you can go after I pee." He laughs and I slide my legs out from under the covers and without saying a word he is dutifully there to help me down. With IV pole in tow, I go to the bathroom.

"Addie?"

"Hmm?"

"It's morning, how are you...?"

"Not puking?" I say with a smile. "Anti-nausea meds. Give it time. I'll be back to morning vomiting in no time." I wink at him and he smiles. "I can still feel it. But the meds are working."

"Good," he says as he helps me to sit down.

"What were you reading anyway?" He blushes. "That bad?"

"No," he shakes his head then leaves the bathroom.

I take care of business and when I go to stand back up, he's there helping me with his iPad in one hand. "Show me," I say and he opens up his iPad. The cover is a men's shirt with a kid's toy keys and the title reads, 'The Expectant Father'. I look at him.

"I thought maybe it would help me to read about dads, versus just reading about you. I ordered two paperback copies that should be delivered to the hotel in a day or two. But I couldn't wait, so I started reading it while you slept."

"And?"

He smiles. "It's helping me feel more comfortable. I guess knowing that I'm not the only one in the world who has gone through this makes it a little easier."

I reach up on my toes and kiss his cheek. "Good, I'm glad."

"Talon had one of the guys bring you your messenger bag, a change of clothes and some breakfast." He helps me back into bed. "I'll get you set up with food and your stuff, then I'll go help Talon."

"Good." I smile as he brings the bed table over, putting my food on top. He opens it up to reveal eggs, sausage, no bacon, some mini pancakes, toast and a bag with syrup, salt, ketchup etcetera inside. I notice that there is like a double serving of eggs and sausage. I smile at my food.

"Eat, sweet girl. Eat so you can come home to us."

He gets out my laptop, plugs it in for me and sets it next to my food on the table. He puts the messenger bag between my legs so that I can access my other stuff as needed. "I need my purse too." He cocks his head at me. "I have some journaling to do," I say with a wink.

He smiles wide. "We have a picture to take too."

My smile back is equally as wide as his. "But not in a hospital gown, we'll do it when I get home."

He kisses my forehead. "I can't wait." He pulls back. "You good?"

"I'm good, make sure I have my phone, and go. I will call when I know something."

"Alright, sweet girl. I'll see you later." He leans down and kisses me softly on the lips. "I love you," he breathes and I smile against his lips.

"I love you too." I kiss him again, and again then finally I pull back. "Now go, I want to eat."

He laughs as he leaves my hospital room.

Shortly after I finish eating there is a knock at the door. "Come in."

"Hey girl," Raine says.

"How'd I know you were roaming around the hospital?"

"Oh you know, it's kinda my job, as your assistant and all."

I snort, "Well, you're pretty damn good."

"Someone is here to see you."

I raise an eyebrow at her just as the door opens and Cami comes strolling in. All high heels, pencil shirt, sleeveless top and jacket slung over her purse. "Hey Addie," Cami says and I think I blush, or panic, not sure which.

"Hi Cami, what are you doing here?"

"Oh I got a call from a little birdie yesterday telling me what happened, about three minutes before I got the call from the studio that you'd collapsed."

"So you hopped on a plane and came to New York?"

She smiles wide. "I did. So should I be saying congratulations?"

"Oh Cami, I'm so sorry…"

"Why are you sorry?"

"You sent me on that bus to do a job and I end up sleeping with…"

"Oh lord, do not apologize for that. Dear god, I am the last person to judge you, I'm married to a client."

"I know, but this is so not like me…"

She laughs, "Listen, I know you've had a rough few days and believe me, I can completely understand." She sits down on the bed. "Let me tell you a story that no one really knows. When I found out I was pregnant with Jaden, I ran away and hid, literally, I disappeared for a long time because I was so afraid of what Tristan was going to think. It was the stupidest mistake I've ever made. You didn't run, you didn't do anything wrong, you haven't done anything wrong, and you're still doing your job. What we do isn't that demanding when we're limited to one client." She tilts her head down. "I know, I've been there."

"I haven't been doing a very good job."

"Nonsense. You've done amazing, especially considering that you've become your own PR Rep with your own celebrity, that's not easy to handle. It's overwhelming at times, but you're doing great. But, given the circumstances, I think you need some help. Raine has agreed to join the tour, assisting you with the band and handling you're own brand building. She's amazing at what she does and she knows what she's doing." I look at Raine who is smiling from ear to ear and I smile too. "She's a decoration around my office because I don't use her like I should and Trinity's assistant can handle me too. You just need to take care of that baby."

I look at Raine and cock my head, she shrugs. "Cami, not baby, babies." I emphasize.

"Oh my god, how many are you having, girl?"

I laugh at her excitement. "Two, just two."

"No wonder you're a mess. God, one for me was enough to knock me on my ass for a while, I can't imagine, two..." she breathes out the last word. "Well then, double congrats. Whose?" She asks gently.

I laugh. "I wish I knew. They're either Talon or Kyle's."

"You little minx."

"Or both... they're fraternal twins, which means two eggs, which means there's a small chance that they could each have one in here."

"Oh my god." She laughs. "Do you know when it happened?"

"Albuquerque based on all the information I can find. That's about the time."

"Oh god, that was right after you left Phoenix." I blush. "I can't imagine how you do it. Dealing with both of them like you do. I commend you for it, really I do. Tristan is a handful as it is. Speaking of which..." she looks to the door.

"Did you leave him outside?" She nods. "Tristan!" I shout and the door opens. Tristan is standing on the other side and I can see Tyson behind him. "Get in here," I say playfully and he comes into the room. Raine slides back into the corner.

"Hey Addison, how you doing?" he asks with a little bit of a blush.

"Better now." I smile. "How are you?"

"Can't complain." He smiles.

"Babe, she's having twins," Cami tells him.

"No way?" He has a big grin on his face. "That's so awesome, congrats Addison."

"Thank you." I blush.

Cami, Tristan, Raine and I chat for a little longer until the nurse comes in to take some blood for some final tests. "Call me. Let's have lunch tomorrow if you're up to it," Cami says with a smile on her face.

"I'd love to." The nurse sets about getting me ready while I talk to Cami. "Have we rescheduled the studio?"

"We did. Marc says he'll do it Saturday morning. Other than the concert, the schedule is clear." She looks at Raine, who nods. "She has all the details you need. Oh, and after the photo shoot with the band, and you get yours done. I've arranged for some private time with the photographer, for you, Talon and Kyle."

"Cami, you didn't have to..."

"Nonsense. It was actually Tristan's idea. When we were pregnant with Jaden, some of our most cherished pictures are from that time. Of course the ones that came after are more so, but we still have several hanging in our house. Soak it up. The session is private, you three, plus the photographer. Who is a very dear friend of mine. We can discuss when to announce, later."

"It won't be until after the tour."

Cami smiles, "We'll shoot for that, but Addison?"

"Huh? Ouch." The nurse pokes me with a needle.

"What are you now? Six weeks?" I nod. "Big clothing isn't going to cover you for very long. What you're wearing now, and how you're lying isn't very flattering, but I think it will have to come out sooner than you want. We will keep a lid on it as long as we can. I promise."

I nod my understanding. "I..."

"Oh I understand, believe me. So we will do what we can and I'm sure your fashion sense will keep you looking normal and not raise too many questions. No one even knows you're here."

"Okay good. Besides, what happened could be twisted into something else, if it got out."

The nurse finishes and interjects, "We'll be back shortly to take you for another ultrasound." She quietly leaves the room.

"Look, let's just get you better and get you out of here. Raine's started working on handling tonight's show, assuming you're not cleared to perform."

I snort. "I doubt Talon and Kyle would let me anyway."

She smiles, "They take pretty good care of you, you know?" I nod. "But if the doctor says it's okay and you feel up to it..."

"Oh, I can handle those two, and as of right now, if I get out of here at a reasonable time, I plan on being there."

"Good to hear," Tristan says.

"Speaking of which, is this going to affect anything else that's in the works?"

"If it does, I'll sue their asses for discrimination," Cami says with a smile on her face. "Don't worry about that now. There's a lot you can still do while you're pregnant and anyone who wants you as bad as they're claiming right now, they ain't gonna care."

"That makes me happy."

"Good, now get some rest."

"We'll see you later," Tristan says behind her as he escorts her from the room. I smile when I see his hand on the small of her back as they leave the room.

"Alright, Raine, what do you have for me?" I ask and we start talking.

chapter 39

"Does it mean anything that you can't see the heartbeats?" I ask the doctor who's doing my ultrasound.

"No, not at this stage. You're measuring great at six weeks and they're both looking great on the ultrasound. But I'd like for you to come back to the hospital next week to have a follow-up ultrasound. We can schedule an appointment for you before you leave. By then we should be able to see the heartbeats and we can check on things."

He pulls the wand out, another internal ultrasound, ugh. He hands me a couple of pictures of both babies. "I'll go ahead and discharge you. Your lab work looks great, your HCg levels have gone up even since yesterday, so that's a great sign. If you feel any cramping, discomfort, or something just doesn't feel right, come back in to the ER."

I take a deep breath, trying not to panic. "Do I have any restrictions?" I ask.

He shakes his head. "No, just get some rest and get back on track with eating and drinking. You may notice some increased urination because of all the IV fluids we've given you and the anti-nausea medicine will be wearing off soon."

"I have a concert tonight."

"As a patron or?"

"As a singer, but I only sing two songs throughout the show. Am I okay to do that?"

He hesitates. "Go with your gut instinct. If you have the ability to back out of it, I would consider it, but if you continue to eat and feel alright as the day goes on and you limit your stress and excitement, I think you'd be alright. Just take it easy," he tells me with a smile.

The nurse helps me back into the wheelchair and takes me back to my room where Raine is waiting patiently, working on her laptop.

"Go ahead and get changed, I'll be back with some care instructions, your discharge papers and we will send you on your way."

"Thanks," I tell her as she helps me up and then leaves the room.

"I'll rally the troops," Raine says as she hops up out of her chair.

"Can I ask you something?" I say to her and she stops in her tracks looking at me. "Are you sure you're okay with all this? The tour and everything?"

"Oh my goodness, are you kidding me? I am so stoked you have NOO idea!" she exclaims with such an infectious attitude that I can feel mine shifting as well. "Besides, Dex has the hots for me."

I snort a laugh. "Sweetheart, I hate to break it to you, but Dex has the hots for anything with legs, a vagina and tits."

"Oh I know, and it's damn fun making him work for it."

"Oh my god, and Cami called me a minx." We both burst out laughing.

"Get dressed. I'll be back in when the nurse comes with your paperwork. Which will be in like three hours." She rolls her eyes and I know immediately that we're going to get along just fine.

An hour later and I'm in a wheelchair, being pushed by Raine and flanked on both sides by Tori and Rusty, and I'm on my way out of the hospital. I haven't called the guys just yet, I'll do it from the car. It's just after twelve so I am left to decide what I want to eat for lunch and I decide on room service back at the hotel. Tori calls ahead to place my order. I have a feeling she's in on this gig and will make sure I eat, even if the guys don't. Once we are on our way, I call Kyle.

"Hey sweet girl."

"Hi cowboy, how are things there?"

"A mess, but they're straightening out quickly. We've got some new equipment and we're coordinating with the venue for some of theirs. We've moved everything over to the venue and the crew and the guys are getting it set up. They're running sound around two, two thirty, at least that's the goal. But enough about what's happening here, how are you?"

"I'm great. I'm in the car on my way back to the hotel."

"Oh sweetie, that's awesome."

"What's going on, Ky?" I hear Talon in the background.

"She's doing great and in the car, they've discharged her."

"Let me say hi," Talon says and I hear the phone change hands. "Hi angel."

"Hi big man."

"You're doing good?"

"I'm great, now that I'm leaving. Tori ordered lunch from the hotel to be delivered to the room. Raine is with me. I want to take a shower and then come down to you guys."

"Nope, you need to rest."

"Talon, please, I'm fine. The doctor said everything is fine with me and the babies. I'm really wound up and…"

"Alright," he says softly. "Eat first, shower, get dressed and have them bring you down here. But Addison?"

"Yeah?"

"You will take it easy once you get here, you hear me."

"Yes big man, I hear you," I say with a smile. He can't say no to me and I love it.

"Alright, I love you, here's Ky."

"Love you too."

They pass the phone. "I know, it's fine," I hear Talon say to Kyle.

"What was that all about?"

"Me arguing with him about you coming down here. Are you sure that's a good idea?"

I love that he's expressing his concern to me. "Listen cowboy, I have been in a hospital bed for twenty-four hours. For the first time, I slept amazing and I am full of energy. I don't want to sit around the hotel room waiting for you guys to come back. So please, let me come there. I will behave, I will listen, and I will not lift a finger. I just want to be near you and Talon."

"Baby girl, you know I can't say no to you."

I smile wide. "I know, cowboy. I love you. I'm going to eat, shower, and get dressed, I'll be there soon."

"I love you too, baby girl."

We hang up and Raine looks like she's gonna gag. "Oh come on, we're not that bad." We both laugh. I hear Rusty snort from the front seat. "Oh not you too, Rusty?" Then Tori snorts and everyone is laughing.

Zoey Derrick

Pressure, pain, heartache, depression and guilt, all washed away compliments of a pretend gag.

chapter 40

Raine hangs out with me while I eat, then leaves to go change and get ready to go with me to the theater where the show is taking place for the next three nights.

After my shower, I pull my hair back into a messy bun, throw on a pair of my button up, drawstring, elastic cargo nylon pants and decide that I need a lot more of these for the coming months. They stretch and fit beautifully. Not wanting it to be too obvious, and since most of my shirts are pretty form fitting, I steal one of Kyle's from his drawer. His shirts are not overly big on me, but they hang lower, giving me flexibility in fluffing for additional hiding.

For the first time, I wear a bra. My nipples seem to constantly be hard and rub against even my tank tops. I slip into my chucks (Converse), and I'm ready to go. Looking in the mirror, with the bra on, my boobs look freakin' huge. Though the tug on the shirt helps hide my tiny pouch that much more.

Once we're in the car, I call Dr. Paige and leave a message with her receptionist, letting her know that Bellvue will be sending over the records from my visit. I tell the receptionist what happened and that I'm alright, valuable lesson learned. I expect Dr. Paige will be calling me later.

I also call my mom.

"Hi mom," I say when she answers the phone.

"Hi sweetheart, how are you?"

"I'm doing good, in New York, how are you doing?"

"Oh you know, same ole here. Just working. Did you know that everyone seems to know about you and your success with the singing thing? People keep coming up to me congratulating me. I had a reporter stalking me a couple days ago..."

"Oh no mom, why didn't you call me?"

"Pfft," she says, "I handled him. I ignored him, mostly, then when I got pissed off I told him to go away. I haven't seen him since."

I laugh, "Oh mom, I'm so sorry about that."

"Don't be, it was fun telling him off."

"Oh jeez, mom." She laughs.

"How are those boys of yours?"

"They're great, taking really good care of me."

"Oh sweetheart, I'm so happy for you."

"Thank you mom, that means a lot to me."

"How are those babies doing?"

"What?" I nearly shriek into the phone. "Mom, how did you find..."

"Oh sweetheart, Talon called me yesterday when you went into the hospital. He was so scared. I could tell he didn't want to tell me, he really wanted it to be you, but I can't resist asking you about them and well, I'm gonna be a grandma."

"Oh mom," I start crying.

"Oh baby, don't cry. I'm really happy for you. Those boys love you with all their hearts. I think it's a little soon in your relationship, but with all the problems you've had in the past, I..." I hear her choke up a little bit, "I'm so happy that this has happened to you times two."

"Oh mom, don't cry, please."

"I can't help it, I'm so happy for you. Now go get that tour done so you guys can come home. I want to see you."

We talk for a couple more minutes and then I have to let her go because we're pulling into the venue. "Hug them both for me, sweetheart, and make them hug you from me."

"I will, love you, mom."

"Love you too, call me soon."

"I will." We hang up.

"Did you know he called her?" I say to Raine.

She shakes her head. "No, but I was talking to Dex when Talon called him. Then Dex turned around and called Kyle. After that Dex shut me out and left. Then the next thing I heard was that Kyle was over at the hospital. I didn't go over there until this morning. I didn't want to intrude and I knew Cami was coming."

"So you told Cami?"

"I kind of had to. I knew with you going to the hospital, either the label or the studio was going to call her and I didn't want the news coming from anyone other than me or Talon and I didn't know if Talon would call her."

"Well, I appreciate that Raine, I really do. I was so scared to tell her."

She laughs, "One thing you need to understand about Cami is that she just goes with the flow and like she told you, she can't punish anyone for dating a client because she's married to Tristan, but she will step up if that relationship becomes a problem, which I don't see happening here so she's not going to say anything. Besides, she's very fond of you."

I smile as we pull up between the theater and the one lonely bus, our bus. Talon and Kyle come bolting out the back door right in front of us. I laugh and open my door.

My feet barely touch the ground before Talon scoops me up into his arms. "Hi angel."

"Hi ace," I say with a laugh. "Happy to see me?"

He smirks. "You have no idea." He plants a kiss on my lips that is full of love and passion and I melt.

Smiling against his lips, I say, "I missed this."

"Me too." He kisses me again, sliding his tongue inside, finding mine. I shiver with desire and he deepens the kiss.

Someone clears their throat. I open one eye to see Kyle chomping at the bit. I start laughing. "You might want to share me," I tell Talon. He sets me down with a laugh and squeezes me to him one more time, then with barely an inch between us, Kyle swoops in.

"Hi cowboy."

"Hi panda," he says with a sly smile.

"Kiss me," I breathe.

"With pleasure." He smirks and plants his lips on mine, hard and fast. Love, lust and devotion pour into me at a pace that leaves me breathless. His tongue slides past my lips and he caresses mine with his. Desire explodes and I moan, melting into his embrace. Our first kiss since his return and it feels like he never left, but that his love for me has grown by leaps and bounds.

I want him, I need him, I need them both so bad. I pull back, my breathing jagged and hard. "We have the bus," I whisper.

He chuckles. "Later, baby, promise."

I melt into his smile and the promise of fulfilling my need for him. Talon comes up behind me, pressing me between the two of them. I can feel their erections probing into me and I turn to putty in their hands. "If you make me wait, I just might explode."

They both laugh. "We have to make you wait. Not because we want to. We have to do the sound check," Talon says into my ear then he pulls my lobe into his mouth. I hiss through my teeth as my clit throbs.

"Mmm, seems we discovered a new hot spot," Kyle teases me.

Talon lets my ear go. "I like it," he says with a lust filled growl.

"Okay, if you're making me wait, we better get going because I'm about three seconds away from sliding my hand down my pants."

"Oh no, you don't. Those orgasms are ours and ours alone." The command in Talon's voice makes my knees weak and they both hold me tightly.

"Yes," I breathe and then they slowly let me go. Each taking a hand in theirs and escorting me into the theater.

chapter 41

Once we're inside and near the stage the guys all stop what they're doing and come over toward me. All except Dex. I watch him as he goes straight to Raine. "Hang on guys," I say holding up a finger and I walk over to Dex and grab him by the ear. "Down boy."

"Hey, come on, stop cock blocking me."

"She's my assistant," I say, letting his ear go. "She's not for you to schmooze."

"Schmooze...? What are you, five?" He laughs. "And I'm not schmoozing, I'm working it."

I shake my head. "I hope she plays hard to get."

"She already is," he growls.

"Good. But she doesn't need to be another notch in your bedpost, Dex."

He leans into me, and whispers, "I want her to be the last notch in my bedpost."

"Prove it!" I tell him in a whisper.

"I'm trying," he growls again. "Now stop blocking me."

I burst out laughing. "It's your funeral."

"Thanks so much." Then he throws his arms around me. "I'm so glad you're back. Fucking missed ya, little mama." I roll my eyes.

"Thanks for bringing him back." For the first time ever, I hug him back.

"Anytime. Now let me go, I got schmoozing to do," he says with a laugh and I punch his shoulder.

I turn around and Mouse and Peacock are standing there like little boys waiting for candy on Halloween. I throw my arms wide. "Come here, boys," I say with a laugh and they both come at me, hugging me and kissing my cheeks repeatedly. "Alright," I say.

"Missed you, Red. Happy you're back," Mouse says with a big smile then he punches Eric in the shoulder.

"Don't scare us again," Peacock says.

"You told Mouse?" I whisper. He nods. I wrap my arms around his neck and hug him. "I'm so proud of you."

"Told Mouse what?" Talon asks.

I pull back from Peacock and I nod, taking his hand in mine. "That I'm gay," he says confidently.

"About fucking time you admitted it, brotha," Dex says from behind me. I raise an eyebrow at Peacock, in a 'see I told you' kind of way.

Talon wraps his arm around Peacock's shoulder with a smile on his face. He taps Peacock's chest with an open hand. "I know, Eric, but you know what?" Eric shakes his head. "I'm glad you finally told me."

"It doesn't bother you?" Eric asks.

Talon lets him go and grabs Kyle, pulling him close and kissing him. Kyle is frozen for a moment, but then I can see him melt much the same way I do when Talon is kissing me. When Talon pulls back, he looks at Eric. "I have no room in my heart to judge you. You're my brother, you're my friend." He holds his hand out and he and Eric grab each other's arms near the elbow, holding on.

I feel like crying, I do cry. "Oh crap," I say out loud. Covering my mouth. Looking for the bathroom something anything. Trash can. I go over to it and wretch.

"Ah hell," I hear Dex tease. Kyle is at my side in an instant, holding my hair and rubbing my back.

"Oh god, I missed this," I sob between heaves.

"Puking?" Kyle says with a chuckle.

"No, you holding me."

I heave a few more times and someone brings up a chair behind me. "Sit, baby girl. I got you."

I put my head in my hands, waiting for the dizziness to pass.

"Just because you've finally come out, doesn't mean it changes anything," I hear Dex tell Eric. "I will still tease you, I will still rib you and I will do my best to keep it strictly to girl ribbing."

"You're a dick, dude," Eric says back and both he and Dex laugh.

"No, you need a dick," Dex says back and I balk, looking over at both of them.

"I think it might be you who needs one."

Dex grabs his crotch. "Got one right here." Both Dex and Eric are laughing and my heart warms.

I see Raine off to the side and she's staring at Dex. She's just as smitten with him too. But I hope she knows what she's getting herself into.

"How you doin', angel?" I smile up at Talon.

"Better. I think I'm making up for not puking this morning and the nausea medicine is wearing off. Downside is, there went my lunch," I pout.

"Kyle, take her back to the bus, get her some food?" Talon asks. "We can handle sound."

"Come on, baby girl." He stands and holds his hand out for me to take, I do and stand up slowly. Talon wraps his arms around me, but he doesn't kiss me. I know why, because I always deny both of them until I've brushed my teeth.

Kyle escorts me back to the bus and I use the facilities, brush my teeth and then take a seat. I can see my purse and messenger back have been brought in. I pull out the journal, log my food, my puking and then close it up. "We need to take a picture," Kyle says. I smile and nod and we go back to the bedroom while the water for more mac n' cheese boils on the stove.

After we're done taking pictures of the pouch, we come back up front and Kyle plays on his phone while he makes me some food. After a couple of minutes he shows me what he did. "Look, baby girl."

I take his phone and look at the picture. He put them side by side and you can definitely see the change, though still subtle, it's there. Along the bottom of the left picture it says, "5 weeks" on the right it says, "6 weeks 1 day"

"That is so cool. It's hard for me to see the changes. I feel them, like with my pants and shirts, but seeing them is hard because I see me every day."

"There was a big change in three days, or I just really missed seeing it."

"Don't do that to me again, please? Pregnant or not, it will destroy me."

He smiles, "I don't plan on it."

"Good."

He serves me my mac 'n cheese and I devour the entire box, plus an entire sleeve of saltines and a bottle of apple juice. Shortly after I finish up, Talon comes onto the bus.

"I have a bone to pick with you, mister," I tell him, wagging my finger at him.

"Oh my god, what did I do?"

My eyes get real wide. "You. Told, My, Mom."

"Oh shit, Talon, why?"

"Because I panicked when you got sick and they took you to the hospital. I wanted to let her know and it just… it slipped out." He looks positively scared that I'm really pissed off. "She wasn't supposed to tell you."

I burst out laughing and he melts a little bit. "You can't tell my mother something like that then not expect her to ask me about them. I called her on the way over and she asked me about the babies and I nearly blew a gasket. When she explained that you'd called her and that you were scared and I can understand why you hesitated to tell her. I appreciate that. Now we have even bigger demands to go to Kansas City when the tour is over." I smile.

"Did she say anything else?" he asks through his eyelashes.

"Nooooo, why?"

"Oh, no reason."

"Talon Carver, what the hell are you planning?"

"Nothing, baby, honest. I promise."

I smirk. "I don't believe you, but I'll let it go, for now." He perks up. I notice Kyle is a little too quiet in the kitchen. "Kyle Black, you'll tell me. Won't you? I know you know, I can see it." He blushes and shakes his head. "I know how to get it out of you."

"Oh no, you don't, you little minx." Talon wraps his arms around me as I stalk toward Kyle. "We promise you'll find out soon enough."

"Talon?" Mills calls from the door of the bus. "The producers are here."

"Shit, I forgot they were recording and filming this week," I say. "Oh good, that saves my arguments."

Talon turns to me. "Arguments about what?"

"Performing tonight."

"Oh no, you're not."

"Ha! You don't have much of a choice." I stick my tongue out at him and he charges toward me. I squeal and go running toward the bedroom. He catches me, pinning me to the bed on my back, hands over my head. His legs are in between mine.

"I do have a choice, and the answer is no."

I flick my hips and his eyes roll up. "You don't have a choice. You can't have a live video without your star." I smirk.

"Yes, we can, there will be plenty of time to film..." I flick my hips again, rubbing my sex against his denim covered cock.

"No arguments, big man. Doc said it was okay. I feel fucking fantastic for the first time in two weeks. All the weight of my pregnancy is gone because I no longer feel like every little thing I do is going to push one of the two of you over the edge. I didn't realize how much that was weighing me down until this morning when I woke up. I actually have some energy, and I want to be on stage singing our songs with you tonight."

He crushes his lips to mine and I moan. "I fucking love you," he says against my lips. I smile. He's such an animal when he says it like that and I know he means it with every fiber of his being.

"I fucking love you too."

"I have to go deal with the producers."

"I know, sorry I got you worked up."

"Angel, around you, I'm always worked up." He kisses me on the lips one more time. Then he kisses down my chest. "By the way, you look like you've grown two cup sizes, what the hell?"

I laugh, "I'm actually wearing a bra."

He perks up. "It doesn't hurt?"

"Oh no, it hurts, but my nipples always seem to be hard, so even against my tank tops they would rub. I thought I'd try this."

"Is it better, baby girl?" Kyle asks and I look over at him in the doorway.

"It is, in that they don't rub, but even covered they're still hard."

"Let me see," Talon says as he tugs on my shirt.

"You, mister, have work to do. You can see them later. Now get."

He pouts, I kiss it away and he lets my hands go as he gets off of me. "I'll be back in a bit." He turns to Kyle. "Don't wear her out too much." He winks and leaves the bedroom.

chapter 42

"Can I see?" Kyle asks sweetly.

I smirk at him. "Why?"

"Because I want to see you."

I laugh, "No, you want to see my nipples."

He smirks and blushes. It's freakin' adorable. I lift up my shirt, reach under my bra, lifting it so my breasts spill out. His mouth drops open and he lets out a rush of air. "They're darker?"

"I have a feeling they're going to get much darker." I smile.

He comes over to the bed, between my legs hanging over the side. I spread them for him. He reaches out for my hands and I give them to him and he pulls me up, then reaches around to undo my bra. He tugs on my shirt and pulls it all over my head. "That's better," he sighs as he slides to his knees. His mouth is right there. I feel my nipples tingle as they harden further. My nipples are still puffy, but with a definite definition at the tips. The color has darkened from the pink they were to a more dusty pink color. He brushes his nose against one and I shiver, leaning forward he takes my silent invitation and licks his tongue across it.

"Ahh," I moan and my panties dampen. "Again," I breathe and he switches sides. Running a wet fat tongue along it. "Don't stop." I moan and he pulls it into his mouth, gently licking and sucking it. Every pull is felt in my clit as it throbs.

His other hand comes up and he gently runs his palm along the now fully hard point. When my nipples are hard, they grow large and long, so the movement caused by his palm adds to the pleasure and pain combination. I moan again and he releases my nipple from his mouth.

"I need you so bad," he groans, "but I'm going to be honest, I don't think it's fair for me to do this without him."

My mind clears of the lustful fog and I look at him. "Is this a permanent choice, you and I don't do anything without him?"

"Oh god, no. I think being sexual one on one is very important for all of us. But yes, I left. Yes, I want makeup sex with you so bad I'm getting blue balls, but I left him too, and I think it's best if we all makeup together."

I put his head in my hands and I lean down, kissing him hard. Silent tears streak down my cheeks. "I think that sounds like an amazing idea."

"Then why are you crying?"

I chuckle. "Because I cry at just about everything now. But really it's because you're putting mine and Talon's needs above your own." I kiss his nose. "Now if you'll excuse me, I need a clean pair of panties." I smirk.

"I'm sorry, I shouldn't…"

I tap his nose. "Don't, it's alright and all the more sweeter because you talked through it, you asked, spoke your mind and your concern. Besides they're pretty great nipples if I do say so myself. If it didn't hurt so much for me to touch them, I don't think I could leave them alone."

"Why does it hurt when you do it versus when we do it?" he asks and it's a perfectly logical question.

"Because, when you and Talon do it, the pleasure is so much more than the pain and the pain brings the pleasure higher. When I do it, it doesn't feel the same. It's like what would you prefer more; your own hand job or mine?"

"Definitely yours."

"It's the same for my nipples and even masturbating. When you two play with it, it's deep and it's intense. When I touch it, it becomes a game of hurry up and rub it out."

"Okay, that's just too weird," he says, standing up.

"Why? Because it's the same for you?"

"Yes, except when I'm doing it for you it's so you can enjoy the show."

"Mmm," I bite my lip. Then lick it.

"Exactly." He smirks again. "Come on, panda, let's clean you up."

Thank goodness for not taking everything into the hotel. Worst case scenario, I have enough here to change if I don't make it back to the hotel. After I'm cleaned up, Kyle and I head into the theater and track down Talon. "You're supposed to be taking it easy," he tells me.

"I'm perfectly fine and fed." I hold up my bottle of water, "Hydrated too."

He comes over and kisses me. "I didn't expect to see you guys so soon," he says with a smirk.

"Kyle said it would be better for the three of us to makeup together."

He looks over at Kyle. "I left you too, not just her."

Talon smiles. "Okay then. You better get back to the hotel to get ready," he tells me then kisses my forehead. "You don't need to do make-up, they have a team coming, they will be here at six thirty for make-up, apparently we're all gonna need it." He rolls his eyes. "I think I'm handsome enough without it." He snorts.

"You are, but the camera will love you more for it," I tell him and he shrugs.

"Go on, take him with you. We're good here. I'll be about another hour then I'll be there. We'll have dinner before we come over."

"All of us?" I ask, skeptical.

"Well, I figure if you have to eat, so do Kyle and I. It only seems fair."

I smile, kiss him and Kyle and I leave for the hotel.

chapter 43

"Kyle!" I shout from the bedroom.

He comes running in. "What, what's wrong?"

I laugh, "Sorry, nothing's wrong. Well, not with me anyway.... Crap, um, can I wear this?" I turn.

"You look amazing," he says. I'm wearing the green plaid skirt they bought for me back in Minnesota, but the problem is the skirt is high-waisted and my shirt is tucked in.

"No, look, I mean really look, down there."

"Oh," he says and I turn again. "Oh um...shit, Addie, already?"

"I know. I thought I could cover it up, but...damn it, I guess not."

"Hey guys!" Talon says as he comes into the room. "Wow, angel that outfit looks amazing on you."

I feel like crying. "Watch," Kyle says and he nods to me, and I turn sideways.

"Oh! Oh!" His eyes go wide. "Shit, Addie."

"Yeah, that about sums it up," I say softly. "Is it really noticeable?"

"It's hard to tell," Kyle says, "he and I are so attuned to your body we know it's there so we see it, all the time. Hang on, I have an idea." I watch as Kyle goes to the bedside table and grabs his phone and pushes a button before putting it to his ear. "Hey Raine, can you come up to the suite? Addie needs your help." There's a pause, "perfect, have them let you in." Another pause, "okay, thanks." He sets the phone down. "She's on her way up. She doesn't know you like we do. Let her be the judge."

"What about your red plaid skirt or your pants, if you're set on plaid tonight. At least the skirt is a low rider and you can wear a different shirt," Talon says, his voice is soft and sweet.

"Addie, why are you crying, baby girl?"

"I got so set on this outfit, I hadn't worn it yet, and then to have to change because I'm showing in it, it's just, it's all happening so fast," I sob out.

Both of them come over to me, Kyle behind me, Talon in front. "Look at me, angel," he says softly and I look up to him. "It's only temporary. Once it's safe to tell the world, it won't matter anymore what you wear. I'm okay with shouting it from the rooftops, but I know you're not and that's okay. I think you're beautiful, Kyle thinks you're beautiful, pouch and all, sweet girl. Remember what you told us?" I shake my head. "It's all worth it."

Those four little words is all it takes to sober me up. He's right, it's all worth it. As I dry my tears, Raine lets herself into the suite.

"Hey..Oh jeez, sorry..." Raine moves to leave.

"No, you're alright." Talon looks at her. "She's having an issue, can you help?"

"Uh, sure," she says.

"She wants to wear this outfit and we're bad judges."

"Uh, okay," she says skeptical. They step back from me and I turn in a circle. "It looks great."

"You can't see anything?" I ask and turn again.

"No, it looks great. I don't know what I'm supposed to be looking for." I turn again, "Oh!" she squeaks.

"Okay, I'm changing," I say resigned.

"No, Addison, really I only noticed because Talon pointed it out."

"No, it's alright Raine, guys, I promise. It's been noticed and that's all I need because I will get self-conscious about it while on stage and that's only going to make it worse. It's alright. I promise," I say with a small smile. "Now go, so I can change." I shoo them all out of the room.

Taking Talon's advice, I go for the red plaid pants with buckles on them and change into one of my black cowl neck shirts that has a band at the bottom and it balloons out a little bit down there. I have a red cami under it and I'm wearing a bra to boot. I pull on my platform boots and I'm good to go. When I leave the bedroom and enter the sitting room the guys are talking to Raine.

I spin around. "Does it look like I'm trying to hide something?" I ask honestly.

"No, you wear shirts like that all the time," Raine says. "Not that I pay attention or anything..." She blushes.

I laugh, "Isn't that part of your job now?"

"I suppose. But it wasn't when I was paying attention though." She blushes again. "But seriously, you look great." She nods, and smiles from ear to ear.

"Addie, you look better in that than you did in that skirt. I love you in skirts but this is just more you," Talon says.

I laugh a little. "Sort of..." I lift the front of the shirt, exposing the fact that my pants are unbuttoned at the top and dip downward.

"It's time to go shopping, angel," he says with a wide smile. "That can't be that comfortable."

"It's not so bad, but in another week, it might be." I smile. All pregnancy angst from earlier is gone from my system. Talon is right, it's all worth it.

"We'll go Sunday," Raine says.

I cock my head at her. "That's what we were talking about, baby girl. Raine has offered to go with you. If you want," Kyle interjects.

I don't know how I feel about that. Not that I have a problem with Raine. "We have a pretty busy few days and Sunday is the only down time we have. Can we wait and see how I'm feeling?"

"Absolutely," Raine says, "but the offer is there. I can help you if you're unsure about something. Besides, I was going anyway. I mean, we're in New York." She laughs, "so if you want to come along."

"I appreciate it. Thank you for wanting to bring me with you."

She smiles, "absolutely. Okay, I'm going to go, your dinner's here and I need to get changed."

"Thanks for your help," I tell her.

She lights up. "Of course."

She leaves the suite. "Why wouldn't you want to go?" Talon asks.

"I don't know. It seems pointless."

"But if you need new clothes…"

"No, I know I do, but if I go up a size, to accommodate them, they won't look right on me, they'll look baggy and I'm not ready to buy maternity clothes just yet. In fact the idea of that terrifies me."

"Aww baby girl, no one said you need to buy maternity clothes, and shopping is entirely up to you, but you seemed really comfortable in the pants you had on earlier, maybe get a few more of those. Just avoid jeans." Kyle comes over and wraps his arms around me.

"It's just hard."

"I know, sweetheart," Talon says as he comes over, that's when I remember what's in my purse.

"Hey, where did my purse end up?" I ask out of the blue.

"Over there." Kyle points to a table along the bedroom wall.

"I forgot about something." I go over and dig them out. I turn back to them, I'd put them together with the first ultrasound. "Okay, sit down."

"You need to eat, angel."

"Shh, I know, I will, just let me show you this first. Then we can eat."

"Okay." They both sit on the couch, far enough apart that I can sit between them. I take my spot.

"This is why I'm changing so fast." I tell them, "This is the first ultrasound, last week." I show them the original Baby A and Baby B pictures. "This is what they looked like this morning."

I show them new Baby A and Baby B picture. "Oh my god," Talon says.

"Look at that," Kyle leans in and continues, "We can actually see them, they're not just blips." By the time Kyle is done, his voice fills with emotion. The images that they're seeing are still just kinda a cluster of dots, but there is a little bit of shape to them.

"See, so they grow, I grow." I look to Talon and then to Kyle. Both of their eyes are wet with tears. "Oh, jeez. I…"

"Shhh." Talon leans forward, putting his fingers to my lips. "We're just happy, angel. It's okay."

"It finally feels real," Kyle says and I look at him. "To see them, actually see them, not just a little dot, it's, wow."

"Just wait, it will only get clearer," I tell them both, fighting my own tears.

"Thank you for showing that to us," Talon says. "They wouldn't let me in yesterday and we weren't there today, but we will be there every time." Talon leans in and kisses me.

"Without fail," Kyle adds.

"Good, because we go back next week, before we leave town."

"Oh?" Kyle says, his eyes clearing.

"The doctor just wants to check again. At this stage, heartbeat detection is very hard, so it's hard to determine just how well they're doing. So he wants me back next week. Raine was scheduling the appointment during a time we were all available before we go to DC."

They both smile. "I can't wait," Kyle says, kissing me. "Come on, baby girl, food!" he says with wide eyes. "Let's feed you."

chapter 44

Two grilled cheese sandwiches, a full serving of french fries and a big bowl of very good chicken noodle soup later, I'm finally stuffed.

Talon tried so hard to eat for me, but he just couldn't do it. He did eat a little bit. I asked him why it was so hard for him and he said that he always freaks out before a show. "Ironic thing about that…until I kiss you before taking the stage."

"What do you mean?"

"I used to freak out, it would take me two or three songs to fully get into it before I'd lose the nerves. Now, when I kiss you and take the stage, I'm totally into it."

"So kiss me, then eat."

He laughed, "I wish it worked. I think a lot of it has to do with you being there. Remember Vegas and your migraine?" I nod. "I was good until I realized you guys had left. I deflated a lot that night. I got it back, but it took a couple songs. Then when you started singing with me, it

269

energized me that much more and now the nerves still fade when I kiss you."

"I had no idea," I tell him.

"Well, now you know." He smiles, "and now we have to go."

Our tradition stands. Dex gives me a super sloppy, back at you for cock blocking me kiss that actually makes me gag, causing Raine to laugh uncontrollably. Mouse and Peacock give me my usual hug and dual cheek kisses.

When Kyle wraps his arms around me, I can feel his thumb rubbing along my pouch, just above my unbuttoned pants. Sending shivers through me. When Talon comes at me, I throw my arms around his neck and I kiss him with gusto. Tongues stroking, and full of as much love and passion as can be conveyed in a kiss.

I can feel his breathing hitch before mine. I stop the smile that spreads across my lips, ruining our kiss. He groans. "Go kick some ass, tiger!" I tell him and he backs up and onto the stage.

"Hello New York!" he yells into the microphone and the crowd goes insane.

I turn around in Kyle's arms. "I want you to do that every show," I tell him.

"Do what?"

"Remind me of our babies."

I take his head in my hands and kiss him with as much passion and love as I gave Talon a few moments ago. "Not fair," he growls as he takes my lips again. I smile and laugh, breaking our kiss.

"It is fair, that's what I gave to Talon, you deserved it too."

He chuckles. "How you feeling, baby girl?"

"Getting tired. This is the first day in like two weeks that I've been awake for an entire day. It's tiring."

He laughs. "That's what happens when you're growing panda cubs."

His words make me smile. It's what I said last night in the hospital. We start to dance to Talon and the band as they play through their set. Then the song before 'Your Eyes' comes on and the crowd starts getting riled up. They know what's coming. Sound guy shows up attaching my microphone.

"You ready, mama?"

I blush. "As ready as I'll ever be."

"Break a leg, baby girl."

"Ladies and Gentlemen," Talon says into the microphone and the band cues up their softer version of 'Your Eyes'. "It is an honor and a privilege to introduce you to the beautiful, amazingly talented, love of my life, Addison Beltrand!"

Deep breath, and go!

Walking out on stage is an adrenaline rush that's better than getting a tattoo. I wave to the crowd, play it up a little bit. When I come to stand next to Talon he wraps his arm around my back and the band kicks up.

'To Be Free' goes amazingly well too. And this time I actually saw a tear escape Talon's eye as we sang. I almost lost it too. That is until I looked at Kyle and I was grounded again.

The greenroom was awesome tonight. There were a few celebrities that came by too. I guess that's what you get being in New York, it's not that hard.

Kyle notices how badly I'm fading. "Come on, baby, let's get you back to the hotel."

"What about Talon?"

"He'll be along."

"Let me tell him," I say with a smile.

I go over to Talon. "Hey angel, whoa, you okay?"

I smile, "I'm fading so fast. Kyle's gonna take me back."

"Aww, okay angel."

I hug him. "Go out with the guys."

"Are you sure?"

"Absolutely, I won't make it back to the room. I am so tired and I'm sorry."

"For what?"

"You'll have to wait another night."

"Oh heavens no, sweetheart, go, get some sleep," He encourages so sure and sweetly, I don't argue with him. "I'll see you in the morning." He brings his lips to mine and I kiss him back with love and devotion. "Love you, angel."

"Love you, big man."

Kyle escorts me to the SUV and we're off. Before we even make the security gate, I'm asleep.

I wake up when Kyle lifts me from the car. "I can walk."

"Nonsense, I got you."

I put my head against his chest and sleep until he lays me down. "I have to get you undressed, sweetie."

He pulls my shirt over my head. "Clothes or no?"

"No," I tell him. He takes off my bra and I feel his hand gently brush along my nipple. "I'm so sorry," I say softly.

"For what?"

"Not being awake enough."

"Oh baby girl, don't be."

"I told Talon to go out with the guys. Go join them."

"No, I want to hold you tonight. I need to be near you."

He sets out to untie my boots. Once they're gone, I lay down and he unzips my pants. "Panties?"

"Off." I lift my hips and he pulls down both my pants and panties. My stomach rolls. "Oh god." I shift my legs off of the bed, nearly kicking Kyle and take off for the toilet.

"Oh no, baby girl…" Kyle comes in right behind me.

chapter 45

He stays with me the whole time. "I'm sorry. I was shaking you too much."

"Cowboy..." I say between heaves, "not your fault."

I know it takes a lot for him to say what he says next. "Okay, baby girl."

I smile, flush and sit down on the lid waiting for the nausea to pass. He kneels in front of me. "Better?"

"Yeah, I think so." He stands up and readies my toothbrush for me. I smile when he hands it to me and I promptly brush my teeth and he helps me stand up to spit out the paste.

"Back to bed?"

"Yes, please." He helps me back to bed and I lay down toward his side. He strips down, but hesitates to pull off his boxers. He always sleeps naked. "I know you're hard and I wish I had the energy to fix it."

"No, it's alright, I just, you're naked and it's hard..." he snorts a laugh, "okay, I didn't mean it that way. But to lay, naked in bed with you isn't easy."

"I have an idea." I roll over, facing Talon's side of the bed. "Take them off."

"Addie, I?"

"Please, let me do this." He climbs into bed behind me. "Spoon with me." He rolls toward me and I lift up my leg, reaching behind me, I grip his erection firmly in my hand and stroke it a couple of times.

"God Addie, that feels so good."

I shift to better line up with him. "Take me, cowboy. I'm wet and ready for you."

"Baby girl, I'm not going to use you to get off."

"You're not using me. I want this too. I just don't have the energy." He doesn't do anything. "Please," I beg.

"I can't say no to you," he growls, taking his erection from me. I lift up my leg. He stops, unable to get the angle right. "Put your leg down."

"No..."

"No, I have an idea." I put down my leg and he bends my knee, pushing it forward so that I roll a little onto my stomach. "Are you okay like this?"

"Yes."

Then he straddles my other leg and I feel him pressing into my sex. He slides in and out slowly. Then when he's all the way inside, he freezes, allowing me to adjust. He puts a hand on my leg, pushing it up just a little more before he leans down. "I'm not hurting you, am I?"

"No, it feels good."

He pulls out and my nipples harden into painful peaks. He's leaning over me as he slides in again. I twist, exposing my breast to him. He hisses through his teeth as his pace increases. He leans down and sucks my nipple into his mouth. "Argh!" I groan. "Faster," I urge.

His strokes are long and I can feel as he uses his hips to push deeper into me. "Oh god, Kyle," I moan. He releases my nipple as he starts to pant above me.

"You feel so good," he says as he continues his long steady pace.

An orgasm is building deep in my core. "Ahh! Fuck! Faster Kyle, please, I'm gonna...ah!"

"Let it go, baby, I'm ready. I need to feel you." My pussy clenches around his cock and he pushes into me harder and faster. "Give it to me, baby girl, let me feel you."

My body locks down and my orgasm races outward. I cry out as my orgasm shatters me. I feel Kyle twitch and then he's exploding inside of me. "Addison," he cries out as his orgasm takes him completely.

He slows his strokes in and out of me and I look at him. There is a look that I've never seen before. It's sad and desperate almost. His eyes are full of unshed tears. "Whoa, what's wrong?" I ask him.

"I just love you so damn much and I can't believe I wasted three days when I could have been with you, been inside you, been loving you. I don't think you understand how awful I feel about what happened."

I reach up and he brings his cheek to my hand, leaning into it. "Don't, please. It was awful, and I never want to feel like that again, but we learned a lot about ourselves in those three days. We've grown stronger because of it. I don't take it back, I won't, and I will not let you beat yourself up over it. We're better because of it."

He kisses my palm. "I love you so much it hurts."

"I know, because it hurts how much I love you."

He pulls himself out and the sensation sends a thrill through me. I don't want to lose the connection. He leans down and kisses me. "Let me clean you up."

I nod and he gets off the bed.

I'm fighting my eyelids when he returns with a warm washcloth and towel. "Open for me, baby girl." I roll onto my back and he cleans me up then dries me. He tosses the towels on the floor then adjusts so that he is sitting on his feet and he leans forward over me. Gently placing his hands on my tummy. "Good night, little ones. Sweet dreams," he says softly against my stomach, then he kisses one side, then the other. "Love you," he whispers. Then he crawls up my body and kisses me softly. I take his head into my hands and kiss him back. He pulls back. "Good night, baby girl." He gives me a kiss, "sweet dreams." He kisses me again.

"I love you. Good night, cowboy."

He lies down next to me, putting his arm out for me to lie against him. I roll over, snuggling into the crook of his shoulder; I slide my hand across his stomach. The arm I'm lying on bends and he is touching the small of my back. I'm holding him to me and he's holding me to him.

Before long, I'm sound asleep.

chapter 46
kyle

"Hey T."

"Oh hey, I didn't wake you, did I?"

"Nah," I say quietly. Talon comes over to my side of the bed; he leans over and kisses me. He rubs the scruff on my cheek.

"How is she?"

"Good. She was asleep before we even got out of the lot."

"I'm so proud of her."

I smile. "Me too, she stayed up all day even after the hospital this morning."

"I was expecting her to leave during the show."

"I asked her after you guys were done if she wanted to go, she said no and that she was okay. I carried her up here. Then woke up after I got her undressed, she threw up."

Talon sits down gently on the bed next to me. "Oh man."

"It didn't last anywhere near as long as it usually does and it was mostly liquid, but she had soup for dinner." He gives me a half smile. "After she brushed her teeth and came back to bed, she refused to let me crawl into bed in my boxers. I was trying to be chivalrous because I was hard." He snorts a laugh. "I felt so bad, then she begged me. I told her I felt like I was using her, she begged some more and you know I can't say no to her."

He smiles. "Neither can I. Don't stress it. She knows what she's doing."

I smile, trying not to laugh, I don't want to wake her. "She does. Did you have a good time tonight?"

"Not really. It was nice to hang out with the guys. Raine came along with us. Dex, man you should have seen him, I think he's whipped, dude. I think he's found the chick to straighten his shit out."

"No way!"

"I think so. Eric seems much happier since this afternoon. I had a feeling it was true, but you know, I needed confirmation from him."

I smile and nod. "Last Tuesday, when you guys were getting ready to jam," he nods, "he was in the bathroom when you confessed to me."

He covers his mouth in shock, "Why didn't you tell me?"

I shrug. "I figured what you did was hard enough, I didn't need to tell you that we weren't necessarily alone. I told him that I knew, because I did. I've seen him sneak off with a guy or two over the years."

He pushes on my thigh. "Why didn't you tell me?" he asks again.

I laugh silently and Addison shifts a little, snuggling in. "Help me lay her on the bed," I tell him and he picks up her arm slowly, then puts his hand under her neck, I move enough that he can put her head on the pillow. She adjusts and snuggles in without waking up. I slide out of bed slowly. "Let's go out here."

He nods and I grab my boxers off of the floor and slide them on and follow him out of the room.

"I didn't tell you because I knew Eric needed to do it. For the same reason you needed to do what you did today by kissing me in front of everyone. I knew that when he was ready he would, but I think we have Addison to thank for that too," I tell him as we sit on the couch.

"Why?"

I smirk, "She told him to tell you then took his hand while he did. They talked last week, the night we went out, that's the reason he left the bar early. He was hoping to talk to her. I told him to. I knew she'd give him the courage he needed. I mean, Dex? Come on, that's not an easy nut to crack."

He snorts, "He knew too. He also helped him look for dudes tonight. I think he needed to do something to keep his dick clean. It was funny to watch."

"She told me to join you guys tonight."

"Oh? Why didn't you?"

"I needed to hold her. I couldn't last night because of the hospital. I just needed to feel her in my arms."

"Dude, you left."

"I wasn't in the right headspace when I walked out the door. As soon as that elevator closed, I knew I'd fucked up."

"Then why didn't you come back right away."

"I couldn't spend the next twenty-four hours looking at her, knowing I was hurting her by not talking to her. I wasn't ready to talk, I didn't yet know how to talk to her and by the time my twenty-four hours were up, I was so drunk that I didn't know what day it was."

He nods, "I've been there, I can understand that. We all have our demons, Kyle. I just hope you were able to tackle them."

"I did. You, her, our babies, are the most important things to me. Losing this family will kill me whether it is long and slow with drugs and alcohol or..." I let the thought drop off.

"That's not going to happen. I won't let it. If I hadn't been tied up in the studio, I would have been out looking for you. We added a drum track to 'To Be Free', so it took longer, which is why I wasn't around. The only reason we're not being fined for yesterday is because she was carried out on a stretcher. She and I have to be in the studio Saturday morning to lay the vocals. Not that I wouldn't have paid the fine to come and find you, but Monday, after you left, somehow she pulled herself together long enough to lay 'Your Eyes', then came back here. So I knew that if I got it done and got her back to the studio, she'd be better, at least for a while. You know the rest."

"She's amazing. I can't believe she could do that."

"Believe it, I have no clue how she did it. I was already panicking about tonight. I didn't know how she was going to be able to perform, how I was going to be able to do it without you there. You've been there from day one. As my boyfriend or not, you've always been there, I don't know how I could have done it without you there."

"I don't know what to say to all that." I put my hand to his cheek, he leans into it.

He shrugs in typical Talon style. "Nothing to say, it's just the truth." He looks to the bedroom door. "Everything's set for tomorrow," he whispers.

"I can't believe Cami was willing to help you out."

He wears a smug look and chuckles, "She's quite the sucker for a good love story. She could fire Addison for being with us, we're Bold's clients, but instead she supports it and she supports Addison. Raine said that she about flipped her shit when Addie told her she was having twins. Cami was so excited for her. Cami's taking her to lunch tomorrow. She's gonna come by the studio and pick her up, take her to lunch and give us a chance to set up. She'll get her make-up and hair done when she gets back. So we should be ready to go by two or so. Did you get it?"

I smile wide. "I did. It's gorgeous. I gave it to Tori to hold on to."

"Oh sweet, okay."

"Are we doing the right thing?"

"Are you doubting yourself?" he asks as he raises an eyebrow.

"No, I'm worried she'll freak out on us."

"After what she's been through, I think she needs it. She needs the reassurance," he tells me.

I lean forward and kiss him. "So do you."

"I do, and you do too. We all do." I kiss him again and he melts under my touch. I don't stop. I adjust so that I'm above him.

"Is it wrong that I don't want to stop?" I ask against his lips.

"No. Don't stop," he whispers and I kiss him again. He runs his hands along my chest. I shiver. I slide my tongue along his bottom lip, coaxing him to open for me and he does. I slip my tongue into his mouth. He moans and I grow harder, as if that was even possible.

He grabs the waistband of my shorts and pushes them down, freeing my cock. Then he grips it in his hand and I thrust into his hold. My mouth comes off of his. "Fuck," I growl.

"I want in you," he says and I shiver as he continues stroking my cock.

"Take me." He kisses me, pushing me back onto the couch. He pulls off his shirt and quickly unbuttons his jeans before taking my cock into his mouth. "Fuck, Talon!" I thrust into his mouth as he licks and sucks me.

I watch him push his jeans down and his cock bounces as he pushes his pants off. My mouth waters. He sucks really hard on my cock and I cry out as pleasure seers through me. He lets my cock go. "Turn over." He moves so that I can flip over. I put my elbows on the back of the couch, arching my back, giving him access.

The next thing I know, his hands are gripping my ass and his tongue is rimming me. One of his hands comes away and then he grips my cock. "Fuck! Fuck!" I growl. Then out of nowhere his finger dips into my ass. "Shit...I'm gonna come. Talon, oh god!"

He doesn't stop and I'm going to explode all over the couch. I begin thrusting into his hand as he works my cock and I freeze up and he lets go. "No, no!" I grumble as my orgasm dies in a moment. My balls fucking ache. All contact with my body is gone until he is standing in front of me stroking his cock. I dutifully open my mouth and he slides in. Gently fucking my mouth.

"Get me wet. I want in your ass," he demands and I begin sucking and licking his cock, I spit on it a couple of times and use my hand to rub it around as my mouth continues sucking. "Fuck!" His reactions only turn me on more. He lets me suck on him a little more before he pulls out. I watch until he walks out of my line of sight, then I feel him wet my entrance. He works it quickly so that he can slide in.

"Talon, god, fuck me," I groan and he presses his cock against my entrance.

He pushes into me. It burns until the head of his cock passes the tight ring and then the pain turns to pleasure and I'm moaning. He starts to slide in and out of me. I'm so close to exploding already that this won't last long. He groans when I take him all the way to the hilt, he pauses and I grind against him. Telling him to move and take me. He takes the hint and begins fucking me. Hard and slow at first then gradually the pace increases.

I know when he's close because he leans forward and grabs my cock, stroking it while he fucks me. "Oh fuck!" I cry out and he moves faster.

"Give it to me Kyle. Give me your orgasm."

"Fuck!" I moan then the pleasure heightens to the point of exploding.

"Now!" he growls and I explode as he releases his own inside of me.

chapter 47
addison

When I wake up Friday morning, I'm surrounded by both the men I love. But I don't get to enjoy it for long; my bladder has other ideas. I slip out of bed slow and steady. For the moment, I'm not running to the bathroom. I grab a peak at the clock on the table, it's nearly seven. Ugh, it's early. But strangely I feel wide awake.

Once done with my bathroom business, still no vomiting, I go back to bed, crawling in between Kyle and Talon. As soon as I lay down they both gravitate toward me while still sleeping and I take so much comfort in what they do even in their sleep.

An arm from each of them slides across my stomach and their hands both wrap around my ribs and they pull themselves toward me. It's so damn cute it makes me chuckle softly.

"What's so funny, baby girl?" Kyle whispers.

"Look at you two," I whisper back. There is light from the living area coming in through the semi open door and light is surrounding the curtains on the windows and Kyle looks down my body. "I got up, went to the bathroom, came back and you both wrapped around me at the same time."

"We can't help it. You're such a magnet we gravitate toward you," Kyle says softly. "How'd you sleep?"

"Great. I just woke up a few minutes ago."

"I'm sorry, I didn't hear you."

"Shh, I haven't thrown up. Yet." He kisses me on the cheek.

Talon stirs next to us. I reach over and run my hands through his shaggy hair. I watch as he nuzzles into my hand. "Good morning, angel." His voice is very sexy, groggy with sleep.

"Good morning."

"Did you sleep well?" he asks.

"I slept great. You?"

"Mmm." He snuggles into me, inadvertently pushing his hips into mine, brushing the back of Kyle's hand in the process. He's hard as a rock. Kyle kisses me on the cheek, then nuzzles into my neck. I turn toward Talon, giving him access. I can't say no, I won't say no. I need them both so bad. He takes my ear lobe into his mouth and I start to pant. I feel Kyle's hand move to what I can only assume is Talon's cock because he moans.

Their mutual hold on me doesn't give me much room to move around. That's when Talon runs a fat tongue over the nipple that's ridiculously close to his mouth. "Ahh," I moan. Kyle releases my lobe and begins licking and kissing his way down my neck. My legs scissor on each other as my clit begins pulsing with desperate need to be touched.

Talon catches on to my ailment and his hand moves down along my stomach. I shiver when his hand glides feather light over my pouch. Kyle continues down to my shoulder then down my chest, seeking out my nipple and I can see him looking at Talon, whose tongue is still licking at me. Kyle begins doing the same thing the moment Talon's finger presses against my clit. Kyle is still stroking Talon's cock.

My back arches as they take my nipples into their mouths. Pain and pleasure shoot through my body. "Don't stop," I moan out and they continue licking and sucking my super sensitive nipples.

Talon's fingers begin moving in achingly slow circles around my clit. It's the worst possible tease and my breath is coming in short bursts. Kyle pulls off of my nipple. "Who do you want, baby girl?"

Talon's finger flicks across my clit. "Talon," I cry out and Kyle takes my nipple back into his mouth as Talon releases the one he has. He shifts, lifting himself up. His hand comes away from my pussy and I whine at the loss.

"Easy, angel. I got you. Kyle's got you." Talon pulls the covers off of all of us and I shiver as the coolness of the room surrounds me. Talon takes his place between my legs and I spread them for him. He lifts them up with his thighs, moving closer to where I know he wants to be buried. I feel his erection fall heavily onto my pussy and slides up along my clit.

"Ahh," I moan. My sex is sensitive.

"Kyle?" Talon says and I look down my body and watch as Talon stroking his cock. An invitation. Kyle releases my nipple and kisses down my body, then before he gets to my pouch he takes Talon into his mouth.

I'm the one that cries out watching Kyle working Talon's cock in his mouth. Thank god it only lasts a couple of moments and then Kyle is guiding him to my entrance. "Take our girl. Love her." My back arches and Talon slowly pushes himself inside of me. Kyle's mini blow job is enough to make sliding in that much easier. Kyle slides back up my body, lifting himself over my body he claims my mouth. Tongues dance, breathing becomes impossible as Talon begins sliding in and out of me. I moan into Kyle.

"I want your cock," I breathe.

"Where?"

I lick his lips, my silent answer is my mouth and he adjusts himself so that I can take his cock into my hand and then finally my mouth. Talon and Kyle moan as my pussy clenches on Talon and my mouth consumes Kyle.

When the pleasure becomes too much to handle, Kyle begins gently sliding in and out of my mouth at a pace similar to Talon. I moan, filled at both ends. Filled by my two beautiful men. I look up at Kyle who is looking down at me. I let his cock pop free. "Take him," I moan. "Take him for me."

His mouth falls open and a rush of breath follows. His body shivers with desire. I look over at Talon who looks eager for Kyle's cock. When he slides off of the bed Talon's pace increases and his finger begins strumming on my clit. I moan. His free hand comes up and gently strokes from my neck, down my chest, he makes sure to capture my nipple as he does. My back arches, my pussy tightens and my body rocks with a pending orgasm. His fingers still working my clit feverishly and without much more build up, my orgasm takes me. Shattering me. Talon fucks me through it, and then I feel him still while I recover. When he leans forward to give Kyle access, he nuzzles into my neck. Kissing and nibbling me.

When Talon begins to breathe heavy I start to feel his erection sliding in short bursts inside me, immediately driving me to another orgasm, I look up to see Kyle looking at me. I know he's inside Talon when Talon cries out and sitting still is no longer an option for him. His hips begin to move in and out of me and along Kyle's cock.

They find their rhythm and my pussy is the receiving end of their connection. Kyle slamming into Talon causes his cock to jerk and my orgasm to erupt throughout my body, building higher as I look into Kyle's eyes. He has a firm grip on Talon's ass as he pounds into him.

"Ahh fuck!" Talon moans and my pussy clenches, milking him as I build quickly toward my third orgasm.

"Talon!" Kyle cries out.

Talon's answering moan is all Kyle and I need as his thrusts increase and my orgasm shatters me. Talon's cock twitches and explodes inside. His animalistic cries into my ear send me higher, followed by Kyle's own orgasm consuming him.

chapter 48

I don't move as they begin the process of extracting themselves. When Talon is clear of Kyle he pulls from me and my body quakes with the emptiness. Talon lifts his hips and then rests his head on my stomach. Above the babies. "Am I hurting you?"

"Not at all." I rub my hand through his hair and Kyle comes back with a washcloth and he gently cleans Talon up. When he's done, Talon doesn't move, just wraps his arms along my body, holding me. "What's wrong, big man?"

"I just love you so much. I missed this. I missed you."

My heart breaks a little. Kyle's absence really took a toll on Talon and it didn't help that I wasn't much comfort to him. I don't know what to say so I just keep stroking his hair. "I missed you too," I whisper.

Kyle comes to lie next to us. He kisses me gently and rests his head on my shoulder then he puts his hand on Talon's cheek. Comforting him too. The moment is so sweet. I could stay like this forever with my two men.

Talon moves slightly, lifting his head and shifting downward. He kisses my pouch once, then again. He doesn't say anything, but I can see the emotion in his eyes as he looks at me.

"It's alright, everything is better now. After this week, do you honestly think there is something in this world that can pull us apart?" I ask him and he gently shakes his head from side to side. "Good, because it can't." I tap the tip of his nose with my finger and turn to Kyle and kiss the top of his head.

All our sentiments are broken the moment my stomach rolls. "Oh no..." I try to move and I am trapped by them, "guys...you..." I swallow, "you gotta move." My stomach heaves. "Now."

Finally they get it and all contact with me is lost, I roll towards Talon's side of the bed. I stop, swallowing. Then I get up and fly into the bathroom. Our tender moment is brought to a halt by morning sickness. Though neither one of them leave my side.

After I regain my strength, Kyle gives me my toothbrush and then Talon starts the shower. "We need to get moving, Kyle," he says.

"What about me?" I pout around my toothbrush.

"You don't need to come right away. We're going to be in make-up for a little bit before they start the shoot. You can stay here, relax and get ready at your own pace, angel."

"I want to come," I pout with toothpaste on my lips and they both laugh.

"Alright. Let's shower," Talon says with a kiss to my head.

I finish brushing my teeth and slip into the shower. Both Talon and Kyle take to washing me from head to toe and I return the favor to each of them.

When we get out, I am dried off quickly, and wrapped up in a dry towel. Then Kyle disappears. I wonder where he went but before I can speculate, he's back, still naked as a jaybird. I look at him, raising an eyebrow. "I ordered you breakfast."

"Oh." I smile. "What did you get me?"

"Oatmeal, toast and a side of sausage. Two glasses of apple juice." He smiles.

"Mmm, thank you." I drop my towel and both guys groan. "What?"

"You have no idea how sexy you are, do you?" Talon says with a wicked grin and I watch as both men harden.

"Oh no, we don't have time" I tease them. "I'll go into the bathroom."

"Hell no, we're just going to sit down and watch," Kyle says as he sits down on the bed. Talon quickly joins him.

"Oh dear god, it's not as much fun when I cover up."

"Says who?" Talon says with a laugh.

I get dressed and pull my hair up. I know that I'll be done up by make-up a little later, so there is no point in getting creative. "Breakfast is here," Kyle calls from the bedroom.

"I'll be right there."

About three hours later and the band is standing around waiting for their photo shoot. Well, Dex is in front of the camera first. I'm surprised by how photogenic he can be, but then again, Dex is a very attractive guy, until he starts talking. Though today he's been pretty mellow. I think Raine really has something to do with this.

When Dex is done, Mouse is up. That's when Cami shows up. "Hi boys," she greets them as she comes into the studio.

"What are you doing here?" I ask with a smile and I hug her.

"We have a lunch date."

"What? Oh!" I squeak.

She laughs. "Come on. Go kiss your boys."

I turn around and Kyle and Talon are standing there with big ass pouty faces. I can't help but laugh. "I'll be back," I promise as I walk over to them. They both wrap me up in their arms and Talon kisses me first.

"Have fun," he says with a smile that makes my panties melt. He kisses me again and then releases me to Kyle, though he doesn't actually let go.

"Enjoy yourself. See you in a bit." He kisses me a little less heated but no less passionate.

"You behave," I tease and they let me go.

"Is Tori coming?" I ask.

"No, we have Tyson and where we're going, everyone's a celebrity."

I leave with Cami. "Where are we going?"

"Le Cirque."

"Holy shit," I squeak.

She bursts out laughing. "Have you ever been?"

"Uh no. Not usually in my budget."

She laughs, "It is now." When we leave the studio, there is a limo out front. "Tristan's joining us, is that okay?"

"Oh absolutely."

"We have some business to discuss."

"Oh dear..."

She laughs at my discomfort. "Good business."

Tyson holds open the door for me and I step inside. I take one of the side bench seats as Tristan is sitting opposite the door. "Hi Tristan."

"Good morning, Addison. How are you?"

"Great, thank you, you?"

Cami climbs in. "You look great by the way," she says to me. They'd already attacked my hair for my photo shoot and it's stick straight and has a fresh coat of new color in it. It's hot pink with streaks of purple throughout.

"Thank you."

"Much better than you did yesterday." She smiles. "Are you still feeling good?"

"Great actually."

She smiles. "That's awesome." The limo starts moving. "I have a folder for you. Don't let me forget to give it to you."

"Oh, what's in it?"

"Your copies of the 'Your Eyes' and 'To Be Free' recording contracts that outline in detail your pay for the recordings, which is more of an advance than anything, and your royalty breakdown based on sales. It's not much, 69 Bottles gets the majority of the available royalties."

"I don't care about that."

"I know, but you still stand to make some pretty good money, especially with 'To Be Free' since it's not on the airwaves yet."

"You should hear their new stuff. It's pretty awesome."

"I'm looking forward to it," Tristan chimes in.

"I have a couple sound bites."

"Really?" he gets all excited.

"I do. We tried to use them in a PR release but the label wouldn't allow it. The recording isn't that great and it's raw. They were jamming around a campfire back in

Philly." I pull my phone out and pull it up. Giving my phone to Tristan, he listens to it.

"That's awesome. I can't wait for the new album," he says with enthusiasm.

"I don't know if I ever pictured you as a fan," I say.

He laughs, "I think the only difference is I don't really get nervous around celebrities. They're human too."

I snort a laugh, "that's my line., " I say.

He and Cami both laugh.

*chapter*49

Lunch with Cami and Tristan was so much fun. We talked shop, talked life and we talked about some upcoming things for me. Tristan came alive as lunch progressed. I gather that he's actually quite shy most of the time, which for an actor is odd.

When we return to the studio, I am whisked away to freshen up my hair and then to make-up. I don't even see the guys before I'm put in the chair. I ate so much during lunch that I have a hard time keeping my eyes open. But my make-up artist is talkative, so it helps. This is what I miss about caffeine and coffee.

After about forty-five minutes, she finally turns me around to the mirror and I'm blown away. "You're gonna have to show me how to do this," I tell her and she laughs.

"So you like it?"

"Absolutely."

"Good!" she chirps and then someone else comes in.

"Hi Addison, I'm Liz, I'm here to take you to wardrobe."

"Oh?"

"Come on," she says and I stand up, my head spins for a minute, but I don't have any nausea, thank goodness. I regain my balance and she escorts me to another room. There are racks of clothing, a rack of shoes and a chest that's open with some jewelry on it. Beyond that there is a screened area for me to get dressed in.

"I'm thinking..." Liz pulls out a sleek black sheath dress, accented with a four inch wide red belt.

It's actually a pretty hot outfit.

An hour and half, plus three wardrobe changes later, I'm finally done with my personal photo shoot. It was so much fun. I understand why models enjoy their job. Then again the photographer is pretty awesome and extremely encouraging.

Liz comes back. "Your guys are ready. Are you ready for another outfit?" I groan. "Come on," she says, leading me back to the room with the clothes. Hanging on the rack is something that doesn't look like clothes. It looks like a wrap of some kind.

"What exactly is that?"

She smiles widely. "If you don't mind, I'm going to have to help you get into it. Do you have issues being naked in front of a woman?"

"Uh...not really?" my voice is skeptical.

"Okay, why don't you go get out of that, and then go ahead and come out. I locked the door so it's just me and you.

"Alright."

When I'm disrobed I come out from behind the curtain and I feel like I need to cover up, but decide against it. I can do this, I tell myself as I walk toward her. "Wow," She

297

says with wide eyes. And I know I blush. "Sorry, you're just very pretty."

"Well, thank you for that. Let's do this thing," I say.

She has the material in her hands. It's solid white and rather long. She starts along my hips, though she dips below my pouch, covering my sex, but leaving my little bump exposed. It looks like I'm wearing a really short skirt. Then she crisscrosses the material behind me, and then brings it back to the front where she covers my breasts with another cross at my neckline. Then she brings one side around my arm to the front, then the other, crossing it again below my breasts then pulling it to the back. She hangs onto it, "Turn around for me." I do and she goes to work tying it off.

She turns the remaining parts of the length of fabric into a bow behind me. I can feel her tugging and straightening it. "Perfect. Go take a look," she says with a smile and I walk toward the mirror.

"Wow," I say as I take in the full effect. Really the only thing exposed is my legs, my tattoos on my arms and my tummy. Which actually looks a lot larger like this. She comes over and puts a purple choker around my neck that is studded with white stones that look like diamonds. The effect is complete.

"You're all set."

"Shoes?"

"Nope. Just as you are."

"Okay then."

"Are you ready?"

"Absolutely."

We leave the room and go back into the studio. The background has been changed to a light blue.

"Hey Addison, wow, you look amazing," Elli, the photographer says. "We're gonna take a couple pictures of just you while Liz gets the guys."

"Okay. I step onto the mat and Elli sets out to pose me. I'm standing sideways with my hands resting below my bump.

"Arch your back," she says and I do. "Lean your head back a little, but keep looking at me." I do. "Perfect, hold that." Her camera starts going nuts. "Smile for me." I smile and she takes some more pictures. "Okay, keep your pose but look down at your babies," she guides and I do. Her camera goes nuts and I can see her moving into different positions, different angles, up high, down low. Then she comes to stand in front of me and crouches down. Looking up at me she starts snapping more pictures. "Less smile." she says and I do my best to lighten up my smile. "Perfect." She snaps away.

"Okay, go ahead and kneel for me." I do, "now sit back on your feet." I sit down, "okay, take back the same pose looking at your babies." She is standing over me, snapping pictures downward. "Hold your babies," she says and I put one hand up top and one below. "Beautiful," she says and snaps away. "Can you stay like that?"

"Yes."

"Okay." She moves around and I feel someone come up behind me and I feel one hand, then another on my shoulder. "Alright guys, look at your girl." She snaps away. My skin is electric with their touches on me. "Put your hands under again, Addison." I do and she snaps some more. "Kyle, why don't you stand in front of her. Talon, stay where you are." Kyle stands in front of me and my line of vision is greeted to black slacks and very sexy dress shoes. "Kyle, hold your right hand out. Addison, take his hand, but leave your other one where it's at." I do, "now look up at Kyle." I look up slowly and I hear clicking of the camera as Elli captures my slow visual orgasm as I take in Kyle's black suit. When I reach his chest, he is in a full tux with a purple vest.

A huge smile spreads across my face. He's freshly shaven and looking sexy as hell. Our eyes lock and Elli goes crazy with pictures. "Addison, stay put. Talon and Kyle, switch places."

Kyle kisses my hand before letting me go and handing me over to Talon, and Elli's camera is going crazy. I look up at Talon, and hiss through my teeth. "My god," I breathe and Elli continues taking pictures. Talon is dressed in the same tux as Kyle, with matching vest and tie. It wouldn't be a shock except Talon never wears anything but jeans, t-shirts and his leather vests.

"I know he's sexy as hell, Addison, but can you relax a little?" Elli says with a laugh. Kyle's hand is now resting on my shoulder and Talon is standing before me, looking down on me. Elli takes a few dozen pictures. "Okay, Talon, take a knee. Kyle, help Addison stand up."

He leans down and helps me up and Talon takes a knee. Looking up at me. Kyle wraps his arms around me, putting his hands under my pouch. "Addison, take Talon's hand." I do and Talon's eyes are full of emotion as he looks up at me. "Kyle, kiss Addison." He kisses my hair while we hold the pose. Elli takes several pictures. "Okay Talon, let's say hi to your babies." He slides closer to me and releases my hand. Both of his hands come gently to my belly and Elli takes several pictures. "Okay Kyle, look over her left shoulder down at Talon and your babies. Addison put your head back on Kyle's shoulder." I do and then I feel Talon's lips against my belly and the camera flies. "Addison, reach back with your right hand and grab hold of Kyle's pant leg." I do, taking away a lot of activity along my stomach.

"Perfect. Hold that." Elli takes several pictures like this. Then Talon pulls back from kissing my belly and Kyle cups his cheek.

Elli continues snapping picture after picture. The guys trade places and we repeat the process. Then both men are kneeling in front of me, with their backs to Elli and I'm facing the camera. Elli moves around from one side to the other snapping pictures, then when she's behind the guys, they both hold up their hands and I take them.

"Addison Lynae Beltrand," Talon says. "I promise to cherish you, love you, hold you and take care of you for the rest of our lives. You mean more to me than anything in this world."

Tears start sliding down my cheeks.

"Addison Lynae Beltrand," Kyle says, "I have never felt more complete than when I'm in your arms. I promise to love you, honor you, care for you, and be your rock."

More tears as they talk to me. Elli's camera hasn't stopped flashing. The guys shift, reaching into their pockets and I want to cover my mouth, but I can't because they won't let me go. Tears streak down my face and drop onto the floor.

Together they say, "With these promises we, Talon and Kyle, ask you to be our partner, our lover and our wife, will you marry us?"

"Oh my god," I breathe and Elli is going crazy with the camera. I can hardly breathe. A million and one things are flying through my mind, but the only resounding thing comes from my lips, "Yes!" I say and they both light up, releasing my hands, I bring them to my face. Trying to wipe away the flood of tears and they open up their boxes and hold them up to me. There is a lot of applause, cheering and whooping, but I can't look up.

In Talon's hands there is a silver ring inlayed with stones. At first I think it's crooked, but the stone is off center.

Then Kyle opens his. It's a matching ring and the stone is off center opposite Talon's. They both pull them free and Talon reaches for my left hand. I give it to him and he slides the ring onto my finger, a perfect fit. He kisses the ring before handing my hand to Kyle, who slides his ring on and they click together, both stones creating a circle on my finger. He kisses my rings. "It's beautiful."

"Not as beautiful as you," they both say together and I laugh cry.

"Get up here," I tell them and they stand, wrapping their arms around me.

Elli continues snapping pictures as Kyle, Talon and I become raw and animated. While they shed their jackets, I am hugged and congratulated. When Cami comes up to me, "you knew all about this, didn't you?"

She smiles wide and nods wildly. "I set up the photo shoot for the three of you. The guys did the rest."

"Well, thank you."

"You deserve to be happy. They love you so much." She hugs me again.

I'm not sure what was hotter, Talon and Kyle in full on tuxedos or when they shed their jackets and roll up their sleeves. It was fucking hot and it took everything I had to not jump them right there in the studio.

*chapter*50

The rest of our New York stay was action packed with studio time, concerts and air time for the band at many of the local news stations. Talon and I were able to record 'To Be Free' in five takes during our studio time. Monday and Tuesday were filled with media obligations. The band had scheduled appearances on the nationwide news shows and it was so much fun.

It took all of Monday before Talon spilled the proposal beans to the world. Though, at Kyle's insistence, we limited the news to Talon and I. We have friends and family who wholeheartedly love and support our relationship, but the world might not see it that way.

When Wednesday rolled around, Kyle took my picture again and added it to the other two he'd taken. Gradually pants are becoming hard to button up. I went shopping with Raine and sent four more boxes of clothes back to my house in LA.

When we went back to the hospital, we were able to see both babies and their heartbeats. Everything is measuring perfectly. The guys cried, which of course means I cried too. It brought me great comfort to see that everything is going well with the twins and the raging morning sickness hasn't let up. Oddly enough, I take comfort in it every morning.

Each night before falling asleep, the three of us made love and then they both would say good night to the babies before wrapping me in their arms.

We left New York for Washington DC, then headed south to Nashville and Greensboro. I continued to sing with Talon at every concert and my fan base has been growing. By the time we reached Florida, the band was tiring of being on the road. The looming vacation was a motivator in keeping everyone's moods bolstered.

By the time we hit Atlanta, Dex and Raine were in a full on relationship and Dex, much to everyone's surprise was faithful to a fault with her. I was happy to see it. Mouse and Peacock stayed close. I tried asking Peacock how things with Mouse were going and he'd just smile a wide, secret smile. We'll see, I guess.

Talon, Kyle and I decided that the best way for us to marry was a handfasting ceremony. They both refused to marry me in a traditional setting since they said it wouldn't be fair to the other one and three way marriage is in no way legal. We plan to have the ceremony this summer.

Once we're back in LA for our break, I take care of some much needed and neglected things, like my overflowing bank account. I spent an entire day with a financial advisor discussing how best to invest my money. I paid off my house, paid off my mother's house, and became completely debt free. It was a surreal experience.

At ten weeks and one day pregnant, the three of us walked into Dr. Paige's office and she immediately fell in love with Kyle and Talon. We were able to hear their heartbeats for the first time. We had another ultrasound and for the first time, they really looked like babies. I started crying when I saw that their sacks had come together and they were touching butt to butt. Dr. Paige measured them and they're both perfect. As for my growing pouch, it's now officially a baby bump and my shirts are looser and my pants are pretty much all elastic waisted. I miss jeans. I refuse to buy maternity pants just yet.

The guys continue to worship me, my body and the panda cubs any chance they can get and I love every minute of it. Morning sickness has now turned into anytime sickness. Though two heaving sessions is usually my max in a day, I occasionally have days of three and four times. I'm quickly figuring out what foods I can and can't eat.

Less than a week after our doctor's appointment, we flew out of LA to Denver for the last two weeks of the tour. The west coast is a different animal when it comes to a crowd and we have a blast. Fatigue continues to be a problem for me, but Kyle has finally learned to go out with Talon and the guys from time to time and I love that. Though more often than not, they're too busy worshipping me.

By the time we reach LA again, I'm twelve weeks along and slowly starting to feel better, with a little more energy. My bump continues to grow and my clothes continue to change. I'll be so happy when we finally spill the beans to the world so that I can stop trying to hide the bump. With two shows left in the tour, the guys are tired and ready to be done. I have to agree with them. It will be nice to stay at home for about a week before I shove off to Nashville to record my duet with Bryan Hayes.

At thirteen weeks and two days, the news breaks that Talon and I are expecting, though we manage to keep the fact that it's twins a secret. Kyle and Talon both come with me to Nashville along with Tori, Rusty, Beck and Mills who are now our regular security team and I couldn't ask for a better group of people to be around all the time.

Talon bought us a house in LA that's gorgeous with a massive master bedroom with a beautiful alcove for the babies to be in once they join our family and Talon has it furnished quickly. I sell my condo, one of the hardest things I've ever had to do, but it didn't make sense to keep it and I didn't want to deal with being a landlord. I don't bring much from my condo when I move into the house because we have all new furniture which includes a custom made bed that is bigger than king size. It's great because some nights it's hard to sleep surrounded by Kyle and Talon when my belly is getting so big and my body temperature runs a little warmer when I sleep.

We spent a week in Nashville while I recorded my duet with Bryan Hayes. From Nashville we headed to Kansas City. My mom was over the moon when I told her we were coming and able to stay for a week. She promptly took the week off from her job, hell bent on spending the week with the three of us and that makes me happy.

"Mom?"

"Yeah, sweetheart?"

"Will you move to LA with us?"

"Oh Addie, I don't know…"

"Listen, we have a guest house on the property, you'd have your own place. We'd happily find you a job, or when the babies are born you can be there, help us, help me."

She starts to cry. "Alright, Addison. I will move to LA with you."

I hug her so hard. The guys join us and it turns into a group hug. Kyle has taken to my mom and I take so much comfort in that. Talon is a little more her favorite, but I think his phone call from New York really connected them. It doesn't seem to bother Kyle, but he's quickly earning his own place in her heart.

My mom and I spend the week shopping and I try to get her to start packing while we're there. She refuses, says that she will take care of it. She plans to come out for the ceremony in a couple of weeks, but doesn't plan to move out there until the weather starts to turn cold. She wants to finish the summer in Kansas City.

She doesn't want to sell the house, and I don't blame her. Talon takes it upon himself to hire a caretaker for the property. This way she can be in LA and the house can be taken care of for her.

This makes my mom really happy, and says that it gives her some place to go during the summers. I teased her that LA doesn't get that hot and she disagrees. It makes me smile. I'll take her for eight months out of the year over a couple of weeks once in a while.

By the time the week comes to an end, I'm super sad to leave her, but with the wedding looming closer, I know I'll see her again soon.

When I'm seventeen weeks and four days along, our new house is the backdrop for a very private handfasting ceremony where we're surrounded by our friends. Peacock and Mouse are finally together and it's amazing to see. I wasn't sure that their relationship would happen, but I guess you can't mess with destiny. Dex and Raine are still together and they're doing great. Cami and Tristan, along with their friends Mick, Beau, their daughter Tyler, Travis and Naomi, who are finally getting married, along with Tyson and Jolene, who's also pregnant with their first child, and Derek and Dacotah. My mom is there along with Talon's mom. Kyle refused to invite his mother to the wedding and when I pestered him to give her the option, he refused, saying that he didn't want the disappointment of inviting her and her not showing up.

Talon finally told his mom before the news broke about the babies. She was extremely happy for him, but I could sense some hesitation from Talon about it. He'd shrug it off and I decided to wait and see how it went when she came out for the wedding. She actually seems genuinely happy about the babies and the wedding. Maybe she just needed some time to let it soak in.

My engagement rings are now worn around my neck because my fingers started to swell and before they got stuck, Talon bought me a beautiful chain to put them on. My wedding band is the same as the engagement rings without the added stone. So I now wear three rings.

After the wedding, I legally changed my name from Addison Beltrand to Addison Carver-Black which is what the twins' last name will be when they're born.

20 Weeks 1 day...

"Are we going to find out?" I ask the guys as we drive to Dr. Paige's office.

"Of course. I say it's two boys," Talon says confidently with a smile and a rub of my belly.

"I say two girls," Kyle retorts with his own rub of my full on belly.

"Ha! I say you're both wrong." They raise an eyebrow at me. "I say one of each."

The guys argue why they think it's their particular choice, and even a little about why they want two boys or two girls. I just sit back and listen. Letting them fight about it is kinda fun to watch. Fourteen weeks ago you never would have guessed they would be here arguing about the sex of our babies.

I decide to settle the argument. "How about we just settle for happy and healthy regardless of what's between their legs? "

"Deal," They both say together.

chapter 51

"Addison, I hate to do this, I didn't want to do this, but we've talked about it already. Your blood pressure is much higher than I want it to be. I'm going to have to put you on bed rest."

"What?"

"Relax, sweetheart, it's probably not going to be permanent. But for now, I want you on bed rest to see if we can't bring down your blood pressure. If it comes down to manageable levels I will release some of your restrictions, but for now, you're in bed for twenty-three hours a day. The other hour you can use for a slow walk, a long bath, or minor activities, but only an hour, no more. And the thing that kills me the most to tell you is no sex."

Talon and Kyle groan. Dr. Paige laughs. "Sorry guys, but the more rest she gets, the less stress she feels, and the sooner she can get back up and move around."

"We will do whatever is best for Addison and the babies," Talon calmly states and Kyle agrees with him.

"Okay then. Shall we take a look?"

I nod with enthusiasm.

"We want to know," Kyle says with a huge smile on his face.

Dr. Paige chuckles. "I will do my best." She lifts my shirt, exposing my tummy again. It's huge. Okay, maybe not yet. But it's getting there. She squirts warm gel on my stomach and sets about scanning my belly. She takes her measurements first then, "Okay Baby A, what are you?" she talks to the monitor as she moves the wand around. Then she clicks a couple of buttons and the image turns brown.

"Oh my god," the three of us gasp as we get a good look at what our babies look like in a 3D image.

"Meet baby A," Dr. Paige announces. "And," there is some clicking and then a humming noise as the screen flickers. She moves the wand downward. "Well, hello there little one," she says. "Meet your daughter."

"Yes!" Kyle says

"Oh man," says Talon.

Dr. Paige laughs.

"One down, now we just need another one," Kyle says with a smirk at Talon, who laughs. I want to laugh but I'm trying to stay still.

There is another beep and another hum when the screen freezes. She's taking pictures. Then she pulls the wand away. Types something into the machine and puts the wand on the other side. "Okay baby B. We know you have a sister, but what does your sister have." The image remains in 3D and though they look the same, there are some tiny differences in their look which only spurs me to think that our one in a million shot of two dads might be more possible.

Dr. Paige continues looking, moving the wand upward. Then I see it before the guys do. "Hi there, little man," I say and Talon laughs, Kyle huffs and I fight to sit still.

"Yep, see," Dr. Page says pointing between his legs. "Baby B is a boy."

I start to cry as Dr. Paige takes a few more pictures and finishes up with the ultrasound.

"Oh baby girl," Kyle says. "It's alright, what's wrong?"

"I'm so happy," I sob out.

The guys are overjoyed because they both get a little of what they want, a boy and a girl. And I'm over the moon because I get to have both. I don't stop crying for some time. "Why are you still crying, angel?"

"Because, for years I was told kids were not in my cards, then to find out I'm pregnant, then to find out it's twins, then to find out it's a boy and a girl, it's all so much. I couldn't ask for more. I'm just sorry I'm on bed rest."

"We'll take care of you," Kyle reassures me.

"I know, but...but damn it, I'm so fucking horny."

I cursed so of course the guys laugh at that. "I know, angel, I'm sorry, I wish I could help. But we need to follow the doctor's orders. If we follow them then there is a good chance you can come off of bed rest before the twins are born."

"I know, but..." I sob.

They both hold me. Which doesn't help my libido. As this pregnancy has progressed, I can barely get enough of these two. Wearing them both down before I'm finally satisfied for like an hour. They don't complain, in fact they love it, and now, nothing. My breasts don't help that horniness any. They've grown a full size and my nipples are losing their puffiness, being replaced by full on nipples and it's kinda hot to look at, if I do say so myself. They've also darkened to a more solid brown color.

The guys have taken to spreading shea butter lotion on my belly at least twice a day and have added my breasts to their routine when a few stretch marks started popping up. I almost always wear a bra now because the rubbing of a t-shirt hurts and not in a good way.

When we get home, the guys help me to bed, strip me out of my clothes and give me my other bra. "Angel?"

I look at Talon and he looks concerned. He shows me the inside of my bra, which is white. Inside the bra there is a brownish tint. "Oh." I look down at my breasts. I cup them both and squeeze downward toward my nipple. "Oh!" I squeak as a liquid comes out.

I wipe it off with my fingers. "I think this is normal," Kyle says. "The book talks about it; the start of lactation."

Talon's eyes light up. I laugh. "Well, okay then."

Kyle gets me a couple of tissues to put between my nipples and my bra because I don't have any pads yet and Talon is severely disappointed when I cover back up. "So not helping, big man," I tease him. "I am so horny and this doesn't help."

"I know, angel, I'm sorry. It's just, well, it amazes me what your body is capable of. To not only see your belly growing but to know you're producing milk that will feed our children, it's just inspiring." I watch as he adjusts himself in his jeans.

I moan and climb into bed. No sooner do I sit down, I have to pee. I groan and get back up. "Where are you going?" Kyle asks.

"I have to pee," I whine and he laughs as I head to the bathroom.

Zoey Derrick

Once I return, they tuck me into bed and I'm tired enough that I snuggle in. Talon becomes my pillow when I snuggle into him, adjusting so that my belly is resting on his side and I close my eyes. Kyle sets out to work on making me lunch. I don't remember much else because I fall asleep.

chapter52
kyle

Talon is standing over the stove making Addison her favorite. He's shirtless and I can't stop the raging hard-on I have while watching him. As he moves and shifts, his muscles tighten and release, god, he's so fucking sexy. "You should stop staring," he whispers with a hint of mischief in his voice.

"How'd you..."

He stops, turns around to face me. "Because every time you stare at me with hunger, I get hard."

My breath catches and he turns back around to tend to Addison's lunch. I walk quietly up behind him, wrap my arms around his waist and my hand slides along his erection. I hear his breathing spike. His hands fumble slightly with the pan. "I can't concentrate when you do that."

I kiss his neck, right behind his ear and whisper, "So don't." I continue kissing down his neck, along his shoulder, my hand glides along his cock and I shiver. It's been a while since Talon and I have been together alone and I'm not one for initiating much of anything, but with Addison off limits, I can't help myself anymore.

Talon's head falls back to my shoulder and his body relaxes in my embrace. I don't stop kissing, biting, and sucking my way along his neck and shoulder while my other hand works feverishly to undo the fly of his jeans. "We can't," he breathes.

"Why?" I counter.

"Because she can't."

"Do you honestly think she would be mad at us?" I ask him.

He shakes his head as my hand slides under the waistband of his jeans, wrapping my fingers around his hard as steel erection. "Ah, fuck!" he groans.

"I need this. I need you," I breathe against his neck.

My words entice him into action and he spins in my arms, my hand pulls free of his pants and his hands cup my cheeks. His lips slam into mine as he pushes me back against the counter. My breath leaves my body in rush and I moan. My hands quickly go back to his jeans pushing them down, springing his cock. I grip it in my hands and pull along his shaft. I feel him shudder and his breathing hitches.

His hands roam along my chest, down to my shorts. He hooks his thumbs into the waistband and pushes down. He grips my cock in his hands and begins kissing down my chest. First kissing one star, then the other. His tongue slides wet and hot against my nipple then he nibbles his way down my stomach.

His cock falls out of reach and I groan at the loss. "Easy, cowboy. I got you," he says right before his hot wet mouth wraps around my cock.

"Fuck," I groan as his mouth and hand goes to work, licking, sucking, stroking. Bringing me closer to orgasm faster than I want to be. "Take me, Talon," I say roughly. "I need you to fuck me." He sucks me into his mouth deeper. "Now!" I growl with impatience.

"A bit demanding, aren't we, cowboy?" he says with a glow in his eyes, one that tells me that I'm about to be turned into submissive putty. He lets go of me and stands. "Turn around," he commands and my muscles liquefy.

I do as he's commanded and immediately his hands are on my ass, spreading them wide. I feel a warm breath of air followed quickly by a fat, wet tongue rimming me. My chest falls to the counter as he prepares me to take him.

He doesn't hold out long. The licking is barely enough to get me going when he pulls back. Just when I'm about to turn around to see what he's doing, I feel the soft blunt tip of his cock pressing into me and I relax as his hand runs along my back. "Tell me, Kyle, how fucking bad do you want me right now?"

I can't breathe, consumed by my desperate desire for him. I push back, pushing my ass toward him and he smacks me square on the soft flesh of my ass. "So bad it hurts," I cry out as he pushes into me.

"Relax, cowboy," he breathes as he leans down over me, covering me, warming and relaxing me with his touch. I feel him start to move, sliding in and out, slow and steady at first, allowing me a chance to get acclimated to his invasion, but it doesn't last long before I'm pushing back against him, silently begging him to take me harder and faster.

He takes my hint as he rears up, grabbing a hold of my hips he starts to push into me harder and pull out faster. "Ah, fuck," I moan as sensations radiate everywhere, I'm nearly ready to explode already.

"How does that feel?" he asks as he continues thrusting into me.

Zoey Derrick

"Fucking amazing...Don't. sStop. God. Please. Ah!" I feel every cell in my body explode, my balls tighten and my muscles lock down. His hand comes away from my hip and he reaches around. Taking my cock in his hand. "Ah, Talon!" I practically scream as he strokes once.

"Fucking come for me, cowboy," he growls. "Ah, fuck!" he moans as he strokes a second, then third time, and on the fourth, I explode at the same time as I feel Talon erupting inside me.

That day isn't the last time that Talon and I will spend alone time together. Not being with Addie will kill us both every day, but she also isn't stupid. We just choose not to tell her, at least not while she's on bed rest.

chapter 53
addison

They wake me up a little while later with food. I get up and go to the bathroom before I lay back down on the bed. Talon props up a crap ton of pillows and I sit against them as Kyle puts a raised tray over my legs. I smile. "How'd you know?" I ask him.

He smiles and shrugs. "It's your favorite." I dive into my mac 'n cheese. Now before you freak out that this is all I eat, chill, because this is what he feeds me when I need comfort food, like now, and my new bed rest situation. I pick up the bowl and start eating. My hand grows tired so I set it on my belly and the guys laugh.

I smile. "What, it works."

That's when it happens. "Omph," I say and the fork rattles in the bowl.

"What..." Then it happens again with all eyes on my belly.

"Oh my god," Kyle breathes as he climbs onto the bed. I move the bowl and nothing happens. I put it back and we watch and wait.

He kicks again. I say 'he' because he was the upside down one this morning. I move the bowl and press my hand to the same spot. It tickles when he kicks again. I grab Talon's hand and press it to the same spot. "Oh. My. God," he says and he has tears in his eyes. I trade their hands, giving Kyle his turn and baby boy doesn't disappoint. Kicking Kyle square in the hand.

After that, both Talon and Kyle sit with me, hands rubbing on my belly. "Get the lotion if you're gonna do that," I tease and Talon gets up, grabbing the lotion and Kyle moves the tray. My hunger has taken over and I work on eating my lunch while they pull back the blankets and lift my shirt. They both massage lotion into my skin and are rewarded with a few kicks from both babies as they set about their task. They both have amazed expressions on their faces. I've felt it before, but nothing like this and nothing when they've been around. The babies have always been quiet when they are around, until today.

23 weeks

I spend the next three weeks following doctor's orders. Eating and sleeping, growing panda cubs. Kyle and Talon continue their nightly rituals of goodnights and kisses to babies in my belly and then to me. Kyle has switched from calling me baby girl to calling me mama or panda more often than not. Which works for me since he will soon have someone new to call baby girl.

In the late afternoons, they both escort me around the yard or around the house for a nice slow walk. It's warm outside now in August in LA. So I take to the house more often than not. I'd called Dr. Paige last week and asked her if I could take slow swims in the pool. She said that the pool could be very relaxing but that I shouldn't move around too much. I took her advice and used it often. Though most of the time I found myself just sitting in the water. It was nice to feel weightless and relax.

Today we go back to Dr. Paige to check my blood pressure. It has come down a lot since she put me on bed rest, but she hasn't rescinded it just yet.

I told the guys that if she rescinds it today that I need a few moments alone with Dr. Paige to ask a couple of questions. They're reluctant, but they finally agree.

Once I'm settled in and waiting for Dr. Paige, the guys are on either side of me. She hasn't done another ultrasound, but the machine is back in the room today. I'm hoping for another look at my babies.

"Hi Addison, Kyle, Talon," she greets us as she comes into the room. She has a mischievous grin on her face.

"I think I like that smile," I tell her.

"You should. Your blood pressure is back to normal. Now, before you go getting all woohoo on me, I want to do an ultrasound and check on the kiddos. If everything looks okay, I will remove your bed rest, but you will still have strict rules to follow," she says with a raised eyebrow and the guys groan. She laughs, "Well, maybe not that strict," she says with a smirk. She sets about measuring my belly, which I can't even look past anymore. It's bad enough that Talon and Kyle have traded off shaving duties already.

"You're measuring a little bigger than I expected you to be, but, that's okay. Your weight is good. You've only gained about twenty-five pounds so far."

"Ugh!" I groan and she laughs.

321

"Hey for twins, that's amazing. Be proud of yourself."

"It's all the extracurricular activity I used to be able to participate in," I say with a smirk and both Kyle and Talon blush.

Dr. Paige laughs. "That's a good possibility. Though at this stage, I'd find a good maternity yoga instructor, if you can, and have them come to the house a couple days a week. It will be good for you and your body, and it will help you bounce back after they're born. Plus it might help wear you out. Though I get the impression these guys have secretly enjoyed their reprieve."

"Dr. Paige," I scold and the guys snicker. "I doubt they've been resting up for my triumphant return to the bedroom."

"Stop it," Kyle says, he's as red as a cherry.

Dr. Paige laughs. "Your secrets are safe with me. Alright, let's have a look."

She fires up the machine and sets about looking things over. She turns the sound up because she knows that the sound of their heartbeats is a comfort to me. She doesn't point out too many things, but she does recheck the genders to make sure she was right the first time. When she's done the guys kiss me, giving me my time with Dr. Paige.

"What's up Addison?"

"A couple of things, one, can I have sex now?" I whine and she laughs.

"Yes, but..." I pout, "one at a time. Don't let yourself get over stimulated. I can imagine the two of them are a handful together, so be wary of overdoing it."

"That, I can handle."

"What else?"

"I haven't shown the guys this in a while." I pull my bra down and remove the pad. I squeeze and clear liquid squirts out. "It only happens, really, when I do this, but, they're boob men, like major boob men."

She laughs, "With your small size before your implants, I'm not surprised you're lactating early. No, it's not a problem, especially if they're into that. But be wary that while stimulation brings it out now, if they start helping themselves, you will start lactating at regular intervals. I recommend getting a pump before you let them have at it. You can freeze it for up to six months. Which doing so now, will help them better bond with the babies and allow you time to rest. Feeding twins can and will be very demanding on your body and your milk supply. Though I don't think that's going to be an issue for you."

"Okay, so what are my restrictions?"

She goes over a list of restrictions and I am still required to rest for no less than four hours a day in addition to a good night's sleep. Though it can be in bed or on the couch. The idea is to lie down when I can and take it easy as often as possible. Also avoid long walks etcetera.

"Last question."

"Shoot."

"I know that I will likely deliver early and that thirty-six weeks is ideal."

"If you can make it to Halloween, it will be ideal. Listen to your body, I know the second trimester is a time where you feel great, you want to get out and do things and be normal, but you've got to listen to what your body is telling you. If it says to rest, then rest. If it says to go go go, don't go go go, but just go. If you feel energized, take a leisurely swim in the pool. The weightlessness will help aches and pains in your body, but don't stay in too long. If you're going out that night or have something coming up, then make sure you rest until the very last minute. Don't wear yourself out. Don't let yourself get to the point of exhaustion. You're fortunate to have the type of job that you don't have to go in everyday. Take advantage of it and if you do have to work, eat and drink lots and rest. You're doing an amazing job growing these babies, don't stress about the things you can't control. Let them take care of you, they're eager to do it."

"Sometimes I feel like I'm taking advantage of them."

She smiles wide. "You can't take advantage of the willing and believe me, they're both willing."

"Thanks, Dr. Paige."

"Anytime. Anything else?"

"No, I'm good for now."

chapter54

"So?" they both ask as soon as we're in the car.

"Mills?" I ignore them.

"Yes, Addison."

"Can we stop at Bel Bambini on the way home?"

"Absolutely," he says.

The guys look happy, yet dejected at the same time. I sigh and smile wide. "The chastity belt is off."

"Mills, we'll go to the store later," Talon says.

"Oh no, this needs to be done because I need a couple of things before you can have at me. Okay?"

"But, but, but," they both whine.

"Look, my milk is coming in and if the two of you are going to go to town on them, I need some supplies."

Talon lets out a pleasurable huff and Kyle groans, neither are bad and my nipples harden and my clit pulses. Shit, I don't know if I'm going to make it home. I'm just as sexually frustrated and horny as they are.

Zoey Derrick

"Besides, I haven't been out of the house except for doctor appointments for three weeks. Let me have just a little fun." I smile prettily at them both and bat my lashes.

They both groan, "Fine."

"Eek!" I squeal in excitement and they both laugh.

"You know we can't say no to you."

Our little trip into Bel Bambini turns into a full on shopping spree. It's the first time that we've actually indulged in buying stuff for the twins. Mills and Tori stand by laughing. We end up walking out with several names written down of strollers, carseats, swings and bouncers. I want to research the best names before I buy anything.

I buy a pump, something that I'd already been researching in my alone time in bed. It's expensive, but it's the best there is. It has both electronic and manual options and the guys kinda cringe. Talon is all too eager to help relieve me of my milk supply. Guys and their fetishes, but when I tell them about storing it for them to be able to feed the babies when they're born, they're very gung-ho on that idea.

Getting home is a challenge, neither one of them can keep their hands off of me. I haven't gotten into their restrictions just yet. I will once we're home.

Ten minutes later we finally pull in. The guys grab the shopping bags and I'm not in the door before Kyle is at my front and Talon at my back, kissing my lips and sucking along my neck. "Okay guys, you have rules." They both groan and I chuckle. "It's not bad. I promise. I am still fair game, but… one at a time. As much as I love both of you and desperately need both of you at the same time, the orgasms are too intense. I'm not allowed to get too worked up."

"Oh, we can handle that," Talon says as he moves my hair to the side. Kissing that sweet spot where my neck and shoulder meet.

I turn in their arms, "And you, be nice to the girls." He gives me a wicked grin that sends a shiver through me making my pussy weep, soaking my panties and my legs go weak. "Take me, upstairs," I moan out. And they whisk me upstairs to the bedroom. I'm naked before we hit the threshold. Hands, mouths, clothes, arms and faces are everywhere in a tangled, uncoordinated mess. My skin is alive and sensitive and their soft caresses send shivers up my spine, rocketing pleasure straight to my core.

I am gently laid out on the bed. Kyle growls as he is the first one to wrap his mouth around a nipple. My back arches and Talon's hands caress up and down my body. The pleasure is so intense and I have missed this so much that I nearly come just from being touched.

Kyle's mouth continues to lick and suck and Talon is watching him, raging jealousy in his eyes. "I have two," I remind him quietly and he doesn't need any more encouragement. He lies down beside me and engulfs my other nipple, just like Kyle, the licking sucking and pulling by both of them is nearly enough to send me over the edge. I try to reach around my bump and fail. Kyle takes my hand and places it on his cock; I take it into my hand and stroke him. He moans again.

I take Talon into my other hand, stroking, pulling and playing with their purple heads. Kyle's hand slips between my legs, spreading me wide. I arch my back and his hand slides between my sensitive folds. My orgasm explodes through my body. My pussy clenching and releasing around nothing but the orgasm is intense none the less.

Kyle releases my nipple and kisses his way down my torso. He kisses along my belly and moves down south, Then his hot tongue seers into my folds, taking my clit into his mouth and I nearly come undone again. My tugs on Talon's cock become harder and he cries out his own pleasure, releasing my nipple. He sits up and brings his cock to my mouth. "What do you want, big man?" I breathe out.

"Your mouth, angel," he growls as I grip it in my hand then teasingly lick the head. He groans. I tease him again and again as Kyle continues licking and sucking on my clit. I feel him slide two fingers inside of me and I explode, moaning around Talon's cock as I finally suck him down as deep as I can. Holding him in place, I stroke along his cock with my hand and Kyle rears up. I can feel the head of his erection pressing at my entrance and desire explodes, radiating outward sending ripple after ripple of pleasure through my body.

I release Talon from my mouth. "Take me, god, Kyle, I need it, I need you." I arch my back again and he slips inside. "Faster, Kyle, I can't..." He slides inside, impaling me and I cry out. I take Talon's cock back into my mouth as Kyle begins fucking me. My pussy is squeezing and releasing him as he strokes along my inner walls, massaging that special spot.

"Talon!" Kyle grinds out as I feel his orgasm hardening his cock further.

"Do it," Talon orders and I explode all over Kyle's cock, his orgasm explodes inside of me seconds later. Talon pops free of my mouth and I can't look away as he strokes his cock. "Take it, Kyle," he demands and I feel Kyle shift before I watch him suck Talon into his mouth and Talon explodes. Kyle greedily swallows his cum. I shudder in pleasure watching the exchange.

chapter 55

That was the first of four times that day, though they let me eat and rest in between. That day also found me opening my eyes and really seeing the love and passion between the two of them. I learned later that they didn't wait around for me while I was on bed rest, but they were afraid to tell me because they didn't want to upset me or make me jealous. I told them that wasn't the case at all.

Despite not talking about them much, the guys in the band are always at the house doing their thing and Talon's studio is nearly done. His goal was to build his own studio so that once the babies are born, he'd never have to be far away.

The guys spend the majority of September and almost all of October in the studio recording the new album. With 'To Be Free's' track already recorded my part is done, but I got to go and watch them a few times and I have to say, this album is certainly better than the last.

Talon's absence is felt by both Kyle and I, but we get by and enjoy every minute we can with him. His goal is to have the album recorded before the babies are born and I commend him for that. The days spent without him around are always made worth it when he comes home at night.

Halloween comes around and I am on full bed rest and have been for two weeks. This time around I don't complain because I'm equal parts miserable and excited to meet my babies.

In the spirit of Halloween, the guys found some body paint and painted my blooming belly into a pumpkin. We had a good laugh about it, took some pictures and Talon later posted it on Twitter with a tag, "This is how we roll on Halloween #BabiesOnBoard #ComingSoon"

On November Fourth, my duet with Bryan Hayes went live and exploded across the airwaves and landed on a couple million mp3 players around the world. The guys celebrated with me by eating ice cream off of my body. The babies hated the cold, which of course egged the guys on some more. Bryan called twice that day congratulating me. I thanked him over and over again for the experience. He asked how I was doing and said he was bummed I couldn't be at the launch party. When I told him I was busy growing babies, he laughed. We became pretty good friends when we recorded our song and both Talon and Kyle grew to like him too. All animosity and jealousy was long forgotten.

On November Eleventh, at exactly thirty six weeks, my water broke at three in the morning and the guys rushed me to the hospital. I could tell that they were nervous but they never let me really see it. Until Dr. Paige ordered an emergency C-section because of fetal distress. We'd agreed that if this happened, because they both couldn't be in the operating room for the delivery that I would go in alone. It killed me to let them go, but rules are rules and despite my begging, they said no. Dr. Paige's concern was the fact that there had to be so many people in the OR already because of the twins.

Emily Grace Carver-Black was born first, followed three minutes later by her brother Logan David Carver-Black. I only got to see them briefly before the tears overwhelmed me.

"Addison?"

Feeling very weak I try to respond, "Hmm?"

"Addison, I have to go in, one of your cysts has bursts. I've got to put you out."

I don't remember much after that.

When I come to, I'm back in my room. I can't see much but I can hear cooing and talking coming from Kyle and Talon and I look over and immediately burst into tears when I see Emily in Kyle's arms and Logan in Talon's. Talon and Kyle have the biggest, brightest, most beautiful smiles on their faces. Kyle notices me first. "Hi mama." He stands up and Talon follows, bringing my babies to me. Kyle comes around the bed, "Who do you want first?"

"Both of them," I say and they lay them gently on my chest facing each other. "Hi babies," I coo at them. I watch the miracle of life before my eyes as they both start rooting around, looking for food.

"Let me call the nurse," Kyle says softly. He has tears in his eyes. Talon too, as I hold our babies to my chest.

"Yes?" a voice comes over the phone.

"She's awake," Kyle says.

"Be right there." The nurse comes back.

I keep talking to my babies as I hold them close and just a minute or two later the nurse comes in. "Hi Addison, my name is Melissa, I'm your nurse. How are you feeling?"

"Happy."

"Good, any pain?" I shake my head. "That's good. You ready to feed your babies?" I nod.

Melissa helps me get set up and feed the twins. They both took to it pretty easy and Melissa made jokes with the guys while I watched them eat. It was so surreal and hypnotic to watch. I realized quickly that being close to them like this would bring me the greatest joy most days.

Once I'm all dried up, or at least I think I am, I change gowns, adding my nursing bra to the mix so that I have some protection against leaking everywhere just as I'm about to take back the babies two nurses come in with Dr. Paige. "Hey there Addison, how you doing?"

"Great." I smile. "They've eaten and I was just about to hold them again."

"Er, okay, we'll hold off on the testing for a while. I need to talk to you about what happened after they were born."

"Are they alright?" I say panicked.

"Oh, they're perfect. I promise." she says with a reassuring smile.

"How long will the testing take?"

"About half an hour," Dr. Paige says.

I nod. "Go ahead and take them now. Then I don't have to be interrupted with them later," I say reluctantly. But it's true, I'd rather not get an hour than have them taken again. Both Talon and Kyle pout as they hand over the twins, then Kyle comes to sit on the bed at my feet and Talon pulls the chair closer to be near me as the twins leave the room. "Okay Doc, talk to me."

chapter 56

"Do you remember what we talked about, the risks of delivery?" I nod. "Well, the cysts that were blocking your tube ruptured when I pulled Emily's placenta out. It caused a lot of bleeding, and it ruptured your uterus." Tears, more tears. "I didn't want to have to do it, I swear I tried, Addison."

I shake my head. "No, it's, it's okay. I...Today I got more than I ever imagined I could have, I got two very healthy babies." I look at Talon and Kyle and they're both crying. They know what this means. "It's okay." I look at both of them and repeat myself, "it's okay." I nod at them. It's a lot to process.

"I was able to leave your ovaries. We will continue with some hormone treatments to help keep your symptoms managed. We will continue to monitor for cysts on your ovaries. It also means that you have eggs for the future, should you want to have a surrogate or other options." She smiles reassuringly at me. I nod. "Now, for some possibly fun news, more for these two."

"Oh my god," I squeak. "No way."

"Yes, way," Dr. Paige teases.

"What way?" Talon and Kyle say together.

"You want to tell them?" Dr. Paige smirks. I nod.

"Do we know which?" She shakes her head. "Okay." I look at both of the boys. I smile wildly. "I gave Dr. Paige permission to run some blood tests on the twins when they were born."

"Addison, we talked-" Talon says and I cut him off.

"Let me finish. All she did was compare the twins against each other. Because they're fraternal twins their DNA and blood types were going to be different, but there are enough differences for her to determine.."

"They don't match," Kyle says standing up, complete shock on his face. "You mean one is," he points to himself "and one is..." he points to Talon. I smile again and Kyle sits back down.

"Now this really makes you having to take my uterus okay." I tell Dr. Paige who smiles. "They each have their own."

"They do." Both of them are in shock staring at each other. "Now the real question is, do they want to know which one is theirs?" She asks playfully.

I'm blown away by the resounding, "No!" that comes out of both of them. "We don't care. We will each raise them as ours no matter what. They're both our babies and we're okay with that," Kyle says with a huge smile on his face.

"Just knowing that we both played an equal role in making them is satisfying enough for us," Talon adds and the subject is dropped.

Three days later, we finally get discharged to go home. I'm still recovering from the C-section and my hormone levels dropping makes me feel sick and weak and emotional. But it's all worth it when I get to hold Emily or Logan or both in my arms, which it's rare that I don't have one of them in my arms all day long.

The guys take turns getting up at night with them, but I refuse to let them not feed from me when they're hungry. So one will get up, change them and bring them to me to be fed while I lay in bed.

When I lay in bed feeding, whoever got the baby out of bed lays awake watching, even if I fall asleep. Emily was born at just five pounds and Logan was five pounds three ounces. By their first week check-up, they've each gained about five ounces and it's a great sight to see.

As I get better from my c-section I become more active, eating is still my number one priority because these two babies eat a ton from me, but my food choices have shifted to healthier options. With the cooler weather, the five of us always take a walk. Putting Emily and Logan into their stroller, we take a nice long walk.

Hate me if you want to, but by their first Christmas, six weeks later, I've lost all of the weight I gained, but I'm working hard to lose the pouch. Though the guys miss having the babies in there, they constantly remind me of the good reasons why I have it and I love them all the more for it.

My mom is a whirlwind of energy around the house, helping with meals, taking care of the twins when I need to rest, though after Christmas, my resting becomes few and far between. It's great having her around the house and she seems happy here in LA.

She has her CPA and has worked as an accountant for years. Talon hires her to handle his own financials regarding the band, paying bills and managing the expenses. It's great to have her working again. Talon's own financial madness is enough to keep her busy a good twenty hours a week. Though with the new album getting ready to come out, I imagine it's going to increase some more. Also, tax season is coming and the entire band is determined to have her do their taxes.

I tell her it's too much and she tells me it's not. Lest we forget that I need someone to do my taxes now. It's great to see my mom feel needed for more than a nanny. Which she's all too eager to do whenever we let her. Which as the kiddos grow older, and I give up some of the feeding duties to the guys, they start dragging me out a little bit more.

chapter 57

In January, Talon has to leave for a week of promotional appearances in New York in preparation for the new album's release. I wake up when I hear Logan whining and see Talon sitting in one of the two rocking chairs in the nursery alcove. He's holding both babies in his arms. I sit up and smile.

"Hey mama," he whispers. I climb out of bed and go over to him.

"Hi big man. He hungry?" I ask and Talon nods. "Want me to?" He nods again and I take Logan from him. "Hi big guy," I say as I hold him up. "Are you hungry?" I smile, and tuck him into the crook of my arm and in a few swift movements, he latches on and I back up into the other rocker.

I look over at Talon who's looking down at Emily, he looks so sad. "Talk to me, big man," I encourage softly.

He looks up at me and I can see a couple of tears streaking his cheeks. "I can't stand this."

"What?"

"I don't want to leave them tomorrow," he admits quietly. "I wish I didn't have to go, or that you guys could come with."

"Don't beat yourself up, you have a job to do. We will be fine and we will all be here when you get back. We'll Skype and everything else while you're gone."

"I just feel like I'm going to miss so much."

I stand up and go over to him. "Better to go now, when they're only eight weeks old."

"Yeah, I just...I've been thinking a lot about my life and where it's going. I don't think I can or want to keep this up throughout their lives."

"What are you saying, Talon?"

"I think I'd rather slip behind the scenes, write songs, produce music, produce your music. This way I can stay here, and don't have to travel around the country away from my family."

"What about the band?"

He shrugs. "I don't want to make it seem like I'm giving up on them, or on us, but sometimes I wonder if their heart is still in it the way it was when we started this gig. But I'd have to talk to them, and it wouldn't be something that would happen right now. We have tour commitments and everything else that we've already agreed to and I can't find anything to get pissed off at them about that we could just break up over."

"I wouldn't want you guys to break up, not like that."

"No, I know, it would have to happen amicably and mutually. It's not something that can happen over night, and I don't want to squeeze anyone out and if they decide to stay together, I'm okay with that, I wouldn't mind if they replaced me. But it's so much to decide on and talk about," he says softly, looking up from Emily to me as I rub

338

Logan's sleeping face. His mouth falls open and he releases me. I tuck back in and bounce him softly.

"You want him back?" I ask and he nods. I turn Logan around so that he can take him back. He rocks them both in the chair. "Talon, if this is what you want, you know I will support you one hundred percent. I don't want you jumping into the decision. You need to remember that they won't be babies forever. Eventually they will grow up and leaving might not be as hard."

He looks down at both the babies again. "I think it would be. But it's a lot to think about and process."

"And not a decision you can make tonight. I know going away kills you, but it's only a few days, you'll be home before you know it."

"I just wish you guys were coming too."

"I know, I wish we were too, but they're so young and flying, I…"

"Shhh, angel. It's alright. I understand and I agree. They're too young. But it doesn't stop me from wishing." He gives me a sad smile.

"I know, big man." Emily starts to stir and whine in his arms. "Here." I lean down and take her from him. "Hi baby girl." I whisper and put her down on the changing table, changing her. Talon gets up and puts Logan in his crib and he comes to stand behind me, wrapping his arms around my waist as I dress Emily back in her pajamas.

I pat his hands and hold him there for a few minutes. Emily starts to cry and I pick her up, much like Logan, she's hungry so I feed her too. Once she's settled, I turn to look at Talon. "Talk to Kyle. He's going to give you better insight into ideas on how to deal with the guys, the contractual obligations and he's great with pros and cons. But remember something for me, big man."

"What's that?" he says softly as his hand gently rubs along Emily's head.

"Do it for you. Don't do it for her, for Logan, Kyle or me. Do it for you. Make sure that giving up 69 Bottles is really what you want and what you'll be happiest with in the long run. If you decide on a solo career, it might not pan out the way you want it to. Writing and producing might not work out either. I don't want you to resent giving up a good thing."

He kisses my forehead. "That's not possible, angel. Trust me. Everything I do, I do for this family, for the band and then finally myself. Besides, I'm pretty sure I'll have a regular customer for writing and production." He smirks at me.

"This is very true." I smile and he kisses me softly as Emily continues eating.

We don't talk much while she finishes and when she's sound asleep, Talon takes her from me, kissing her sweetly and then putting her to bed. "Come on, mama." He grabs my hand and leads me back to bed. As we approach, I realize that Kyle's awake. It doesn't take me long before I'm engulfed by both of them. Each one having their way with me.

We've only been back at the sexual aspect of our relationship for about a week, and they've indulged every chance they could get and I love it! I love them, wholly and completely. From now until forever.

epilogue

Next week, Emily and Logan turn one. I can't believe a year has gone by so fast. But tonight, tonight is all about me. Well, sort of.

In January after the twins were born, after Talon and I had our talk about his future with 69 Bottles, I signed a record contract with Vicious Records and by March, inside of Talon's studio, I recorded my first solo album. With a lot of help from Talon, who became my writer and producer. I'm musically inclined when it comes to singing, but I suck at writing music. So Talon has taken care of most of that for me. There was a time when I would have called you crazy for predicting what would happen, but in the middle of April when my first single, 'Now and Forever', hit the airways, it hit the Top 40 for more than six weeks. Reaching number two. Hey, what can I say, not bad for a first solo song, right?

When the single was released for sale, I made the Billboard Top 100, though I didn't reach the top. I was actually kind of glad about that, I rather enjoy the fact that Talon and I together hit the number one spot with 'To Be Free'.

Part of my signing with Vicious was that I wouldn't go on tour until after the first of the next year. I needed Emily and Logan to be at least one and I needed them to be weaned completely, the upcoming tour gives me that excuse, though the twins will be traveling with us and I have a lot fewer appearances on my tour than Talon and the guys did on theirs.

So about tonight, I am attending my second awards show since releasing my first album and being with the band. The first one I walked the red carpet because I was picked to present and perform during the show. Which of course was awesome. No need to mention that Talon was my guitarist that night. No one knew, which tells me that there is a definite separation between me and 69 Bottles. Though they too performed at that award show. Tonight however, I am performing, presenting and lastly, a nominee. Well, Bryan Hayes is the reason I'm a nominee. Our duet has been nominated as Duet of the Year, Song of the Year and Video of the Year.

Everyone seems to think we're going to win, but I'm skeptical, better to be that than expectant and lose.

Talon and Kyle walk the red carpet with me. Talon is in the vest, shirt and pants of a Brioni tux. Having ditched the jacket completely, his sleeves are rolled up and the top button is open. Regardless, he's still sexy as hell. Kyle, on the other hand, is in an Armani tux, vest and all, looking amazingly handsome. I should mention that somewhere along the course of the last year people started putting two and two together that we were three and not two, it might be the fact that my name is Addison Carver-Black. We received some backlash for it, but in the end all was okay. I guess it helps that we try our hardest not to flaunt it in front of people. Kyle is mine and 69 Bottles' full time manager now, which of course keeps him super busy, but he never complains and is constantly coming up with new ideas for both 69 Bottles and myself.

So back to the red carpet. They're both with me tonight. Though they don't kiss me or do anything to invoke the comments, other than have their arms around me for pictures. I stand there with my arms behind their backs too.

Now that you're drooling about Kyle and Talon, I should tell you that I'm wearing a custom made Vera Wang, that is black, sleeveless and very short. I am rocking the purple hair again and I'm wearing my favorite purple suede platform pumps and my hair is cascading down my back, about two inches longer than last year.

As the awards ceremony gets started, I get ridiculously nervous and I am really sad to say that I will be backstage when the first award is announced, Duo/Duet of the Year, so I won't have the privilege of hugging and kissing Talon and Kyle if we win. I will have just been on stage with Bryan singing the song. Which is another reason why I don't think I'll win.

Our performance goes perfectly. Though we hadn't performed it very much together, we've done it a few times since recording and releasing it. We practiced a lot this week. Then comes the nerves. I could perform, have no problem doing that, but this makes me down right fucking nervous.

Bryan comes over to stand with me. "How you doing?"

"I feel like I'm going to puke."

"Good, glad I'm not the only one," he says with a laugh. "Great job tonight." He smiles.

"You too."

"And the nominees for best duet are..." I start bouncing in my shoes. I can't stand here, argh, I want to fucking run around.

"And the winner is... 'Never Kiss Goodbye', Bryan Hayes and Addison Carver-Black"

At that moment my entire world fuzzes. I'm not sure I can tell you what happens next, all I know is that Bryan escorts me back to the stage. I spot Talon and Kyle standing in the third row and everything balances back out. They hand Bryan and I our trophies and Bryan takes the envelope. And steps up to the microphone. "How you doin there, Addison?"

"Oh my god," I squeal.

"Me too." He turns back to the microphone. "Thank you all so much for this wonderful honor. I'd like to thank Addison for joining me on this project along with..." He struts spouting off names of people at his label and those that helped us with the song before handing me the microphone.

"Oh my gosh, I didn't, oh dear. I need to thank Bryan for coming to me for this duet, it was so much fun working on this project with you. I'd also like to thank Cami and my crew at Bold, along with Talon and Kyle for helping me through all this..." yada yada and like a dutiful professional, I thank a lot of the people I worked with at Bryan's label and the fans for loving the song and I manage to do it without getting cut off.

When we get backstage, Bryan hugs me. "Congratulations Addison."

"No no, thank you, and congrats, you deserve it."

He smiles, "So do you."

"Hardly, you wrote it, you came to me, I just sang along with you."

"But we wouldn't have these if you didn't do that." We have to give back our trophies and because of additional nominations we're being returned to our seats. Thank god. But I will have to walk the press line eventually.

When I get back to my seat Kyle and Talon are positively bouncing with happiness for me. They can't take their hands off of me. The song ends up winning video of the year also. I don't claim that trophy, I'll get one, but I had no part in the video production, which is who accepts the award. The ceremony continues through group, male and female vocalists to get to song of the year and then finally artist of the year, which Bryan is also up for. At least this time I get to hold Talon and Kyle's hands through the process. Thank god.

I can't stop bouncing, it sucks, I'm so damn nervous. Then it finally comes to the nominees and I magically settle down, knowing that cameras are on me and Bryan who is sitting in front of me.

"And the winner is...'Never Kiss Goodbye', Bryan Hayes and Addison Carver-Black."

I turn first to Kyle who stands me up in his arms. Then turn to Talon who whispers into my ear, "I am so proud of you." I quickly hug and shake hands on my way out of my row to find Bryan ready to escort me to the stage. Bryan and I go through our rigamarole of thanks once again, and I add a couple of people I forgot the last time, then throw in kisses for Logan and Emily. One day they'll see this.

Bryan turns around and wins the Entertainer of the Year award too. All in all he walked away with like five trophies and on my third duet, before my first album was even in my mind, I've won three.

I don't get to see Talon and Kyle for some time as I walk the press gauntlet backstage. Bryan is right behind me, since we were the last winners and we pose occasionally for pictures together. At the end of the press gauntlet I am handed two bags. One contains packaged trophies, engraved, from what I'm told and the other is a rather expensive Louis Vuitton weekender bag. It's ridiculously heavy and I didn't expect that.

When I'm finally done backstage, I go in search of Kyle and Talon, who are both standing in front of a bank of reporters. I can't hear what they're talking about and my entrance isn't a surprise because all of the reporters start shouting for me, but I don't care. I make a beeline for both of them and they stop what they're doing and wrap me up in a huge hug. Talon lifts me off the ground and kisses me. Then Kyle takes over, repeating the process. The flashbulbs go nuts and Kyle takes all the stuff from my hands.

We stay in the press line a little longer and I answer some questions before we finally make our dash to the limo. We have two after parties to attend tonight.

When we're in the limo they both attack me with kisses and praise and everything short of fucking my brains out on our way.

"It so surreal," I'm finally able to say aloud.

"I can only imagine," Talon says.

I turn to him, "You'll get your chance, trust me. Besides, I don't necessarily feel like these are really mine. I mean, Bryan is huge and the reason for the nominations."

"Don't say that, mama. It's not true. You worked just as hard on that song as he did."

"I know, but still. It doesn't mean I'm not ridiculously happy about it, it's just, I don't know. Ask me tomorrow when I'm at home, playing with the kids then I might have a better idea about how I really feel about it."

They both smile and agree to do so. I call Nadia, our nanny to check on the kids, who are sound asleep already, but I figured that. She said they did great going to bed without us, which is not something we do very often. We've always been very good about having at least two of us there to kiss them good night, except on nights like this. I miss them terribly.

The after parties are a blast and I leave with more stuff. Talon makes some new contacts in the business and I think his prospects are looking up.

**** *Another Year Later* ****

Emily and Logan are turning two and let me tell you what a wild ride this last year has been.

This year was Talon's and 69 Bottles' year. They released two albums and toured twice. My first solo tour started this last February, though it wasn't entirely solo. I opened for 69 Bottles. Most cities we played two nights because tickets sold so fast they had to add more. The twins came with us in a new bus designed specifically for our family with only two bedrooms. One for us and one for the twins.

Though now it is obvious to me which one belongs to whom because they each have features that are distinctively Talon and very distinctively Kyle. Ironically, Talon had wanted boys when we played that game two years ago and Emily is his and Logan belongs to Kyle. Though I know they both know whose is whose, there is no difference in the love and attention they give both kids.

After the tour was over we returned to LA. I recorded my second album and Talon and the guys recorded their fourth. Which ironically enough, Vicious released them a week apart. We traded spots on the Top 40 charts, both of us dancing with numbers one and two for over three weeks. I took number one the first week, because my album came out first and 69 Bottles took the next week. Again we danced. Now eighteen weeks after that, both albums still remain in the top 100. Who would have thought.

Our next music awards show we all went together, all as nominees. I took all but one of my awards and 69 Bottles took all of theirs. It was such a rush.

When we got home that night, we made love for hours, thank god for Nadia, oh and my mom.

Dex and Raine got married this year and they're expecting their first child. Dex has grown up so much, you almost wouldn't recognize him. Now that gay marriage is legal across all fifty states, Mouse and Peacock married also. They are searching for the right surrogate. It breaks my heart a little because I would have loved to do it for them, but I can't.

Jess, bless her beautiful heart, and I have become extremely close friends over the last year or so. She's constantly hanging around with Mouse and Peacock. I tease her all the time about her own little threesome relationship, but she swears it's not like that at all. "I'm going to do it," she tells me one day.

"Do what?" I ask her as she helps me get beers and drinks flowing for everyone.

"Be their surrogate."

"Oh my god, Jess. That's... are you sure?"

She laughs. "Absolutely. I'd do it for you too, if you ever wanted to you know..." She lets the thought trail off.

"I'm so happy you're going to do it for the guys, they deserve it, they need it. But Talon, Kyle and I have decided that the twins are enough for us. Part of that is because of the fact that neither one of them can decide on who the father would be." I laugh. Those argument were quite fun. Watching them argue about it. "What happened with

Logan and Emily is a miracle, and we wouldn't want to put a surrogate through twins."

"I'd do it," she says with a warm reassuring smile.

I hug her. "You're the best, you know that? Why don't you get through it with your guys first, then we'll see." I smile.

"Sounds great."

"Oh and Jess?"

"Yeah."

"If you need anything at all, call me, I'll be there."

She smiles wide and we go out to join the rest of our guys.

Tori and Rusty are together and Beck finally has a woman of his own. Mills on the other hand is meant to be the bachelor of this group, but he's perfectly happy about that.

After releasing their fourth album, 69 Bottles broke up on mutual terms. Talon is pursuing and maintaining a very successful solo career. Eric and Calvin (Peacock and Mouse) decided that there was more to life than being in a band and Dex, well, he's still drumming for Talon. The crazy bastard will never give up on music. Though over the years I've learned that Dex was never about the money or the fame, it was strictly his love of music that kept him going. Though up until Raine, you would have thought it was the women warming his bed.

Emily and Logan are two peas in a pod. One thing that can be said about twins and what they're capable of is a lifelong bond and though their dads are not the same, those nine months growing together gave them a bond one could only wish for in a sibling.

Today is their second birthday and while I long to have another baby, I'm ridiculously happy with the miracles that I do have and more than that, I think I just miss being pregnant. Who wouldn't when you have two loving husbands who coddle you for nine months?

Sitting at the table, looking out across the lawn, I watch my husbands, playing with the kids. As a woman you couldn't ask for more from the men you love. They are loving devoted fathers who spend all of their free time playing with their kids. Sometimes I actually have to kick them out of the house just so I can have my time with them.

Our extended family is expanding and ever changing and growing. Cami and Tristan now have two beautiful children. Derek and Dacotah have one now and another on the way, and though I haven't asked her to confirm it, Cami says their having twins.

Two and half years ago I started this wild journey as a loner, capable of spending all my time with a book or two, cooking and just being me. Then came a bus, a band, a twelve week tour, twenty-five cities, thirty-seven shows and one wild ride that has provided me with friends, family, two beautiful children and two husbands who worship the ground I walk on. A girl who never thought she deserved to love again, to be loved, is the most loved woman in the world.

ARE YOU READY FOR DEX?

Taming Dex
Coming Late April/Early May 2015
Be on the lookout for Pre-Order Coming Soon!

SQWEEE! You've made it to the end, which means you enjoyed Redeeming Kyle, now I BEG of you to please take a few minutes and add your review to the retailer where you purchased the book.
I LOVE to read what you have to say about my books so Please, PRETTY please, leave a review for me to read.

Zoey's Bio:

Zoey Derrick is a Best Selling Author of Contemporary, Erotic, Erotic Romance and Paranormal Romance from Glendale Arizona. She was once a mortgage underwriter and she now writes full time.

She writes stories as hot as the desert sun itself. It is this passion that drips off of her work, bringing excitement to anyone who enjoys a good and sensual love story.

Not only does she aim to take her readers on an erotic dance that lasts the night, it allows her to empty her mind of stories we all wish were true.

Her stories are hopeful yet true to life, skillfully avoiding melodrama and the unrealistic, bringing her gripping Erotica only closer to the heart of those that dare dipping into it.

The intimacy of her fantasies that she shares with her readers is thrilling and encouraging, climactic yet full of suspense. She is a loving mistress, up for anything, of which any reader is doomed to return to again and again.

Stalk Zoey on Social Media.

Printed in the USA
CPSIA information can be obtained
at www.ICGtesting.com
LVHW091105041224
798305LV00016B/64

* 9 780099 625981 1 *